The Ungovernable series:

Zero Day Threat
Jailbreak
Time Bomb
Insider Threat
Firewall
Trojan Horse
Security Incident
Threat Agent
Attack Path

FIREWALL

R.M. OLSON

ISBN-13: 978-1-7771778-9-8

To my kids, who all want to grow up to be Jez,
despite my best efforts.

FIREWALL:

A security device designed to block unauthorized access to or from a system.

1

"Jez Solokov." The man's face was twisted in an ugly sneer, his breath puffing out in cold white clouds in the early morning Prasvishoni air. "You have a lot of gall coming back here. Guess you didn't expect we'd get word of it."

Jez gave him an easy smile, even though every muscle in her body was tight with adrenalin. "Figured you'd miss me, Dima."

Behind her, down the narrow, dirty port street, the grungy city gate was just visible.

The man's eyebrows lowered. Beside him, easily visible against the dark walls of the alleyway that led onto the street, his companions, a woman and another man, wore similar expressions. Jez wasn't entirely certain she recognized either of them.

"Never thought you'd be back, Jez," said the woman. "Figured that once you'd run off on Dima and on me both, you'd know better than to try that." She pulled a heat-pistol from her belt in an easy motion that was suddenly familiar—

"Alina!" Jez said with delight. "It's been a while. Didn't know you knew Dima."

Alina stared at her for a moment. Jez grinned.

"Come on, it's been a long time. Can't blame me for not

recognizing you right away. Anyways, you always said I was a good kisser. Thought you'd at least want to try it out again before you shot me."

"You weren't that good of a kisser," the woman muttered sourly.

Jez shrugged. "If you wanted to practice—"

Dima glared at her in exasperation, then at Alina. "I was under the impression," he said icily, "that we're here to kill this idiot, not plaguing flirt with her!"

"Sorry," said Jez, sounding not even a little bit sorry.

"You're going to be a hell of a lot sorrier," he growled, and levelled his pistol.

Jez didn't wait for him to aim. She dived forward, the heat from the blast searing the air over her shoulder and the blow-by heat almost scorching her skin. Dima managed only a half-bitten-off curse before she'd landed him on the ground. She managed one very satisfying punch right in the middle of his mouth before Alina and the other man—she was actually pretty sure she didn't recognize him, although if she'd been drunk enough at the time it was possible she was wrong—yanked her off Dima.

Alina's pistol was coming up, and Jez rolled out of her grip, grabbing for Dima, who was still on the ground, and jerking him around between her and the pistol. He twisted in her grasp, trying to bring his own heat pistol to bear, and she grabbed for it, trying to yank it from his hand before he could actually kill her with it. He tightened his grip and swore, lunging to his feet, then grabbed her by the shoulder of her jacket, hauling her up after him.

"You're damn well going to regret messing with me, Jez Solokov," he gritted out through his teeth. "You think you can—"

She bit down hard on his wrist, and he yelped and dropped her. She landed on her side, rolled, and kicked out with both feet. There was a delightful crunch as the heel of her boot connected with his kneecap, then he grabbed her ankle and twisted. She lost her balance and fell hard, landing face-first on the dirty concrete of the alley.

"Tae," she muttered into her com, "you could hurry it up, you know." She twisted violently, rolling over and letting her momentum and body weight jerk her ankle free of Dima's grip. She jumped to her feet and kicked again, and this time she connected with his stomach. He cursed, losing his balance and falling hard into the wall, his heat-gun skittering away down the alley, and Jez spun just in time to knock Alina's wrist up so that the heat-blast aimed at her chest left a round blackened mark on the dirty pre-fab walls of the building behind her.

"I though we'd got along fine," she grunted, dodging Alina's knee to her stomach. "I mean, sure we didn't exactly see eye to eye, but —"

"You plaguing idiot," Alina snarled. "You took off, told me you'd be back when you were done your run. And you never showed, and here I was worried about you and waiting around. And then what happens? The cops show up, they're looking for a Jez Solokov who's wanted for smuggling, and then I spend the next ten months being hauled into the station twice a week to be questioned, and the whole time I'm worried sick about you. And then I find out you just took off because you felt like it."

"Oh." Jez frowned slightly. "Yeah, guess that's fair." She paused a moment. "Why does Dima want to kill me?"

"Just give me a minute," Tae's voice hissed in her earpiece. "I'm getting hooked in as quickly as I can." He paused. "Whatever you're doing, it's working. The guards are all watching the alley. I think I could march a parade through the gates and they wouldn't look up."

"Same reason, except you also cost him half his damn fortune."

She shrugged, and ducked out of the way as Dima's fist missed her jaw by millimetres. "Hey now, not my fault the load wasn't worth what he thought it was. I pulled the job for him fair and square, just like he paid me to."

"Before I met you, you plaguer, I had plenty of credits and good prospects," Dima gritted through his teeth. "After you left, I had nothing."

"Not my fault. You were a worthless bastard before I slept with you, figure that wouldn't change afterwards. I mean, I'm hot, but I'm not that hot."

He snarled and lunged for her. She sidestepped, and caught a fist in the ribs. She gasped, spun, and managed to deflect the blow the third man had aimed at her jaw.

"What the hell's your problem?" she gasped at the stranger. "Pretty sure I never slept with you. Or else I was really damn drunk."

He feinted, and she ducked, and then a fist caught her from behind, sending her staggering up against the filthy wall of the alley. The man gave her a nasty grin.

"Nothing. They're just paying me enough to make it worth my while."

Dima grabbed her by the collar, and as she tried to twist free, he shoved her back into the wall, his eyes boring into hers.

"You dirty plaguer," he growled softly. "You filthy bastard. You think you can just show up here again without consequences?"

She attempted a shrug. "That's what I usually do. Didn't notice until now? I mean, you always were a bit slow on the uptake, but—"

He slammed her backwards into the wall, and she winced. She'd have a bruise for sure this time.

"You—" she began, and then she stopped abruptly.

There was no mistaking the feel of the small, snub-nosed pistol shoved up under her ribs.

She cut her eyes away from Dima. Alina stood beside him, smiling, but it wasn't a friendly smile.

Why the hell had she got together with this girl anyways? Probably not one of her smartest moves, in hindsight. Still, at least Alina was hot. She had no idea what she'd ever seen in Dima.

"Jez Solokov," said Alina softly. "I've waited a long damn time for this. You're going to give me all the credits on your credit chip, you're going to pass them over right now. And then I want to see you beg for your life. I want you to beg me and Dima to forgive you for all the crap you pulled. And maybe, just maybe, if you have enough credits and you put on a good enough act, we'll just beat the living hell out of you and let you crawl away home. But I promise you, when we're done, there won't be anyone in Prasvishoni who'll want to sleep with your dirty carcass."

Jez grinned at her absently, tapping her com inconspicuously against the wall behind her.

Pilot's code.

Tae had damn well better be paying attention.

Tae. How long is this going to take?

His voice hissed through her earpiece. "Got it. You better get out of there."

"Jez?" Alina's voice had taken on its familiar tone of fury mingled with complete exasperation. "Are you even bloody listening?"

Jez took a deep breath and gave Alina a beatific smile.

Then she threw herself to one side, wrenching free of Dima's grip on her collar, and knocking the muzzle of the gun away from her with one hand as it went off, scorching a smouldering black mark into the wall beside her. With her other, she reached into her jacket pocket and yanked out a small, deadly-looking weapon. She grinned, pointed it at her momentarily-stunned attackers, and pulled the trigger.

Nothing happened.

Dima smiled.

Jez swore, turned, and ran for her life.

She slapped her com as she ducked around a corner, a heat-blast scorching the air behind her.

"Ysbel! What the hell? Your gun didn't work!"

"My guns always work," Ysbel responded, in her thick outer-rim accent. "I don't make mistakes with my guns."

"Yeah, well unless you made this one as a decorative piece—"

"You took the gun I told you to take, right?"

She shrugged, and ducked around another corner. Her ribs throbbed where she'd been hit, and she could already feel a bump rising on the back of her head where Dima had slammed her into the wall. "I grabbed the one on the damn table."

Through her earpiece, she could hear Ysbel's heavy sigh. "There were two guns on the table, you idiot. I told you that. And I told you to take the one with the black grip."

Another heat blast, and Jez yelped and dodged to one side, the corner of her jacket smouldering.

"Dammit Ysbel, you knew bloody well I wasn't actually listening to what you were saying!"

"Fair enough," said Ysbel. "I suppose I should have seen that coming."

"Jez. Are you alright?" Tae cut in, his voice tight with worry.

"Define 'alright,'" she gasped.

Ahead of her, the alley she was running down narrowed and

turned. She slipped around the corner, but the sound of her pursuers' boots on the concrete were much too close for comfort.

"Are they shooting at you?"

"What the hell do you think, Tae?"

"Alright, listen." Ysbel's voice was tight now as well. "The gun you have, I think it has all the components, it's just not hooked up yet. What you'll need to do is take the panel off the side of the heat sink. Can you do that?"

The alley turned again. It was narrowing further.

"Jez." Lev's voice over the com was cold, but there was an undercurrent of worry in it. "I grabbed your location from your com. The city's boarded that alley up. You're going to hit a dead end in about thirty seconds."

"Would have been nice to know that five minutes ago," she muttered.

"Hold tight, Jez," said Tae. "Ysbel and I are on our way. We'll be there as quick as we can."

She slapped her com off. No way in hell they were going to get here before Dima and Alina did.

Ahead, at the end of another tight turn, she saw the dead end Lev had warned her about.

"Listen, Jez. Can you get the heat sink panel off?" Ysbel's voice came through her earpiece, sounding more worried than ever.

There was no way she was getting past that barricade, not with a defective gun.

"Hate to tell you this, Ysbel, but I'm basically crap at putting heat guns together. For the record."

"Well, Jez, perhaps this would be a very good time to learn." Masha was clearly speaking through her teeth. Jez skidded to a stop, and shoved herself up against the wall of the alley, dropping her hands to her knees and bending over to catch her breath. Footsteps pounded down the alley behind her. They'd be there in just a couple seconds.

She grinned to herself and straightened, pushing even farther back against the wall.

Dima pelted around the corner, and she stuck out one leg. He hit it, tripped, and went down, his heat-gun spinning off across the cement. Alina was only seconds behind him, not in time to stop, and as she rounded the corner, Jez was already swinging. She brought the butt of the useless heat gun down sharply across Alina's temple, stepped back, and, as she collapsed, landed an elbow in the centre of the stranger's forehead as he rounded the corner. He stopped, staggering slightly from the blow, and she dropped him with the butt of the pistol, which was actually coming in a lot more handy than she'd expected. Dima had staggered to hands and knees, and she kicked him hard. His jaw snapped shut, and he crumpled back to the ground. Jez glanced around, sprinted for the dropped heat pistol, and yanked it up as Alina blinked and stirred.

"Alright, you bastards," she said, grinning like a maniac. "Guess you're going to have to find someone else hot enough to shoot at. I mean, guess I never got off on shooting at people with heat guns, but —"

"Jez," Alina growled. "Believe me, this has nothing to do with—"

"Ah, just keep telling yourself that," Jez said with a grin. "Anyways, hate to disappoint you, but—"

Two skybikes rounded the corner, and Tae slid off his almost before it came to a stop. His dark, wavy hair was falling across his face, like always, and his ragged street-kid clothing made him look even younger than his twenty years, but his heat gun was steady.

"Jez, are you—" He was breathless.

"All good, tech-head," she said, shooting a grin at him over her shoulder. He frowned.

"Looks like you got a little more beat up than 'all good,'" he said.

She shrugged. "Part of the job."

"Get on, you idiot," Ysbel said. "We'd better get back." Honestly, Ysbel, with her shaved head and flat expression and very impressive muscles, could probably have scared the hell out of these bastards even if she hadn't been carrying a modded weapon that could probably burn holes in concrete.

But she was.

"Nice to see you again, Dima, Alina," said Jez with a cocky grin. "And, you other bastard, not sure I enjoyed meeting you, but wait until I get a damn stun gun that works."

She swung up behind Ysbel, and Tae, still holding his heat pistol steady, mounted his own bike, and Jez sighed in satisfaction as her erstwhile attackers' angry curses followed them down the alley.

2

Lev took a deep breath and closed his eyes for a moment.

"Lev?"

He looked up across the *Ungovernable's* conference table at the calm, competent-looking woman sitting across from him, and tried not to think about the spike of sick, desperate panic that had jolted through him when he'd heard the heat-blasts over Jez's com, pulled her location and seen she was going to hit a dead end.

"Yes, Masha?"

She'd be fine. She was always fine, and besides, she'd made it very clear that it was none of his damn business.

Masha studied him wryly for a moment. "I'm quite confident that they would have mentioned it if Jez had been killed, Lev. And further, if you don't start to pay attention to what you're doing, it's entirely possible that not only Jez, but every one of us, won't live through the next week."

He gave her a flat look and turned back to the holoscreen in front of him, trying to force his mind to focus on the lines of text.

Boots sounded in the corridor a few minutes later. And despite everything, his damn heart almost stopped beating when he didn't see Jez, and then restarted again when she sauntered in behind Tae.

She was sporting a bruise along her jaw, an angry red against her tawny skin, and her short, dishevelled black hair was cut through with dirt and gravel, but she wore the same cocky grin she always did.

He shoved down the urge to jump to his feet and grab her by the shoulders, look her over for injuries, pull her into a tight, relieved embrace.

He took a deep breath.

It was fine. She was fine, and he'd be fine, he and Jez had had a discussion, like adults, and they'd mutually decided that—well, whatever it was that they'd been before was a mistake, and the best thing possible to do was to get on with their own separate lives. He'd explained it to her in as logical a way as possible, and she'd agreed, and that had been that.

"Strap down, kids," she drawled over her shoulder as she disappeared into the cockpit.

Tae gritted his teeth and grabbed for the nearest restraint, and a moment later the ship rose delicately into the air, then shot through the open doors of the hangar bay at a speed that made Lev wish he'd skipped breakfast that morning.

"Lev?" asked Masha, once the *Ungovernable* broke through the atmosphere and they were surrounded by the sweep of shallow space. "Would you please put the coordinates through to Jez? Once she's set a course, I'd appreciate if we could have a short discussion."

Lev pulled up his holoscreen, trying not to think about the empty copilot seat next to Jez in the cockpit, and swiped the coordinates through to the ship's com.

A few minutes later, Jez sauntered out of the cockpit and dropped into a seat, a blissful smile lingering on her face.

"Going to do a hyperdrive jump in a few minutes, but figure if you eggheads wanted to talk—" she shrugged.

"Jez?" asked Masha briskly. "Are you alright?"

She shot them all her cockiest grin. "I'm always fine."

Lev sighed and glared at her. "Jez. You said you were fine the last time you were hit by a heat-gun."

She shrugged, still grinning. "Yeah? Well maybe I was. Anyways, I'm good. Hell of a lot better than what I figured I'd be, seeing that Ysbel gave me a defective damn gun."

Ysbel looked up from her seat, narrowing her eyes. "I did not give you a defective gun, you idiot. I told you exactly which gun you should take, and you completely ignored me and took the gun I hadn't finished working on yet."

"Like I said," drawled Jez.

Lev drew in a long breath, fighting down the lingering, irrational panic.

"Ysbel? Tae? I assume you dealt with the tracking on the city gate?" Masha glanced at Tae, her face pleasant.

Tae gave a slight smile. "Honestly, I think we could have paraded down the street with flags and whistles and the gate guards wouldn't have noticed. They're not going to know we left. In fact, they're not going to know anyone leaves through that gate until they find the spoof we set."

"That's excellent to hear," Masha said.

Lev managed a smile. "At any rate, it should give us a head start."

"Well," said Jez, leaning back with a smirk. "Guess that bastard Dima was good for something after all."

"Jez, you were just about shot in a damn alley," he said through his teeth, even though he knew that it would make no difference whatsoever.

She rolled her eyes at him, and his stomach flip-flopped, which was actually ridiculous, and he refused to think about it.

Ysbel turned back to the table. "So, Masha. What is it you want to talk about, considering that in a few standard hours we'll be visiting the mafia krestnaya and possibly all be killed?"

"Thank you, Ysbel. I'm glad that there is someone in this crew who has managed to keep her mind on our current situation," said Masha, her voice carrying the slightest hint of a barb. "Now." She pulled up her holoscreen and flipped through to the list Lev had sent her earlier that day. "Tae, as I promised, your street-kid friends are as safe as it's possible for them to be at present. As the apartment we've housed them in is frequented by people who tend to have family in the government, I suspect that we no longer have to worry about police interference."

Tae turned to Masha, raising an eyebrow. "How did you get an apartment in that complex anyways?"

She smiled slightly. "I did work for the government for some time, and it happens that I do have some connections. I'm not quite as unlikable as all that."

Tae gave a reluctant chuckle, and Jez snorted in amusement.

"Guess it depends on who you ask, you bastard," she drawled.

Lev gritted his teeth and drew in a long breath.

"Grigory Korzhakov, on behalf of the mafia, promised to keep Peti safe for at least three weeks, and as we are ahead of schedule, I believe that problem has also been resolved," Masha continued. She paused a moment. "As you are all aware, however, those are not our only pressing concern."

Lev felt a familiar jolt of worry at the thought.

Two and a half weeks. That was how long it had been since the government had managed to flood Prasvishoni, and the entire crew of the *Ungovernable,* with the particles of programmed metal dissolved in gas that would enter through the victim's lungs into their bloodstream. The metal that, almost certainly, had already congealed in each of their brain stems, in a high enough quantity that all it would take to kill any one of them was a few strokes of a keyboard. And not only them—every person in Prasvishoni. It was, he had to admit, a brilliant scheme, if you happened to value the ability to control mass amounts of humanity with minimal effort and didn't mind killing them to make that happen. You could track any person in the system, find them, and shock them, or disable them, or kill them with a few dispassionate keystrokes.

And of course, there was the additional downside that he'd helped develop it, inadvertently, as a young university student. And that Evka, the professor he'd been working with at the time, who he'd considered both a mentor and a friend, had tracked him down three weeks before and almost killed Jez, because she'd found them both asleep on his couch, Jez in his arms, and decided that planting a subcutaneous explosive under the skin at the base of Jez's skull would be a good way to convince Lev she wasn't joking when she told him to leave this alone.

And Jez wasn't going to be used as a motivating factor ever again. That fact was the hard, solid, immovable object against which every single damn one of his objections foundered every time he drifted into a daydream about Jez.

Which, honestly, was happening much less often these days.

Only once every couple minutes or so.

"Lev?"

He shook his head and brought his attention back to the table. Masha was looking at him, one eyebrow raised.

"Yes, Masha?"

"I asked, what is your opinion?"

He sighed. "I apologize. I—had my mind on something else."

"I gathered that," she said, her tone a mixture of coldness and wry amusement. "Although I'm certain that there are many things that are demanding your attention, I would appreciate if you could possibly spare a moment or two to the problem of how long we have before we are all killed, and what solutions may have presented themselves to you over the last weeks."

He managed a rueful smile in return. "I'm sorry." He gathered his thoughts for a moment. "I—believe that we will have a few weeks yet. Knowing Evka, she'll be intrigued by both the virus Tae hacked into the system, and my modification to the equation they're using to run it. Furious, of course, but intrigued. I suspect she'll attempt to pick out the changes I made, and believe me, I made that very difficult to do. In addition, someone will have to find a way to pick out the changes that Ysbel made to the chemical equation for the composition of the gas. But Evka is—very smart."

"And coming from you, that's saying something," Ysbel muttered. "Alright, so we have a few weeks before this very smart professor of yours kills us all?"

"In fairness, I don't think she'd do it only for the chance to kill us all," he murmured.

Ysbel rolled her eyes. "Well, I'm sure that will be a great comfort to us all when we all get an electrical shock in the brain stem, yes?"

He shot her a slightly-irritated glance. "Ysbel. I am aware of the danger. Believe me, between Tae and me, we've explored every option that either of us could come up with to somehow disable the system, in-between working on how to keep the damn mafia from shooting us all down when we show up on their ship. I'm afraid we don't have a great deal of time to figure something out."

Jez leaned back in her chair, grinning. "I still say we find her and set off one of Ysbel's explosives. Bet she'd have a harder time doing whatever the crap she's doing with all your numbers and crap if she's trying to do it in pieces from the bottom of a damn crater."

He sighed. "Yes, Jez, and, if you recall from the last fifteen times you suggested some variant on this theme, we have absolutely no idea where the government is keeping her, and even if we did, I'm positive it would be virtually impossible to reach her. She will be well aware, and will have made everyone in the government well aware, that we will be trying to stop whatever it is they're doing."

Jez shrugged, shooting him that sharp grin that always twisted his stomach. "Thought Tac made it look like we were all inside that damn building we blew up."

"Yes, and if you recall, Evka knows me," he snapped, more harshly than me meant to. "I'm fairly certain she won't have been fooled by our little stunt."

"Yeah? Well, maybe next time you can try working for someone who isn't a murderous bastard."

He narrowed his eyes, but Ysbel held up a hand. "Alright, you two." She turned to Masha. "So. We're leaving tomorrow for wherever it is those coordinates that Grigory sent to your com lead, correct?"

"Yes," murmured Masha. She hesitated a moment. "Lev, I asked if you'd come up with any solutions to our problem with Evka, and the Vyernist Protocol, as I believe the government is calling the program. However, I have been doing some research myself. I—am not certain what Grigory wants from me. It was worth enough to him that he was willing to track us down, which could not have been easy, and kidnap Tae's friend, in order to get me to agree to come. But, as I said, I have been doing my research. As you likely all know,

Grigory Korzhakov is a man with extensive contacts in the government. Depending on what he wants from me, it's just possible that we can use him in stopping this government program. If he knows about it, I doubt he's much happier about it than we are, so it is a distinct possibility." She glanced over them. "Lev, you've checked the coordinates, I assume."

She paused meaningfully.

He dragged his eyes away from Jez, jaw still clenched, and sighed. "The coordinates lead to a position in deep-space that is, to all extents and purposes, lawless. It's technically outside the legal jurisdiction of the Svodrani System because of a shift in the placement of the wormholes over the centuries since the System borders were set. There's very little out there, but since it is outside the Svodrani System legal jurisdiction, it tends to be a place where some of the more legally questionably businesses have set themselves up. Weapons runners, for instance, gambling ships—"

Jez perked up slightly at the mention of gambling, and he shot her a disapproving glare. She smirked at him.

"So there's no guarantee that he won't kill us as soon as we leave the system?" asked Ysbel.

Lev shook his head. "There's no guarantee of anything. However, if Grigory had wanted to kill Masha, there were several less-complicated ways of doing so than inviting her to his ship, and therefore I think I can say with a reasonable amount of certainty that he has something other than our immediate murder in mind."

"Well, that's a relief," grunted Ysbel sourly.

"Very well," said Masha, glancing around. "We'll be there shortly. I suggest we prepare ourselves. Whatever we're walking into, Grigory Korzhikov is a dangerous man. Ysbel, I'll leave it to you and Tanya to finish the precautionary plans we discussed. Lev, Tae, if either of you come up with any additional insight regarding our government problem, please come discuss it with me immediately. Jez—" She paused.

Jez was grinning widely. "Don't worry, Masha, I could fly my beautiful angel to whatever coordinates you wanted me to, fast asleep and pass-out drunk."

"I am certain you could," said Masha, pinching her lips. "However, I would prefer that you not give us a demonstration."

Jez shrugged, still grinning. "Well, just because I like you, you dirty bastard, I won't get drunk on the ride over, how's that?"

There was a small, unfamiliar twinkle of humour in Masha's eyes under her stern expression that Lev was certain hadn't been there before, and he was fairly certain that he never would have seen it directed at Jez's last comment before they'd pulled the university job.

"That's sufficient, Jez. Thank you."

Jez leaned back again luxuriously, grinning, and Lev scowled.

Damn it, they'd both decided this was for the best.

And it damn well was for the best.

"Come on, Tae," he said, shoving his chair back abruptly and getting to his feet. "Let's go through everything one more time, see if there's anything we missed."

Somehow, he managed not to look at Jez as he made his way off the main deck and into the conference room, where he and Tae had set up their workspace.

Crack this government program, find out how to outwit Evka and stop all of them from being killed, get Tae's friend Peti back from the mafia—there were plenty of things to worry about that didn't involve Jez, the way she smiled, her loud, inappropriate laughter, the infectious, reckless, irreverent joy of her.

The heat of her body pressed against his, the spark in her dark eyes, her perpetually-mussed black hair, just long enough for him to tighten his fingers into while he was kissing her—

He bit back a groan.

He was being ridiculous. He'd made his decision, and so had she, and they were just crewmates and that's all they needed to be.

It had been two and a half weeks, and he was almost completely over her. He was concerned about her, of course, in the same way he was concerned about Tae and Ysbel and Tanya and Masha, but no more.

And he conscientiously ignored the fact that no matter how concerned he was about Tae or Ysbel, he'd never once woken from dreams of them curled up against him, blinking up at him, sleepy-eyed and tousled and smiling softly, and not been able to fall asleep again for the rest of the damn night.

"Lev?"

He looked up. Tae had already pulled back a chair and taken his seat, and was watching him with concern.

He managed a small smile. "Sorry." He pulled back his own chair, and tried to ignore the worry in Tae's eyes. "You're right, we'd better get to work."

Ysbel looked up from the array of weapons components spread out on the ground around her as Tanya climbed down the ladder to the *Ungovernable's* storage bay, where Ysbel had set up her workroom.

There was a tension in her wife's posture that hadn't left since they'd returned, two and a half weeks ago, to the hangar bay where their children were hiding, and found a boyevik soldier from the mafia waiting for them.

Peti had saved them, had volunteered to go with the mafia in exchange for them protecting Tae's street children and little Olya and Misko. But … but even the thought of what might have happened made her nauseous.

She couldn't blame Tanya.

"Are you alright, my love?" she asked quietly, as Tanya crossed over to her.

Tanya gave a short nod, but didn't speak, and for a moment Ysbel was tempted to press her for an answer.

But that was one thing she wouldn't do. Whatever it was Tanya was upset about, she'd tell her when she was ready, she'd known Tanya long enough to know that.

But had she? a small voice in the back of her mind whispered.

How well did she still know her wife, after five and a half years?

It was a strange feeling, this mix of aching familiarity and tentative reticence, knowing her wife like she knew her own self, and at the same time not knowing her at all.

"Tanya?" Ysbel asked.

Tanya smiled, but the smile was strained. "Yes, Ysi?"

Ysbel stood and crossed over to her wife. She ran her hand through Tanya's smooth brown hair, still short from prison, and down her back, feeling the tension in her muscles. "It's alright," she whispered. "We'll figure this out. How many impossible situations have we gotten out of so far?"

Again, Tanya tried to smile. "I know. But—Ysi, I know about the mafia. Believe me, there were plenty in that prison. I spent five and a half years trying to keep our children safe from them. And now—" she paused. "We're flying straight into their arms. And you didn't even ask for my thoughts."

Ysbel frowned. "I did. I told you—"

"Telling me is different than asking what I thought."

Ysbel closed her eyes wearily for a moment. "Tanya. My love.

What do you want me to do? We can't let Peti stay there, you know that. Not after that girl gave herself up to keep our children safe."

Tanya sighed and turned away, the muscles in her slender frame tight. "I know. And I would never ask you to do that. I would never ask you to send the others in on their own, and you know I would never leave you to do this without me. But this?" She gestured around her. "This isn't just getting Peti back now, is it? When did we start talking about Grigory being able to help us figure out this problem with Evka?"

"Tanya." Ysbel bit back her frustration. "Listen to me. You breathed in that gas. Our children breathed in that gas. It will kill them. What do you want me to do, let that happen? I can't. I can't let them hurt you again. So what do I do?"

Tanya closed her eyes for a moment, and for the first time Ysbel saw the exhaustion in her posture. "I don't know, Ysi," she said at last, quietly. "I don't know what we should do. I can't ask you to leave these people. They broke us out of prison. I owe the fact that I have you back to them. But—but Ysi. I'm your wife. You can't solve this by leaving me out of it. I don't know what we need to do, but at least I need to have a say in it. These are your children, yes, but they're my children too."

Ysbel pulled Tanya towards her, and finally, reluctantly, Tanya leaned into her, allowed Ysbel to hold her. "I'm sorry, my love," Ysbel whispered. "I'm sorry. But I need to do this. I need to protect you."

"Even if it means working with the mafia?" said Tanya, her voice soft against Ysbel's shoulder. "Even something I've told you I don't want to do? Something I don't want you to do?"

Ysbel could feel Tanya shift in her arms, and she tightened her grip. "It might not come to that, my love."

"And if it does?"

Ysbel just held her, and didn't answer.

Because the truth was, it didn't matter. She couldn't watch these people she loved more than her own life be killed. Not again. And she'd do whatever it took, it didn't matter what it was.

At last Tanya pulled away, and gave her that smile that wasn't really a smile.

"I'd better go. Make sure the children aren't getting into trouble." She turned, and Ysbel looked after her as she left, something twisting in her chest.

Something had happened to her wife, ever since that day two and a half weeks ago, and she wasn't sure how to fix it.

Or rather, she knew how to fix it. But the price might be Tanya and the children's lives, and that was a cost that was infinitely too high.

3

Jez narrowed her eyes and glared out the front window of the cockpit at the massive ship looming in front of them, right on the coordinates that Masha had set into the holoscreen.

It was almost too big to be called a ship, really—a small station, practically, and even from here she could see the credits it must have taken to keep it up here, the smooth panelling that could absorb the impact of meteoroids and space junk without losing their lustre, that could take the crap and the radiation and the slow, creeping assault of deep-space parasites and hold them all at bay.

And even then, even through the smooth sheen that whispered of credits and luxury, she could see the small signs of rot, the way the spaces between the panels were pitted and ugly, the places under the fins where no one would normally see.

And right about now, unless she guessed wrong—

Half a dozen ships appeared on her holoscreen, bursting out from behind the massive station-ship like sparks from an explosion, and she grinned to herself. They were fast, she could tell that already, and if they didn't have enough firepower to take down any damn long-haul in the system, she missed her guess.

She let her fingers rest loose on the controls, her grin spreading wider, her breath coming just a little quicker.

Because hell. This was the kind of thing she lived for.

"Jez," Masha murmured.

She shot the woman a quick smirk over her shoulder. "Don't worry, you bastard. I know what I'm doing."

"Jez—" Masha was speaking through her teeth. "We are here as invited guests. I'm not certain how long that will last if you start shooting at them."

Jez sighed and rolled her eyes. "I wasn't going to shoot at them, OK? I mean, unless they decided to shoot at me first, in which case —" She grinned wider. Masha sighed and tapped the com.

"Masha Volkova. We're here by invitation. Grigory Korzhakov requested my presence."

"Send in the invitation code," came a cold voice over the com. Jez rolled her eyes again.

Bastard sounded like he'd like an excuse to shoot them down, and to be perfectly honest, she would absolutely love to see him try. An aching, itching restlessness had crawled under her skin over the past two and a half damn weeks, and she refused to think about why, but the point was, if she didn't get to do something soon, she might actually explode into a million pieces.

"I'm sending it through now," came Masha's pleasant voice.

"Confirmed," the voice said over the com. It was probably slightly less cold now, but honestly, not enough so that you'd notice. "I'll send in a pilot ship, and send flight instructions to your com. Please follow exactly. If you deviate from the planned course, you will be shot down without hesitation."

"That's what you think, you plaguers," Jez muttered under her breath.

"Understood," said Masha, her voice still pleasant. She tapped the com off and shot Jez a look.

"I wasn't going to do anything," Jez grumbled.

Masha was still watching her appraisingly.

"Look, if you want to bring the damn ship in—" she snapped.

"No," said Masha. "I do not. However—" she paused a moment. "I have no idea what Grigory wants with me. But if we intend to try to use him to put a more permanent halt to the government's Vyernist Protocol, it will require some amount of patience. Will you be able to do that, Jez?"

Jez grinned, even through the nervous tension that bubbled through her, making her fingers ache and her legs twitch with the need to move, to do something, anything. "You know me. I can do basically anything."

Masha was still studying her. At last she shook her head ruefully. "I've known you long enough to know what I can and cannot expect. And therefore, I'm not expecting miracles. However, if you could see fit to not shoot anyone or incentivize anyone to shoot at you for the next twenty-four standard hours, I would appreciate it."

Jez glanced over at her reflexively.

If she were being honest, this new side to Masha, where she was actually not a complete bastard, was something that would take some getting used to.

Still—well, she'd never actually realized what it would be like, having someone as thoroughly competent, and thoroughly terrifying, as Masha on her side, for once.

It was actually kind of nice.

"Figure I could give it a try," she said finally.

Masha actually shot her something that looked, almost, like a small grin. "I suppose I can live with that."

Jez's holoscreen flashed for a moment, and a long string of

characters scrolled over it. A moment later, she had visuals on one of the ships, sleek and deadly, that was going to guide them in. She glanced down at the flight plan, took a deep breath, and nudged her beautiful angel ship forward.

The pilot ship brought them into a small hangar bay on the belly-side of the station-ship, and she set the *Ungovernable* down gently on the bare metal floor as the bay doors slid shut behind them. The airlock hissed as it pressurized, and then the voice over the com said, "You're cleared to disembark. Please leave all weapons aboard your ship, and come out slowly."

"You have an interesting way of greeting guests," Masha said into the com in her blandest tone. "If you recall, Grigory extended the invitation. And he mentioned nothing about a requirement to disarm."

"You'll leave your weapons on the ship," the voice repeated, the tone slightly harder.

"And how does Grigory intend to guarantee our safety?" asked Masha, in that same pleasant voice.

"You're here on Grigory's private ship." The voice was cold with menace. "You'll do as you're told."

"That is one option," said Masha, noncommittally. "My other option, of course, is to ask my gunner to deploy the ordinances that are loaded under the base of my ship. If Grigory has done his research, which I'm certain he has, he will be aware that my gunner has a certain talent in the matter of explosives. It would certainly take out this hangar bay, that's a given. I suspect it would also breach the hull of the ship and weaken the exterior paneling across the entire structure." She pulled up the holoscreen on her com with a swift gesture, and Jez instantly recognized the familiar wording scrolling across the screen.

Lev. Of course. Of course the plaguer had all the specs to the station-ship within half an hour of their hyper jump into its space.

She took a deep breath and forced her hands to still against the controls.

"I note that you have a lockdown protocol to block off the back of the ship. However, it was rather short-sighted of you to construct the airlock at the juncture between the two segments. Grigory wouldn't, perhaps, lose his entire ship, but I suspect he'd lose everything in those two sections."

There was a long moment of silence from the other end of the line.

"You'd destroy your own ship," the voice said, but there was a note of uncertainty in it that had not been there before.

"Perhaps," said Masha pleasantly. "Although those of us inside would likely survive it. We do have rather impressive shielding. Still, I certainly wouldn't want to risk it, unless I had no other viable options."

There was another long pause. Finally, a different voice came over the com, older and deeper than the first, with a slight rasp to it, as if its owner had inhaled some chemical gas and hadn't managed to cough it out before it had burned his lungs.

"Masha Volkova," he said, and out of the corner of her eye, Jez saw Masha stiffen, just for a moment. Then she smiled and relaxed, but her hand clenched around the the arm of the seat tightly enough that the tendons stood out on her wrists.

"Grigory Korzhakov," she said, in that calm, bland voice. "I wasn't aware that your boyeviki would try to threaten me the moment I arrived here. I was under the impression that it would be in our mutual interest to establish a friendly relationship. But perhaps I was mistaken?"

"Masha," the man said again, a faint note of humour in his tone. "I see I didn't underestimate you. Could you tell me, please, why you chose to arm your ship with an ordinance that would take apart my station ship?"

"Of course," said Masha pleasantly. "It was because you are a man who is virtually untouchable, and you've asked me onto your own private ship in a space that is completely ungoverned by anyone but you. And I am not a stupid woman."

There was a long moment's pause. At last, Grigory said, "I am aware of that. But you don't come onto a person's ship, if they've invited you there, and bring your weapons. You know that, Masha."

"And you don't generally invite someone onto your ship by kidnapping one of their acquaintances," said Masha briskly.

"Listen, Masha. I will give my word that my people will not draw their weapons on any of you. I do want to speak with you, and I think you'll want to hear what I have to say."

"I have made rather a long trip to hear what you have to say," said Masha. "And I do appreciate you giving me your word. In return, I give you my word that none of my people will draw their weapons."

There was a long moment of silence.

"You are stubborn." Grigory's voice had lost its humour.

"I do apologize," said Masha politely.

"Are you doubting my word? I am used to at least some respect from people who talk to me."

"I have nothing at all but respect for you," said Masha. "And with all the respect due you, are you doubting mine?"

There was another long pause.

"Alright. Fine. Bring your weapons. But I had hoped this discussion would get off to a more productive start."

"I see no reason in the world why it should not," said Masha, all bland politeness. "I am, of course, interested in nothing but full trust and complete transparency in all our dealings."

Jez almost snorted at that.

"My people will bring you to my office," Grigory said grudgingly, but there was a note of something that might have been respect under the annoyance in his tone.

Masha smiled to herself and tapped the com off, and Jez watched her, one eyebrow raised.

"Yes, Jez?" said Masha, glancing over.

"You know, I think you might be able to give me a run for my damn money at getting under people's skins."

Masha raised her own eyebrows. "From you, Jez, that is high praise indeed." She stood and checked her heat pistol, then tapped her wrist com to the general line. "I believe you all heard the conversation. I'll meet you at the entrance to the loading ramp. Please do not draw your weapons unless there is at least a credible threat to your life."

"I assume you mean," said Ysbel, a hint of humour under her heavy outer-rim accent, "a credible threat to our lives other than the normal credible threats to our lives, like something in our heads that can kill us as soon as the government figures out how to break Lev's code, or being blackmailed aboard the ship of the mafia krestnaya, or—"

"That is correct, Ysbel," said Masha pleasantly. She glanced over her shoulder once at Jez, then pulled open the cockpit door and walked briskly out towards the loading ramp.

Jez glanced around the cockpit one last time.

The tension in her muscles that always seemed to come whenever she contemplated stepping outside of her perfect cockpit and her lovely, graceful ship was already tightening her chest.

She took a deep breath.

It would be fine. She'd been grounded in Prasvishoni for basically ever during their university job, and at least here she wouldn't be grounded, not really. She was still in deep space, still on a ship, even though it was a ship she wasn't steering and couldn't control. But it would be fine.

Anyways, this was the mafia. Probably wouldn't be boring, at the very least. She'd never flown for the mafia, not even in her smuggling days, but some of Lena's pilots had, and they told stories that made Lena look like a damn angel in comparison. Maybe she'd get lucky, and someone would draw on her. She could use a fight right about now, to be honest.

She closed her eyes for a moment, then took one last regretful look around her exquisite, flawless cockpit, trailing her fingers across the controls one last time. Then she followed Masha out to the loading ramp.

When she arrived, the others were already there. Ysbel and Tanya stood to one side, the children between them. They'd discussed, back on Prasvishoni, leaving Olya and Misko behind with the street kids, but Tanya had flatly refused.

"The last time I left my children, they were almost killed," she'd said, in a tone that did not invite discussion. "I am not doing it again."

And to be honest, Tanya was probably the deadliest person on the crew, and Ysbel was a very close second, and if the kids weren't safe with them, then there was probably nowhere in the system they would be.

"Hey Misko," she said, grinning at the six-year-old who was currently scowling at the world. "You remember what I taught you this morning?"

Tanya shot her a look that could have started wet concrete on fire.

"Perhaps now is not the time," Ysbel murmured.

"You're all a bunch of scum-sucking plague-eaters," Misko repeated with relish.

Tanya's expression grew, if possible, more threatening. Jez grinned at her.

Tae sighed in exasperation. "Look, can we just focus on the fact that we're all about to march into the mafia's headquarters, and Masha's already made enemies with the krestnaya of the entire damn mafia outfit?"

Lev didn't say anything, but looked supremely irritated, which was basically all he ever did these days anyways.

Masha shot all of them a cool glance before she hit the control and the loading ramp hissed open and lowered gently to the ground.

Half a dozen mafia boyeviki were waiting at the base of the ramp. As promised, none of them had weapons drawn, but there was a look on their faces like they sincerely wished they did.

Jez understood the feeling. Honestly, her hand was itching for her heat pistol.

Masha strode down the ramp first, and, after a quick glance around, the others fell into step behind her.

"Follow me," one of the boyevik grunted, gesturing curtly with her chin, and Masha nodded pleasantly. The woman turned, with a suspicious glance over her shoulder at them, and started off, and the other boyeviki fell into a loose semicircle around them. Their guns weren't drawn, maybe, but Jez's muscles were tight, and there was an itch behind her shoulder blades, because she'd run with Lena's crew long enough to know damn well how little that meant. She could see the subtle hints—the hands thrust into a suspiciously-heavy pocket of a jacket, the calculating way their escorts spread out around them —a couple shots each for the grownups, probably, maybe take the kids out with one.

If Grigory wanted them dead—well, even with Ysbel's weapons, they didn't stand a chance.

The woman leading them paused in front of the airlock and typed something into the controls, and the massive doors hissed open. Then they followed her through into the body of the ship.

Despite the adrenalin pumping through her, Jez couldn't help but stare. She'd never in her life seen a ship like this. Hell, she'd never imagined a ship like this. The corridor floors were covered in smooth panelling, made to look like dark, rich wood, and the walls were painted in muted colours and decorated with artwork that didn't look like anything Jez had ever seen before, but probably cost a hell of a lot of money. The ceilings were high, not the low, cramped spaces she was used to, and there were skylights opening out onto the deep black of space.

For a moment, she ached, irrationally, for the familiar, smooth, low-ceilinged corridors of the *Ungovernable*, the soothing sweet musky smell of crystallized wood sap from its paneling, the odd ways the hallways bent and the comfortable imperfections of the paneling.

She sucked in a deep breath.

Must be going soft. She wasn't actually used to missing anything.

Well, OK, that was wrong. Honestly, since she'd first set foot in her gorgeous ship she'd missed it like a constant ache in her chest every time she stepped off it. But she was usually too distracted to notice.

The corridor was absurdly long, with the occasional door to one side or the other. But when they passed through another set of blast doors and turned one final corridor, it became instantly obvious where they were going.

Ahead of them, at the end of the hallway, was another door, made of real wood that matched the luxurious dark floor panelling. It was polished until it gleamed, and the frame around it was plated in solid gold. Or hell, maybe it actually was solid gold. She'd never actually been a mafia krestnaya—maybe Grigory got off on that sort of thing.

The woman who was leading them tapped respectfully at the door.

"Yes?" came the raspy voice they'd heard earlier.

"Sir. I've brought Masha Volkova to see you. Along with her ..." She glanced back at them, appearing somewhat at a loss for words.

"Of course. Let them in."

There was a *click*, and the woman turned the golden door handle and pushed it gently open. She gestured them inside.

"Thank you," said Masha, with a polite nod, and she stepped past the woman into the office.

Jez took a deep breath, and followed.

The first thing that struck her, as she stepped inside, was the thick, heavy, almost oppressive weight of opulence that gleamed from every surface and seemed to permeate the air itself. From the thick plush carpet on the floor to the small and clearly invaluable trinkets on the desk to the desk itself, heavy and made of a solid, expensive-looking wood inlayed with gold, the entire office reeked of credits.

The second thing she noticed, which probably should have been the first thing, actually, were the five bodyguards, standing unobtrusively against the walls, weapons out of sight but bulging menacingly from their pockets and holsters under their jackets.

And finally, she noticed the man sitting behind the huge, opulent desk.

And the moment she met his eyes, she knew, gut-deep and without question, that this was Grigory.

There was nothing about him, taken separately, that would have set him apart from the people around him. His black hair was going to grey, neatly trimmed and falling to his shoulders, his face slightly creased with age, the muscular bulk of him almost hidden under his dark jacket and black shirt.

But one look at his face told her exactly who this was.

There was a cold cruelty in his eyes, scowl-lines on his face, a simmering rage behind his calm demeanour. He had an arrogant set to his posture that showed he belonged on this luxurious ship.

Hell, belonged on it? The whole damn thing belonged to him.

And every instinct in her body told her that this wasn't a person you'd want to cross.

Well, unless you were a hell of a lot more stir-crazy than even she was right at this moment.

He looked up at them and smiled, a perfunctory sort of smile that did nothing to disguise the hungry ruthlessness in his face.

"Masha," he said, standing and pushing back his seat. "I'm so glad you could make it. Are you going to introduce me to these others?"

"Of course," said Masha, all politeness. "This is Jez, Lev, Tae, Ysbel and Tanya, and their children, Olya and Misko."

"You bring children into my office, Masha Volkova?" Grigory said with amusement, looking down at them.

Olya seemed to have come to the same conclusion as Jez about this man, and she stood between her mothers' legs, holding tight to her younger brother, eyes wide and frightened.

One look at Tanya's face, though, and Jez knew that Grigory wasn't the only person in that office you wouldn't want to cross.

"As I recall, you brought children onto your ship previously, which is why we are here having this discussion," said Masha, her voice polite, but businesslike. "Peti?"

"Of course," he said smoothly. He turned to one of the bodyguards and made a quick motion with his head, and the woman left the room out a door behind the desk. Out of the corner of her eye Jez caught the slight stiffening in Tae's posture, the way his breathing had gone shallow and quick. And then, a moment later, the woman returned leading someone behind her.

There was a dark hood over the figure's face. Behind Jez, Tae sucked in a quick breath and Tanya made an almost involuntary move forward.

The guard stepped back, and Grigory gestured, a small smile on his face. "Go on. Show them. As my friend Masha said, she's kept her end of the bargain."

One of the guards pulled the hood back, revealing the terrified face of a girl Jez recognized from weeks ago, in a hangar-bay in Prasvishoni. Tae started forward, but Tanya grabbed his arm.

"Show them. She's fine." Grigory was still smiling expansively. "You're fine, aren't you, little girl?"

Peti gave a small, frightened nod.

Jez felt slightly sick.

There was steel in Masha's voice when she spoke. "So," she said. "Do you hood all your guests? You told me—"

"She's fine." Grigory waived a dismissive hand. "She's been treated well, look at her. She was half-dead from starving when we picked her up."

"Nevertheless, I'd like to talk to her alone."

"Of course. As soon as we're done meeting here. She will be waiting just outside the door. I have nothing to hide from you." He nodded at the guard, and Peti was pulled out of the room.

Jez glanced back. Tae's face was strained, his fists clenched.

She didn't know much about Tae's life before he joined the *Ungovernable*, but she knew that Peti and that other kid, Caz, had been basically the closest thing he'd ever had to family.

"So, Masha," said Grigory after a moment. "As you can see, I've kept my part of the bargain. She's safe, and will be sent back to Prasvishoni the moment we are finished here, if you like. And now," he gestured to a chair across from his desk, "I believe we have something to discuss."

"So I have been informed," murmured Masha, but Jez knew her well enough to see the tension, almost hidden, in her posture, the tightness in the muscles of her jaw.

Jez glanced around the room quickly.

As far as she knew, Masha hadn't told the others. Jez hadn't either —for some reason, she hadn't said anything about the conversation she and Masha had had weeks ago in a dark corner behind a university building they were on their way to break into.

Masha's parents had been killed, she'd said. Murdered. By the government, and the mafia.

And the man back at the hangar bay had called Masha something —Mari, he'd called her.

If she told Lev, he'd probably be able to figure it out, find out exactly who this Mari person was and how she'd turned into Masha, and what had happened to Masha's parents. But …

Well, but somehow that would have felt strangely like a betrayal. Because Masha hadn't had to tell her that. She'd done it because— well, Jez still wasn't exactly certain why, because it didn't actually make sense, but it had almost felt like she'd done it to make Jez feel better. To trust Jez with her own painful secret, after Jez had told hers.

And so she hadn't mentioned it, the entire two weeks they'd been preparing for this. She figured Masha'd tell if she felt like it.

And Masha never had.

And now, standing in the office of the mafia krestnaya, perhaps the most powerful person outside of the Svodrani System government, and looking at Masha, Jez wondered if maybe she'd made a mistake.

She shrugged inwardly.

If she had, well, probably a little late for second thoughts now.

She couldn't seem to hold back her grin, and nervous energy pulsed though her like a damn heartbeat.

"These people," Grigory gestured at the rest of them. "They are your people, Masha?"

"They are my associates," said Masha calmly.

Grigory studied them, his eyes narrowed. There was a look in his eyes, a calculating look of someone who believed killing them would be as easy as snapping his fingers, and for just one moment Jez was desperate for him to damn well try. She shot him back her best cocky grin, every muscle in her whole body on edge. He paused, looking at her a little more closely. She gave him a wink, and his face darkened slightly.

"And I assume you find them useful?" he asked again after a moment, directing the question at Masha.

She gave him one of her bland smiles. "As I said, they're my associates. They do have certain talents, and we've worked together for some time now. I value their contributions."

Grigory glanced over them again, expression showing nothing of what he was thinking.

"Alright," he said at last, leaning forward, his hands on his desk. "Masha. I will get straight to the point. You want something. It's been, what, three, four months? And in that time, you've destroyed my relationship with Vitali Dobrev, you've set off an arms race between me and the government, you've broken thousands of political prisoners, including my people and people belonging to my rivals, out of prison, and you've taken out Lena's entire smuggling cartel." He smiled expansively, but there was a cruelty in his face. "And I am looking for a way to re-set the balance."

He leaned back in his seat, lacing his fingers behind his head. "When you pulled your stunt with Dobrev, both the government and I tried to use you to our advantage. And we were both left looking the fool. I can't help but respect your intelligence, even as I suffer from it. And so the balance of power has shifted, and both the government and myself are scrambling to find the advantage, and desperate people will do desperate things, and, as always, people will die." He studied Masha as he spoke, as if trying to gage her reaction, but of course the damn bastard looked as calm as if she'd just woken up, eaten a good meal, and sat down for a morning of paperwork.

"Of course, I'm telling something you already know, aren't I? None of this was an accident. But you know something else too. The government is planning something. They want an advantage. And I believe you know what they are planning." He leaned across the desk. "But then, I'm also certain you know how badly they want to kill you. You're very smart, yes, but they are very, very powerful. Me though? I'm not like them. I admire what you've done. And I would like to discuss how we can help each other."

Masha looked at him for a long time, and again Jez noticed that faint, unfamiliar tension in her. "Grigory," she said at last. "You are correct. I know a great deal about what the government is planning to do to angle for power. I'm very certain that I can give you information that you would find pricelessly valuable. But—" she paused a moment. "I will unfortunately need some answers from you before I do that." She glanced behind her, her eyes brushing over them, and for a moment the look on her face almost jolted Jez.

It wasn't her normal pleasant expression. Her face looked dead, as if there was no emotion there because there was no emotion in her whole body.

"This is going to be a very long conversation, I'm afraid," she said blandly, turning back to Grigory. "And we've had a long flight. Perhaps you could find a place for my colleagues to rest and refresh themselves while we talk?"

Something cold prickled in Jez's stomach.

She'd never seen that expression on Masha's face before. But knowing what she knew—well, she wasn't certain what Masha was planning, but she had the sudden, uncomfortable feeling that it probably wasn't anything good.

Grigory didn't take his eyes off Masha's face, and Jez got the sense that he was trying to read her just as hard as Jez was, and with just as little success.

At last he nodded. "As you say. You've had a long flight, and I'm certain our young guest would like to catch up with her friends before we send her home."

"Masha," said Lev in a level tone, stepping forward. "Perhaps you should come back with us. I'm certain you're as tired as we are. The conversation will go better, I believe, after you've refreshed yourself."

Masha turned to him and studied him for a long moment, with that same unfamiliar expression on her face. At last she shook her head.

"I appreciate your consideration, Lev, but no. I believe I will be fine."

Jez glanced between them, and for a moment she didn't know if

Lev would push the issue, and what Masha would do if he did.

And she realized, suddenly, that she didn't know Lev, not nearly as well as she thought she did. Because the Lev she'd thought she knew, the Lev she'd kissed and harassed and—well, and almost maybe started to have feelings for—no, she wasn't going to think about that, because that had been a mistake, maybe the worst damn mistake she'd ever made in her life, and that was saying something—since their job in the university, had been replaced by this Lev, cold, and clinical, and completely devoid of any emotion other than a sort of distant curiosity.

And she had no idea what this Lev was capable of.

Lev and Masha were still watching each other, neither dropping their eyes, and she could feel her muscles tensing. Then, at last, Lev turned aside with a wry smile.

"Very well, Masha. As you say, you are in the best position to judge that."

Grigory was glancing between the two of them, but now he nodded, and gestured with his head to two of the guards.

"Take them to the guest suites, please," he said. "Give them the amber suite, I think. Take our young guest there as well, I'm sure they'll be happy to see her."

The guards stepped forward, and one of them motioned for them to follow him out the door, while the other fell into place behind them. Grigory tapped a button on his desk, and the lock on the heavy door clicked, and for the first time Jez realized they'd been locked in, and the thought sent an irrational jolt of panic through her. Then the guard pulled open the door and led them out.

They walked back down the oppressively-luxurious corridor a few metres and through another door, and then they stepped through into a wide, open space that skirted the edge of a large room.

Suddenly, Jez forgot her panic.

Because this? This was beautiful.

It was a gambling hall, but a gambling hall like nothing she'd ever seen before. The tables were a rich green stone, the carpets the dark of deep space, with patterns of gold threaded through them that ran up the columns like spreading vines. And yes, the last time she'd seen spreading vines they'd been trying to actually eat her, but still … The walls were shades of the same blue-black as the carpet and, and there were markers on the tables for all the gambling games she knew and some she didn't. And she'd been pretty certain she knew them all. To one side was the long, low bar where bottles of not just sump, but all sorts of drinks, most of which looked like something that would cost almost too much to actually drink but she'd damn well love to try, were laid out temptingly in dark bottles, and delicate glasses hung from the low ceiling of the bar.

OK, so this wasn't her beautiful ship, and she wasn't flying.

But hell, it was a close second. And every part of her, every restless nerve in her body, wanted to stop right where she was and sit down at at one of those tables.

She could feel the grin spreading across her face, so wide she could hardly contain it.

"Jez," muttered Ysbel warningly.

She realized she'd already come to a stop, staring longingly at the gorgeous, elegant tables, with the smooth gambling tokens she could almost feel in her hands.

"You play?" asked the guard behind her, amusement in her voice, and Jez almost started in surprise. She turned, still grinning.

"Have done, once or twice."

The guard gave her a speculative look, face slightly amused. "I'm guessing you never played in a place like this."

"Nope. Backwater kabaks, mostly."

The guard raised her eyebrows. "Well, here we're used to people who can handle a loaded credit chip, if you take my meaning."

"Ah, I can always pay what I play," said Jez. She was still grinning, and the sight of the gambling hall was a little bit like a drug, and she could sure as hell use a drug after the last couple weeks.

"Well," said the guard, "maybe if you end up staying a day or two, the boss man will invite you down here. It's happened before." She shrugged slightly. "Might be a bit much for you, if you've only ever played in backwaters, but …"

Jez's cheeks hurt from grinning, but she couldn't stop. "Well, you know what they say, never know 'til you try."

Tae sighed and grabbed her elbow. "Jez. Come on. We're not here to gamble, for the Lady's sake."

She rolled her eyes at him, then shot a wink at their guard over her shoulder. "You ever want to throw some tokens—"

Tae shook his head and pulled her forward after the first guard.

It took only a few minutes more to arrive at what must have been the guest quarters, but honestly, Jez was hardly paying attention. Because if she had to be on this damn ship, she wanted to be back there in the gambling hall, and yes, she knew she probably wouldn't be this desperate for gambling chips and something to drink if it wasn't for the fact that she was so completely stir-crazy that she might actually go out of her damn mind, and if it wasn't for the fact that—well, anyways, if it wasn't for the fact that even looking at that damn idiot Lev still made her stomach twist uncomfortably. And she wasn't sure if it was because she still couldn't stop thinking about how it had felt to kiss him, or if it was because she was going to actually be sick. Because there was that other thing too, the morning she'd woken up in his cot in the *Ungovernable*, with her head nestled into his shoulder, his arms wrapped around her and that lost look on his face even in his sleep, and she'd looked up at him and for half a moment she was going to kiss him awake, slowly, and maybe they'd lock the door and they wouldn't leave his cabin for the rest of the damn day.

And then she'd remembered, and she'd thought she might throw up.

Because she'd actually come into his room the night before—before he'd stopped her, asked her in that desperate, pleading tone she'd never heard from him before, if they could talk in the morning, and she'd fallen asleep with him holding onto her like she was the only thing keeping him sane—she'd actually come to tell him that they were done. That she couldn't do this, and if she tried she was going to screw it up and hurt him because that was just what she did in relationships, and the problem was she actually cared about him, and so she couldn't do it.

And so she'd told him, or at least started to, and funny thing was, before she could, he'd told her something similar, with that sort of cold, distant look on his face he'd basically been wearing ever since the university. That it was probably better if they weren't together, better for both of them. And hell, they'd both been right, it was better, it was basically one hundred percent better.

And there was no damn reason why even the thought of it made her want to cry, which made her want even more to head down to the gambling hall, since the only other option was maybe just explode.

"Go on," said the guard who was leading them. He unlocked the door and gestured them inside. "There's a lounge with some food and drink, and bedrooms around the side. You can wait for Masha here."

"Thank you," said Lev, in that polite, detached voice, and stepped past him into the room. Tae caught Jez's quick glance behind her and grabbed her arm again.

"Jez. Relax," he said in a low voice. "It's going to be fine. Masha's not going to lead us into a trap. Just get in here."

She took a deep breath.

The guards had called it a guest suite, but she wasn't a damn idiot. This was a plaguing prison.

Still—

She closed her eyes for half a second, then followed Tae into the room, and tried not to hear the sound of the door locking behind them.

4

Lev stepped back as the door closed behind the guards, and let Tae step around him.

Peti stood against the wall. Lev bit the inside of his cheek, something tightening in his stomach. Her hood was removed, but the stark fear on her face was still apparent, and Tae walked towards her like he wasn't sure if he was awake or dreaming.

"Peti?" Tae said at last, reaching out to touch her arm.

For a moment she stood still, posture so stiff she could have been made of stone. Then she collapsed against Tae, shoulders shaking in silent sobs, and Lev realized with a jolt just how young she was— sixteen at the most.

Tae clutched her like he was drowning, tension in every line of his body.

"Peti," he whispered, voice choked. "Are you alright? Really? Did they hurt you?"

Peti pulled back, blinking hard. "I'm fine," she said in a low voice. "Caz? The other kids?"

"Safe. All of them," said Tae. He glanced around quickly at the rest of the room, and Lev followed his gaze.

Ysbel and Tanya were in the centre of the room, the children

46

huddled between them, and Jez had that trapped, reckless look in her eyes that generally meant trouble for everyone, and he almost reached out to put a steadying hand on her arm, then realized what he'd been about to do just in time.

"Well," said Ysbel at last. "I hope Masha knows what she's doing."

Tanya said nothing, but her face was pinched, her expression hard.

"I'm certain she has everything under control," Lev said, his voice mild. He glanced at Tae as he spoke, raising his eyebrows meaningfully. Tae frowned and gave Lev a quick nod. He pulled Peti over to one of the seats and sat her down, huddling down next to her so their bodies shielded his com. Jez seemed to pick up on what they were doing, because she sauntered over and stood casually in front of them, leaning up against the wall and grinning in that lazy, dangerous way she had.

"Olya," he said, "are you and Misko hungry? It looks like they have some desserts out on the table."

She gave him a skeptical look, one eyebrow raised. Then she said, in her primmest voice, "Yes, uncle Lev, I'd like some desserts, thank you."

"You and Misko help yourself," he said. "But please don't make trouble."

He couldn't help but smile to himself as she slipped away from her mothers.

Of course she'd catch on. Leave it to Olya to figure things out quicker than most adults would have.

He glanced over at Tae out of the corner of his eye as Olya spooned a colourful gelatinous substance onto Misko's plate.

There are three cameras, Tae tapped out over the com in pilot's code. *Enough bugs that it's going to be difficult to spoof them all. I need a minute.*

Lev moved nonchalantly closer to Tae, and noticed Ysbel and Tanya doing the same.

Behind him, Olya tilted Misko's plate just a little too far, and something that looked a bit like a rainbow-coloured pile of vomit landed on the expensive carpet.

"Misko," Olya scolded impatiently, as Misko managed to plant a foot in the centre of the still-jiggling rainbow disaster. He grinned, then tried it again with the other foot.

Tae looked up, his face grim, but triumphant. "Got it," he said in a low voice. "Camera watching this corner of the room is spoofed, and I got the bugs tied into it so they'll hear a spliced loop, but fuzzed out so it'll just sound like a temporary malfunction."

Lev glanced over and gave Olya a small wink. She grinned at him, sighed dramatically for the camera, and grabbed for her younger brother, who slipped out of reach, giggling hysterically and leaving slime-coloured footprints behind him, like a large, two-legged slug.

Lev shook his head slightly.

Olya was the only eight-year-old with whom he'd ever had a close interaction, but he was fairly certain that by the time she hit about fifteen, she'd be ready to run the entire system on her own.

He pulled up a seat as close as he could to Tae and the others. "Peti?" Tanya asked as they sat. "Are you hurt?"

The girl looked at them warily, then back at Tae.

Tae put a hand gently on her arm. "Peti, it's fine. They're safe, I promise."

"I'm alright," she said at last, in a low voice. "They didn't hurt me. I thought they would."

For a moment, looking at the kid, Lev felt his chest tighten slightly.

She'd thought they would. Of course she'd thought they would, he would have thought the same thing in her place. And she'd gone anyways, because it was the only thing she could think of to save her brother and her friends and Misko and Olya.

"But—" she turned back to Tae. "Tae, you have to get out of here. You all have to get out of here now. You have no idea what they're like. They're—I learned things about them, Tae. They—I don't know what your friend is talking to them about, but we have to get out."

"I know," said Tae softly, but Lev could hear the steel in his tone.

"What is Masha up to?" asked Tanya softly, and there was an echoing note of steel in her own tone. "I don't like this at all."

"I don't like that she asked us to leave," said Lev quietly. "I know Masha has her secrets. She's always had her secrets. But this?"

"I'm not having anything to do with the mafia," said Tae, his voice tight. "Peti's right. I know Masha thinks they might have information on how to stop the government's program, but I have a feeling whatever they want in return is going to be more than any of us want to pay."

Lev glanced over at Jez. She'd been uncharacteristically quiet.

"Well," she said at last, "figure the least we can do is wait until that bastard Masha comes back and tells us what she's up to."

"If she tells us what she's up to," Lev said quietly.

She glared at him. "Listen. Masha keeps her secrets, OK? I get it. But … look, she's always pulled through so far. Figure it's worth at least giving her a chance."

There were a few moments of silence as they looked at each other. There was a tight unease in Lev's stomach.

He'd always trusted Masha, up until now. Kept an eye on her, yes, but when push came to shove, he trusted her.

But there had been something about the expression on her face when she asked for all of them to be escorted from the room. There was something here he didn't understand, and he had a feeling that whatever it was was about to become very, very important.

"I don't know Masha, and I don't know what you know about the mafia," said Peti, looking around at the rest of them. There was defiance behind the fear in her expression. "But listen to me. These people are murders. If you get sucked into this—Tae, you'll never get out."

Lev glanced around at the others. Ysbel was still wearing her stoic expression, and Tae, Tanya, and Peti all looked concerned.

And for some reason, he couldn't read Jez's expression, and that was unaccountably disconcerting.

"Ysbel," he said quietly. "What happens if they try to keep us here?"

Ysbel gave a small smirk. "Then I suppose we blow up his ship."

Jez glared at her. "That's my damn ship you're talking about too, Ysbel."

"Well, pilot-girl, I'm pretty sure your ship is safe, because I'm pretty sure that mister Grigory Korzhikov isn't going to want his ship cracked wide open to deep space."

Lev sighed. "Has Masha let anything slip to anyone about what she's planning here?"

There was another long moment of silence. Jez looked slightly uncomfortable, and he frowned. "Jez?"

She glared at him. "Listen, genius-boy—"

There was a tap on the door, and they all jumped. "Stand up," Tae hissed. "Get the chairs back."

There was a moment of mild chaos as they jumped to their feet and shoved chairs away, and then the lock clicked and the door swung open.

One of Grigory's guards stood there, and behind him stood

Masha, as cool and calm as ever.

"What exactly is going on here?" asked the guard, eyeing the spot on the carpet that now looked like a multicoloured invertebrate had spontaneously exploded, as the children chased each other around the edges of the room, both of them now laughing hysterically as they slipped in the goo that Misko trailed behind him.

"I'm certain whatever it is, they have it under control," said Masha pleasantly. She stepped past the guard into the room. "Thank you for your assistance. I will call you the moment I need your services." She smiled at the guard, and the guard gave what looked like an almost-involuntary smile in return, and once again, Lev caught himself wondering how Masha did what she did. Then he stepped out, and Masha closed the door gently behind him, then turned and surveyed the room.

"Well," she said. "It appears your time was not uneventful."

"Aunty Masha!" shouted Misko, hurtling across the room towards her. Lev hid a smile as she somehow managed to catch him without getting rainbow-coloured goo smeared across her pilot's coat.

"Hello Misko. How are you?" She glanced over quickly at Tae, and Lev followed her gaze. Tae tapped, *give me two minutes.*

"Masha," said Lev loudly, stepping forwards. "So. It appears that Grigory didn't actually kill you?"

"No, he thankfully did not," said Masha calmly, taking a napkin from the table and wiping down Misko's hands. "However, he did have a rather interesting proposal he presented to me."

Lev raised his eyebrows.

Why tell them on camera? Why let Grigory know that she intended to brief them?

Masha was playing her game, whatever it was, and he had no idea what the rules were, but the stakes—

He glanced involuntarily back at Jez.

The stakes were a hell of a lot higher than he was willing to risk.

Jez was right—after three and a half months, and more near-death experiences than he really liked to think about, Masha had always come through for them in the end.

He just wished that it wasn't such a damn gamble every time as to which side she was playing.

"I'm glad to hear it," he said, keeping his tone neutral.

Masha smiled at him, then glanced over at Tae, who was still bent over his com screen.

Tae looked up and nodded, his face tight. *I have it back on the spliced loop,* he tapped. *We can talk over in the corner, like before.*

Masha released Misko to wreak havoc with Olya, and the adults brought their chairs back into position. They took their seats, and Masha looked over them.

As usual, Lev could read nothing from her face, but there was an unexpected hardness behind her eyes .

"Grigory's offer," Masha said at last, "was that we—or I, at least —join him."

There was a long moment of absolute silence.

"And I assume you told him where he could put that offer?" grunted Ysbel.

"No," said Masha simply. "I agreed."

The silence stretched.

Lev glanced at the others, his heart pounding more quickly. Ysbel looked suspicious. Tanya's face was set, her mouth pressed into a tight line. Jez frowned warily. And Tae looked like Masha had slapped him in the face.

"Explain," Lev said quietly.

Masha smiled at him, but the smile didn't reach her eyes. "Of course." She paused a moment. "After our Vitali job and then the prison break, Grigory wanted to propose an alliance. Both the government and the mafia are currently struggling to gain an advantage, and he saw us as an opportunity."

Tae shifted slightly, as if about to speak, but she held up a hand. "Tae. A moment please. After he made his offer, I explained what has been happening in Prasvishoni. What the government has planned with the Vyernist Protocol. And he and I—discussed ways in which he may be able to assist us." She paused again for a moment, and Lev found his heart was beating even faster than it had been, from nerves or anticipation or both.

Because he knew Masha.

He didn't know if he could trust her. He didn't know how much she was keeping from them. But he was very, very certain that she wanted to solve their problem almost as badly as he did.

And they were going to succeed, somehow, because, like Masha, he didn't actually care what it would take.

As had happened so often over the past two weeks, a memory flashed in front of his eyes, Jez lying on his lap blinking up at him sleepily, soft smile on her face. Panic spiking through his brain as he grabbed for the com, trying desperately to solve the riddle his old professor had set for him before the explosive she'd planted in Jez's neck went off, a soft *pop* and Jez's body going limp, her bright, intelligent eyes dimming to a flat, dead sheen, her blood soaking through his clothing and into his skin. He'd woken to nightmares of that imagined sound, over and over and over.

And every damn time, he swore that it would remain a nightmare, that Evka would never, never do that to Jez, or to Tae or Ysbel or Tanya, or to Olya, or Misko, or Tae's street-kid friends. She'd never threaten someone he loved again, because he'd find a way to stop it, and stop her, and he'd tear down the entire system to do it.

"And he said," said Masha at last, quietly, "that he could help."

"How?" asked Lev, in that same cool voice.

"He intends to take back his power in the system government," she said quietly. "He had planned to invite a select few government officials out to an event that will appear to be a legitimate financial symposium, and woo them over to his side without raising suspicion. He has been severely weakened, more than he wants to admit, by our actions, and this may be his best and possibly last chance to re-establish his connections in government. He's desperate for it to succeed. And so he's asking our help to pull it off. My connections in government are what he's after, specifically, but I believe he'd also welcome your skills at strategy, and Ysbel's ability to create a threat if necessary. And in return, he's offered to invite the woman who is in charge of the Vyernist Protocol—the Minister of Innovations and Development—to the symposium as well. And once she arrives, he's offered to kill her."

There was another long moment of silence.

Lev's mind was racing.

Masha wasn't telling them everything, he wasn't naive enough to think that for one moment.

But—what she'd described wasn't a terrible plan, as plans went.

Agree to work with Grigory in pulling off whatever scheme he wanted their help with.

And in return, Grigory would kill the people in charge of the government program to control the system.

It wouldn't stop the Vyernist Protocol, not permanently, not yet. But it would slow it down, give them time. He knew how this government worked—take out the person with knowledge of how to deal with the program, and there would be months of paperwork and infighting as the Central Committee and Counsel of Ministers tried to decide on who would replace her. And then, once she was finally replaced, it would be even more time before the replacement would be able to get all the people who'd worked on the program to trust them enough to give them the information they needed, and then the paperwork, and then getting the program up and running —it could give them months. And by then he'd have found a solution, one way or another.

"Lev?" asked Ysbel finally. "Would that work?"

He looked at her for a moment.

Once upon a time, perhaps, he might have believed he wasn't the kind of person who'd work with a man like Grigory.

But—well, but two and a half weeks ago, he'd stood in the basement of a government building, rigged to explode. Full of people—some who'd tried to kill them, yes, but more, many more, who were just doing their jobs, trying to make enough credits to feed themselves or their families for the month.

Lev had been willing to let them die. Tae had tried to evacuate the building, and Lev had stopped him.

Circumstances had intervened, of course, and the building was evacuated before it exploded. But in that moment, Lev had realized he was much, much more like his former mentor Evka than he'd ever imagined.

And perhaps, after all, that was precisely what was needed.

He gave her a faint smile. "Yes, Ysbel. That would be effective." He turned back to Masha. "Masha. Tell him we'll need to kill the Minister's two assistants as well."

Masha nodded, still watching him. "And if I did that, and he agreed?" she asked at last.

"Then I would agree to his proposal," said Lev quietly.

Jez, laying on his lap, her blood soaking his clothing and the couch and spattered across the floor in a faint mist, her restless, wiry form still, her eyes open and sightless.

He'd burn the damn system down if that's what it took to stop Evka.

Tae stared at Lev, ice coating his chest.

Lev wasn't looking at him. He was looking at Masha, and there was that faint smile on his face that Tae had seen there only a few times before, and every single damn time it meant that Lev was going to do something that Tae knew he was going to regret.

He'd known Lev for all of a few months. But he'd trusted him with his life more than he'd imagined trusting anyone.

And he wasn't entirely sure he knew who Lev was anymore.

He glanced over at Peti, and saw the same horror on her face that he felt.

He shoved back his chair and stood abruptly. "No. Masha. I'm sorry. I'm not doing this."

Everyone turned to look at him. He shook his head sharply.

"This is the mafia! I've seen what they do. I know plenty of people who decided to take them up on offers, and not a single one of those people is still alive." He turned to Masha. "Masha. You said you'd worked across from the mafia before. You must know this as well as I do."

She was silent.

Ysbel raised her head. "Tae. I understand you're upset. But Grigory may be the answer to our problem."

He opened his mouth, and she held up a hand. "I'm not saying we work with the mafia long-term. But he is asking for our help with one project. We work with him this one time, and all of us leave with a benefit. In prison, we used the prison gangs to make what we needed to happen, happen. I don't see why it should be different here."

"Because in prison, we weren't working with the damn prison gangs!" he exploded. "Lev turned them against each other, and we let things take their course. We didn't grab a bunch of pin-guns and start killing people for them."

"And was it really all that different?" Ysbel asked quietly.

He glared at her. "Yes. It was."

"Well," said Jez at last, and he looked over quickly. There was an odd look on her face, and she was watching Masha. "I don't know anything about any of that crap. I'll tell you, I'd rather work with a swamp rat than with the damn mafia. But—" she paused a moment. "But I suppose—I mean, look. We've done a lot of crap together so far. And so far—I mean, Masha's worked with this bastard before. If she's going to vouch for this plan, guess I'm willing to give it a try." She reverted to her usual sharp grin. "And if things go sideways, guess we've all got our heat pistols."

Tae stared at her in disbelief. "Jez. Are you seriously saying that if things go badly, we can shoot our way out of here?"

She grinned at him. "Never know 'til you try."

"I—actually, yes, I do know! There's no way you could—"

She smirked and patted her jacket pocket. "Guess you haven't seen Ysbel's latest mods."

"What I saw," he grumbled, "was you grabbing the wrong damn pistol off the table two days ago and almost getting shot down."

"Yeah? Well if you remember, I'm still here, and they're back in Prasvishoni nursing headaches, so—"

He glared at her.

"Tae," said Lev, turning to him. For just a moment he thought he saw the Lev he remembered, the thoughtful expression and piercing gaze that he recognized from months of working with him, and for just a moment he relaxed despite himself.

"Tae, listen," Lev said. "I understand how you feel. But this may be our best chance. It may be our only chance. You know as well as I do that we haven't had any success in stopping the Protocol so far. This gives us time. This saves Caz and the others. This saves all of us." His expression was intent, his voice mild, like it always was.

Like it had been that day two and a half weeks ago, when Tae had been about to turn on the alarm in the building they were about to blow to pieces, to warn the hundreds of innocent people, government workers and support staff and people who'd gotten caught up in it somehow, to get out of the building, and Lev had put his hand over Tae's and said in that same, mild voice, "No, Tae. I'm not going to let you."

Lev had been willing to bring the building down on all of those people, kill them without a second thought. And the thing was, Tae couldn't even blame him. He might have wanted to do the same thing, in Lev's situation.

But he couldn't trust him anymore, either.

He shook his head slowly. "No. Look, I agree, we need to figure this out. But not like this. Not working with the mafia. I won't do it."

Lev was still watching him, that mild expression on his face. Ysbel turned towards him as well, looking at him thoughtfully. Then she turned away, back to Masha.

"Masha," she said quietly, and even though she didn't look at him, he knew she was talking to him as much as she was to Masha. "I don't like this. I don't like the mafia. But my family has breathed in this gas. Tae's friends. My students in the university. And I will do what it takes to stop it. But, I understand that this will not be everyone's choice. So I'm with you, but only as long as those who don't agree are able to leave."

There was something cold in Tae's chest, and something choking in his throat.

"Yeah," said Jez. "Like I said. I don't like this, but hell, figure working with these bastards can't be a whole lot worse than working with Lena. And if it is, I'm out. But tech-head's damn well not going to have to work with them if he doesn't want to."

"Of course," said Masha, after a moment. "I would never expect that." She turned to Tae, and gave him an appraising look. "Tae. I do understand your position. And so, I believe that perhaps the best option at this point is if you took Peti back to Prasvishoni to rejoin the other street children. I'm certain I could talk Grigory into allowing Jez to take you back, and then returning. You could wait for us there."

Tae stared at her, and then glanced at the others.

Jez was watching him, Ysbel was staring straight ahead, and Lev wouldn't meet his eye.

Damn it. Damn it to hell. They actually meant it, they actually meant for him to go back to Prasvishoni, stay somewhere safe until everything blew over, if they succeeded, or if they failed, until the government killed every last one of them.

He'd known plenty of people who'd thought they could work with the mafia, whose bargains had been no less desperate than Masha's. And every last one of them was dead.

He glanced helplessly at Peti. She was staring back at him, but it had been so long since he'd spent any time with her that he couldn't tell, anymore, what she was thinking

Damn it to hell.

He closed his eyes for a moment and took a long breath. "Look,

Masha," he said, and the harshness in his voice surprised him. "I'm not going to leave you all to get killed, OK? I won't help the mafia, but I'm not leaving."

Masha raised her eyebrows. "There's no shame in—"

"I'm not talking about shame!" he snapped. "I'm talking about the fact that we're crewmates, and I'm not going to let you all get killed. I'm not going to have anything to do with the mafia. I won't help them, and if you ask me to, I'll refuse. You can tell them I'm your soft, useless cousin who you couldn't get rid of, I don't care. I won't lift one finger to help the mafia. But—" he gritted his teeth, hating the words before they even came out of his mouth. "But I'm not leaving, OK? You're not going to get very far if you can't even spoof their damn cameras."

There was another long pause. Everyone was staring at him, but he kept his gaze focused on Masha.

"Very well," she said at last. "Thank you, Tae." She stood. "Well, with that settled, perhaps, Tae, you might see fit to un-spoof the audio? Now that we have our responses to Grigory's proposal worked out, we can set them out again for the benefit of those who happen to be watching on the security camera feed. I will discuss with Grigory getting Peti back down to the others safely without disclosing where those others are staying. No point in giving him additional leverage."

Tae turned away, back to his corner, and tapped something quickly into his com as the others returned to their designated places.

A tight tendril of worry had wrapped itself around him, and squeezed tighter by the moment.

He'd lived on the streets long enough to know—you never deal with the mafia, not unless you wanted to end up face-down in an alley with your insides cooked solid from a heat-gun blast. What they offered street kids back in Prasvishoni was hard to pass up—security, protection from the police, enough food and credits to keep you from starving. But he'd never been tempted. Because he'd watched the kids who were recruited, watched their careers, before they inevitably ended up dead on the street somewhere.

And no matter how desperate he was, he'd never have been able to do what the kids who let themselves be recruited did, the sheer, sick violence they visited on anyone the mafia wanted punished, before they ended up a victim of it themselves. He'd seen what they left behind—body parts hacked off, victim's faces carved up like decorations, people shot with so many heat-blasts that they were hardly recognizable as human, but in such a methodical way that somehow, they were still alive, milky eyes staring out of charred flesh.

He shuddered.

And here they were, and Masha and the others had made their bargain.

He honestly couldn't think of a way that this situation could be any worse.

But judging from his past experience with this crew, he was certain he'd find out in short order.

5

Jez grinned at the man sitting across the table from her. He was middle-aged, with a stern face, dark skin, and dark hair going to grey, but even the padding of easy living on his face and body couldn't hide the lean muscle beneath.

He lowered his brows, giving her a glare that he probably thought was intimidating. But hell, she'd grown up with Lena. This plaguer needed to up his game.

Around them, the soft noises of the gambling hall were somehow on their own the sound of ridiculous opulence—the smooth, buttery tumble of gambling tokens dropping onto padded tables or smooth stone, the high, light *tink* of ice against delicate glasses, the soft liquid swish of alcohol being poured, and swirled, and sipped. The light here was low and rich—not the flickering gutter of artificial lights running short on will to live, but a soft, understated light that had been dimmed purposefully, creating a soothing half-twilight that made you think of late evenings in warm places. The rich colours of the room, the deep greens and blue-blacks and rich reds and gold, everywhere gold, saturated every surface like water.

Honestly, when this idiot said he wanted to talk, she hadn't been sure she'd be able to convince him to bring her here. But then again, she'd always been pretty damn good at finding places to gamble. Turns out this time all it had taken was their newfound status as honorary friends of Grigory, and her wide-eyed admission that she'd never played in a place like this.

And if he thought that meant that he could cheat her out of a quick few credits—well hell, she wasn't in the business of going around correcting people.

She gave the man a quick wink, and his brows lowered further. He tightened his hands around the smooth gambling chips that she could practically feel between her fingers.

"Hey now, you scared of gambling against someone you don't know?" she asked lightly.

He leaned back into his chair, studying her. He was still holding the damn gambling chips, and there was something inside her, something restless and bubbling and reckless, that needed those chips, needed to be able to do something, because she couldn't handle this.

"Jez," he said, voice slow and ponderous. "Your name is Jez. Last name?"

"Figure that doesn't really matter, does it?" She was still grinning, but her muscles were twitching, every part of her desperate to move. If this damn idiot wasn't going to play, he could at least have the decency to let her know, so she could go pick a fight or something.

He smiled slightly. "Don't worry, Jez Solokov, we've heard of you. You have a bit of a reputation, you know." He paused, studying her, rolling the smooth tokens between his fingers. "A pilot. Worked for Lena, then went off on your own. Bit of a trouble-maker."

She smiled easily. "Well see, figured being a trouble-maker wouldn't be a problem in the damn mafia."

He gave her a smile that was slightly fatherly and looked almost genuine. "Jez. Your friend Masha has vouched for you and for the others, and the krestnaya has said that he would like to work with you. But he is as aware as I am of your reputation. And so he told me it wouldn't be a bad idea for me to teach you a thing or two about how the mafia works—he isn't in the business of keeping people safe who don't follow the rules." He leaned slightly forward on the table, and Jez's heart rate sped up, her hands spread with anticipation. She could feel the comforting weight of the heat-pistol in her pocket, although she wasn't completely sure she'd get to it in time. He was heavy with muscle, but he looked like he could move fast if he needed to.

He smiled, the expression on his face slightly amused. "I'm not going to try to beat you, Jez. I'm only going to teach you some manners."

She gave him a quick smirk. "Yeah? Had a few people try to do that over the years. Never worked out very well."

He'd almost certainly try to grab her, and yes, she could almost certainly get away, but she wasn't sure she could do it without a cracked rib, and honestly, it hadn't been long enough since her last time breaking her ribs that she was anxious for a repeat. But then, it couldn't possibly be worse than doing nothing. Anyways, she was pretty damn sure she could at least break his nose to remember her by, which, yes, wasn't breaking ribs, but would give him a nice face to show to his damn boss—

He sighed. "Jez." He leaned forward, placing his forearms heavily on the table, and she watched him suspiciously.

Probably couldn't move very fast from that position, so maybe he wasn't planning on beating whatever the mafia considered to be 'manners' into her.

"You grew up in a smuggling operation. I understand that. But here in the mafia, it's different. If you are going to be working with Grigory, you have to understand that." He paused. "The most important thing here is respect, and if you can't learn respect, you are going to end up dead. Grigory is Krestnaya. You address him like that. When you meet him, you call him boss. You understand?"

She grinned. Her foot was tapping against the leg of her chair, and her fingers tingled with adrenalin. "Well, but here's the thing. I don't call anyone boss, you bastard. Ask plaguing Masha about that one if you want."

His face hardened. "Then perhaps this would be a good time to learn."

She shot him an innocent look. "Well, how about this? We play a nice, friendly game. You win, I call Grigory boss, every damn time I see him."

The man stared at her. "Do you even know who I am?"

She shrugged. "Nope. Don't have the foggiest. Does it matter?"

He was still staring. "I don't have to gamble with you for this, you know. You will call Grigory boss and treat him with respect, or you'll end up floating out in space without a space suit."

She shrugged. "I mean, he could try."

The man was still staring. At last he shook his head. "Alright, and if I were to agree with you, what happens if you win?"

She glanced around and raised her eyebrows. "I get to come in here whenever the hell I want. And, you buy me a drink. And, I don't call anyone on this damn ship 'boss.'"

He sucked in a long breath and glanced around the room, then down at the tokens in his hand.

"I mean, I get that you might be a bit nervous and all. You may as well just admit it," she said.

He turned back to her, his face now completely hard. "I asked if you knew who I was," he said softly.

"Yep. And I told you I didn't have a damn clue."

"I am Fyodor Yanovik. I'm the one who runs this gambling hall. I make Grigory a lot of money, and you should be very, very flattered indeed that he asked me to teach you manners rather than one of his less understanding people."

She shrugged. "Guess it makes sense that you're scared. I mean, you have a reputation to keep up, right? Shame to lose it to a little no-name smuggler pilot who learned to gamble in kabaks."

He narrowed his eyes. "Has anyone ever told you that you are very, very irritating?"

She gave him an innocent look.

He sighed heavily. "Very well. We gamble. One game." He pushed a pile of tokens across the table to her, and she slid them through her fingers, sighing in ecstasy.

This was more like it.

Maybe she'd live through this damn scheme of Masha's after all.

Twenty minutes later, Fyodor was glaring down at the tokens spread in front of him on the table, a look of disbelief on his face.

"You cheated," he said, looking up finally.

She grinned and shrugged. "Or maybe you just had a crap hand. Happens to the best of us."

"You cheated! And I didn't even catch it."

She shrugged again, helpfully. "Like I said, we all get a run of bad tokens now and then. And then there's me—beginner's luck and all that."

He shook his head. "I don't know what you are, Jez Solokov, but you're no beginner."

She grinned. "Guess I'm not calling Grigory 'boss.' You want to explain that to him, or should I?"

"I—" he broke off, still shaking his head. "I don't think that you understand the purpose of our little talk. I am not going to explain to Grigory that you will not call him boss, and if you try to explain that, you'll end up dead."

"Yeah? Well I think Masha won't be to happy about that, so—" She shrugged again. "Anyways, figure I'll take my chances." She paused a moment. "Also, pretty sure you owe me a drink."

He sighed and got up from the table, returning a few moments later with a delicate glass of something that bubbled and fizzed against the roof of her mouth, and tasted delightfully strong.

She grinned at him. "Alright, so, Fyodor. Any other manners you want to teach me?"

Two and a half hours later, she wasn't actually drunk, but she was a hell of a lot more muddy-headed than when she'd started. Also, she knew a whole damn list of what Fyodor liked to call manners, and had promised to follow exactly zero.

Fyodor had started drinking as well by the time she'd won her third round, and she figured he was at least as drunk as she was.

"So, you bastard," she said, grinning at him as he glared down once again at the table, as if somehow he could glare the tokens into coming up with a different total. "Guess I'm not going to be changing my behaviour all that much."

He turned his glare on her. "How did you do that?"

She shrugged. "Told you. Beginner's luck."

"I don't have to keep my side of the bargain here, you know. You cheated."

"Hey now, don't play what you can't pay. Besides, if I'd cheated, figure an experienced gambler like you would have called me out on it when you caught me."

"I am calling you out."

"You never caught me. You're just guessing."

He narrowed his eyes, which were, she noted, noticeably glassy. He must have drunk more than she'd thought. "A good cheater lets the other person win once in a while. To keep from being detected."

She shrugged. "Good thing I'm no cheater then. Guess I'd be a pretty crap one." She couldn't stop grinning, and honestly, it had a lot less to do with the alcohol than it did with the memory of the look on his face every time he lost a game.

He was wrong. She could have let him win once or twice. Hell, she'd been tempted to, just for a change. But the way his eyes bugged out of his head and then narrowed, darting back and forth between his tokens and hers as if trying to figure out how she'd done it—she gave a sigh of satisfaction and glanced back up at him.

Honestly, she hadn't been able to help it.

"Someone is going to kill you one of these days, Solokov."

She gave him a slightly-drunken grin. "Hell, people have been trying that for about twenty-three years now."

"Yes, well now you're on the krestnaya's ship. You're right in the centre of the headquarters of the mafia. And you have just finished telling me that you don't intend to follow any of the rules I set out for you, for your own protection." He was still glaring at her.

"Yep." She scooped up the tokens and held them out. At last, grudgingly, he held out his hands, and she poured the tokens into them. "Don't know what you're talking about, anyways. We just had a couple friendly games here. Nothing to lose sleep over. Just be glad we weren't playing for actual credits."

He was still scowling. "I think I would have preferred to be playing for credits."

She shrugged. "There's always next time, you bastard."

He slammed his free hand down on the table. "No. There's not going to be a next time. And I told you, over and over, you do not call members of the mafia 'bastard.'"

"Guess I do." She gave him one parting grin and turned, ever-so-slightly unsteadily, and sauntered out of the gambling hall. She shot Fyodor a glance over her shoulder as she left. He was still sitting where she'd left him, glaring at the tokens in his hand and the row of empty glasses on the table. She gave him a wink.

"I'll see you 'round," she said cheerily. "Seeing as you've told me I'm welcome here whenever the hell I feel like it."

He half-stood. "I never—"

"Got to pay what you play," she said, shaking her head at him in mock-admonishment. "Can't have people thinking you'd stiff them."

He sank back in his chair, glowering at her, and she made her way down the hallways to the guest quarters.

Yes, she was slightly drunk, and yes, she'd probably made an enemy of someone who was clearly in the good graces of Grigory Whoever-the-hell-he-was, but honestly, she felt about a million times better. She'd needed something like that.

She held her key-chip up to their door, and when the lock clicked, pushed it open. She hit the button on her com—well, it took her a couple tries to remember which one it was, but it was a lot better than it could have been—to activate the spoof Tae had set up, then shut the door carefully behind her and let out a long breath.

"Jez?"

She looked up sharply. Lev was sitting at a table, a holoscreen pulled up in front of him, and he was glaring at her with a mixture of annoyance and concern.

She gave him a slightly-drunken grin. "Yeah, genius?"

"Jez?" He stood, frowning. "Are you al—" he stopped abruptly. "You're drunk," he said flatly.

She grinned at him again. Honestly, she'd probably be snapping at him at this point, normally, but the combination of alcohol and the warm satisfaction sitting in her chest made her slightly less snappish than she'd usually be.

"Damn right. But don't worry, genius. Fyodor stopped buying me drinks half-way through, and I didn't make him keep going." She glanced back at the door speculatively. "Could have, you know. Maybe I'll go find him, tell him he owes me a few."

Lev's expression had turned a shade of disbelief. "Fyodor Yanovik?" he asked after a moment. "Jez, please tell me that you didn't manage to irritate Fyodor Yanovik."

She gave him a contemplative look. "Nah," she said after a moment. "I don't think irritate is the word. Bastard looked like he wanted to throw me out the airlock by the time we finished."

"Jez!" He came over to her and grabbed her by the arm. She jerked out of his grasp and almost overbalanced, barely catching herself against the wall.

"Jez, sit down," he said through his teeth. She glared at him, but the adrenalin and alcohol were still buzzing pleasantly through her brain and she discovered she couldn't be quite as irritated as she'd normally be.

She dropped into the chair he pulled up, still grinning. He shoved a ration pack at her.

"Eat something, you idiot. I'd prefer having this conversation with you at least somewhat sober."

She shrugged, and ripped the packaging off the rations pack. "Well, genius, if I was sober right now, probably wouldn't be talking to you. Because I'm going to be honest, you've been an absolute bastard lately."

He stared at her for a moment, irritation still clear on his face, but at last his expression softened, and he shook his head ruefully.

"To be fair, Jez, you've been a bit of a bastard yourself."

She cocked her head at him as she took a bite of the rations pack. "Well, maybe," she conceded, "but I'm always a bit of a bastard."

He was still watching her, but at last she saw a reluctant smile tug at his lips. "I'm not going to comment on that."

She smirked. "See? There's a reason I call you genius-boy."

His smile widened slightly, then, with an effort, he scowled again. "Alright, now that you're sitting down and I'm not worried you're going to actually fall over, would you mind explaining how you got Fyodor Yanovik to the point that he wanted to throw you out the airlock?"

"What, don't want to just guess?" she asked, taking another bite of the rations pack. "Figure you could come up with something good."

He sighed in exasperation, but there was still the hint of a smile on his face.

It was actually kind of nice. She hadn't seen him smile in a while. Since—

Nope. She wasn't nearly drunk enough to think about that yet.

"Yes, Jez, you're right. I could probably come up with about a dozen ways in which you could have, over the course of two and a half hours, convinced a mafia avtoritet to get you drunk, and then irritated him to the point where he wanted to throw you out the airlock. But I'd rather know what actually happened."

"Hey, he's drunk too," she said. "Figure he's more drunk than I am, because I'll be honest with you, right now I'm just barely drunk enough to want to keep talking to you, you plaguer."

"Jez—"

She rolled her eyes. "Fine. He told me Grigory asked him to teach me manners. So I convinced him that we should talk over a nice friendly game, seeing as there was a gambling hall right here on the ship. And he said that he could only bring members in there, and I asked why he was so afraid to play with some pilot who'd learned to play in kabaks in backwater zestavas, and he said—"

Lev's face was growing gradually more and more disbelieving. "Wait. Please tell me you didn't—"

"Probably did," she said, leaning back with a grin. "Anyways, he said he wasn't afraid, he was trying to protect me from myself, and I said if that was the case, figure I deserved whatever I got, so why not have a friendly little game? And finally he agreed. And I figured he was going to try to beat the hell out of me, which, I'll be honest, he probably could have, but anyways, apparently he thought he could teach me manners by just talking to me." She shrugged. "So I told the bastard I'd do what he said if he won the game. And if he lost, I wouldn't, and he'd let me use the gambling hall whenever the hell I felt like it, and he'd buy me a drink."

"You didn't call him a bastard. Please tell me you didn't call him a bastard." Lev's expression was one of resigned horror.

"Yep. Sure did. Can't honestly remember how many times, but hell," she shrugged. "Like I said, he stopped buying me drinks about half-way through, mostly because he was buying them for himself. Also, turns out I'm not going to follow any of his manners. Figure he was drinking so much because he didn't want to explain that to Grigory."

Lev was still staring at her. At last he sank into his own chair with a sort of resigned exhaustion.

"Jez," he said at last.

"Yeah?"

He just shook his head for a moment. "The problem with this, Jez, is that in a few hours, when you've sobered up and you've finally had time to think about what you've done with a clear head—you're not going to feel any differently about it."

She smirked.

He sighed, still shaking his head. "Jez. Listen to me. Fyodor is a very dangerous man. He would almost certainly throw you out the airlock without a second thought, if he didn't do something worse. He likely only has not done so because Grigory believes that Masha and Ysbel and I will be useful enough to him that he's instructed his people not to actually kill any of us unless necessary. I am, unfortunately, of Tae's opinion that if our usefulness ever wears off, Grigory will waste no time in getting rid of every last one of us."

She raised an eyebrow at him. "Alright, genius, explain to me how that's different than any other thing we've done in the past few months." She paused a moment. "Or, basically anything I've done my whole damn life."

He was still shaking his head, but again, there was that hint of a smile beneath his exasperation.

"Well, Jez," he said, after a long moment. "I suppose you're right. I wish you hadn't done what you just did, but—" he held up his hand before she could protest. "But, you're a grown woman, and you've managed to survive so far, although I honestly am not certain how, so I suppose there isn't much I can say about it. Other than, you might want to at least be able to act sober by the time Masha gets back." He paused again. "And. Um. I—suppose I should say sorry. For being a complete bastard."

She frowned at him.

He looked like he actually meant it.

"Um." She said. For the first time since she'd headed down to the gambling hall, she somewhat regretted the fact that her head wasn't as clear as it usually was, because honestly, she wasn't entirely sure she knew what to do with a Lev who wasn't being a complete bastard. "I. I mean. I'm sorry too."

He smiled slightly. "Well." He paused. "It isn't like we can't—I mean—"

"No, we—just because we aren't—we don't—" She found she was stumbling over her words, something strange twisting in the pit of her stomach. This was definitely not a conversation she could have drunk. Hell, she wasn't sure it was a conversation she could have sober, not now, not with Lev. She stood abruptly, and almost fell over. He caught her arm, and damn it, why did his touch send tingles all the way up her shoulder and down her body?

She was definitely too drunk too deal with this right now, or else not nearly drunk enough.

"'M going to lie down," she mumbled, jerking her arm out of his grasp. She certainly wasn't drunk enough for that, but it sounded like a hell of a lot better plan than staying out here for even one second more.

"Jez," he said quietly, dropping his hand.

Reluctantly, she turned.

"I'm—sorry," he said. "Friends?"

She paused for a long moment. Then, at last, she turned, sitting back down again.

"Yeah," she said. "Friends."

He gave her a small smile, and somehow she found herself smiling back. And that cold, empty place in her chest, that had been there ever since he told her they should probably be done, seemed to shrink, just a little.

At last he turned back to the table, pulled his chair back around to where it had been, and tapped his com, pulling up his holoscreen again. She watched him surreptitiously as he worked.

Maybe—well, maybe if Lev was going to stop acting like a cranky old man, there was just a chance she'd be able to handle this thing after all.

And she didn't have to think, right now, about what that might mean to them not being together anymore, because they were just friends, that's all it was.

And anyways—Fyodor had promised her full access to the gambling hall, so there was always that.

6

There was a loud knock, and Lev stood, tapping Tae's spoof on his com off, and walked to the door to their suite.

When he pulled open the door, a woman stood behind it. He glanced her over quickly, and she did the same to him. She, however, made no attempt to disguise the unimpressed look on her face.

"You're Lev," she said at last.

He nodded politely. "And you, I assume, are Marta Babanin."

She frowned at him. "Grigory informed you I was coming?"

He smiled noncommittally.

"Then perhaps Grigory told you the reason I'm here. You're invited to dine with him tonight."

Lev raised one eyebrow. "No. I wasn't aware of the reason for your visit. I'm honoured."

He watched her as he spoke.

Grigory hadn't told him she was coming, but Lev was conversant enough with the mafia hierarchy to recognize her instantly. She was an avtoritet, not a high-ranking one, but still— Whatever this was, it was important, if she'd been sent as a messenger.

And an invitation to dinner.

Either there was something the krestnaya wanted his help with, or he was going to be murdered. He wasn't entirely certain which, and at this point it was beginning to seem like the two things were relatively interchangeable.

"The dinner will be in—" Marta glanced at her com. "One standard hour. Down in the dining room off the gambling hall." She glanced him over once more, letting the distain bleed through her expression. "And please, try to dress the part. I'll instruct my people to have proper clothing sent up."

"I appreciate it," he murmured. "As you might suspect, I neglected my dinner wardrobe over the course of running for my life these past few months."

She gave him a look that told him very clearly she doubted he'd ever had a dinner wardrobe.

Which, in fairness, was entirely correct.

He gave her another bland, pleasant smile, and closed the door as she turned away.

A suit of clothing arrived soon after—dark trousers and a dark, embroidered vest of a fine, soft material, a white shirt of something even finer, and soft, high brown boots—and he stepped out of his room just as the door banged open and Jez sauntered inside. She was grinning, as usual, and he decided not to ask what she'd been doing because quite honestly he wasn't sure his nerves could handle knowing.

She glanced over at him, then did a double-take, raising her eyebrows. "Well, genius-boy. Least we know you clean up nice."

He looked at her in surprise. She seemed to suddenly realize what she'd said, because she turned away quickly and wouldn't meet his eyes.

He watched her for a moment, that familiar tightness in the pit of his stomach, then, shaking his head, stepped out the door.

There was a boyevik there waiting to escort him. Of course there was. And the threat of the man's weapon beneath his vest was almost hidden enough not to draw attention to itself.

The boyevik nodded politely and gestured him forward, and Lev walked down the opulent corridor, somehow forcing himself not to look over his shoulder.

If Grigory wanted him shot, he wasn't stupid enough to think it would make a difference whether or not he saw it coming.

When they reached the gambling hall, the man beckoned him through to the dining area. "Go on. Grigory will join you shortly."

A server in a blue-black uniform with gold trim that matched the ambiance of the room beckoned him forward, and he followed through the main room, through a discrete door, up a small staircase, and through a heavy curtain into a room that almost made him stop dead in astonishment.

Jez would have loved this.

The skylights were uncovered, and stretched the length of the room, so that it almost felt like you were sitting outside the ship, surrounded by deep space. The many-coloured swirl of a nebula spread off to the starboard side of the ship, the stars glowing from all sides. He'd been out on a space-walk only one time, and it had almost ended in his death—but he still sometimes had a momentary spike of longing for the peaceful, icy black, the beautiful, deadly vastness that could, perhaps, kill you from yearning almost before it could kill you from cold.

And this—this was as close as you could get to that, without dying.

Although considering he was meeting Grigory Korzhikov for dinner, not dying wasn't a given.

The server gestured Lev to a seat, bowed slightly, and stepped back through the curtain.

There was a chance, of course, that Grigory had set this up to murder him—gas him, like the administrators in the University of Prasvishoni had tried a few weeks earlier, or something much more deadly and much more painful.

His muscles were tense, and he made a conscious effort to relax them.

He didn't actually believe that if Grigory intended to kill him, he'd choose this time and place. Of the thousands of ways Grigory could have him killed, this seemed a rather impractical option. Besides, Grigory had invited him with a purpose.

And Lev had his own purpose for accepting.

Besides not being shot by Grigory's boyeviki, although that had admittedly played a part.

Still, he had an unreasonably hard time forcing himself to lean comfortably back in the seat, rather than sit perched tensely on the edge.

The bodyguards came in first. There were five of them, and they took their positions around the sides of the room in a no-nonsense way. Then a woman came in, with an insignia on her vest that marked her as one of Grigory's personal bodyguards. She asked Lev to stand, and he did. She waved a scanner over him, checked it, then gestured him to take his seat again. Then she took her place behind the chair at the head of the table, the one directly across from Lev's chair.

The curtain was pulled back, and Grigory stepped into the room.

He smiled at Lev, the grey streaks in his beard hardly noticeable in the soft light of the dining room.

"Lev." His voice was hoarse, but there was a note of cold amusement in it. "It is so good of you to join me."

Lev gave a respectful nod of his head. "It's an honour."

By rights, he should have called the man Krestnaya, or at the least, boss, but somehow he couldn't bring himself to do that, and so he chose instead to omit a title completely.

Grigory would possibly notice. But at the same time, there was nothing inherently disrespectful in the way he'd spoken, so it was unlikely to cause comment.

For the moment.

He wondered how long it had been that he'd started making these calculations, instead of doing the smart thing right off. If he was being honest, it probably had some connection with when he started working with Jez. She had a way of rubbing off on you.

Grigory took Lev's hand. "I'm delighted to meet with you, boy. Your friend Masha speaks highly of you, and I decided I had to speak with you myself." He gestured around the table, and the people who had entered behind him took their seats. He recognized them at once, from government files—the woman's medium build, pale skin, and brilliant red hair identified her immediately as Yana, the packhan of the mafia's military arm. The other, who identified as non-binary, was Zhenya, the packan of the security arm, and the other member of the mafia trifecta. Zhenya had a slender build, dark hair, and a slight beard, and was supposed to have been one of the deadliest of Grigory's boyeviki, long before they ascended to their current rank.

Grigory pulled back his chair and sat. Yana and Zhenya sat as well, and, after what he judged was a respectful pause, Lev took his own seat.

Grigory smiled at him, then turned to the server. "Please. Take my friend's order first."

Lev bit back a grimace. He'd had more experience than he'd ever wanted with ordering food at the table of a deadly crime boss, and the last time it had ended with him choking down some sort of centipede, which he'd vomited up onto said crime boss's courtyard a few minutes later.

That had, admittedly, been mostly Jez's fault. The centipede, that was—the vomiting had been all him.

"Sir?" the server said. He touched his com, and a three-dimensional screen appeared, the dishes rotating slowly to show their mouth-watering contents off to best effect. Lev glanced them over quickly, and touched one he was fairly certain would contain no centipede to speak of. The server nodded, then turned to Grigory.

"And you, sir? The usual, I assume?"

"Yes, thank you," said Grigory, in his gravely voice. Yana and Zhenya ordered, Yana's voice harsh and slightly jarring, Zhenya's words so soft that Lev couldn't make them out. The server seemed to, however, because he bowed again and slipped out the curtain.

Grigory smiled at Lev. "I must admit, I'm a bit disappointed. Vitali led me to understand you were a much more adventurous diner."

Lev froze.

Grigory chuckled. "Ah Lev. Vitali and I are not on the best of terms professionally any more, and more's the pity. But he couldn't help but brag to me about his clever nephew. We've known each other for years on a personal level, your uncle and I."

Lev forced his hands to stop trembling. "Vitali spoke to you about me?" he asked, keeping his voice carefully neutral.

Grigory leaned back in his chair, a wide smile on his face. "He did. He spoke of you quite highly."

"We—parted on difficult terms last time we met," Lev murmured.

This was true, as he was fairly certain that knocking out one of his uncle's guards, helping break the rest of the crew out of his uncle's prison, leaving, meanwhile, if he knew Jez, all sorts of havoc in their wake, breaking into his uncle's most secure vaults, taking down his security system, stealing his prize ship, blowing up half his compound, blowing up an additional number of his ships who were pursuing them, and also, by the way, stealing a staggering number of credits, would qualify as 'difficult terms.'

"Ah, yes, he did mention you left something of a mess behind you," said Grigory. He was still smiling broadly, but the ever-present menace behind that smile set Lev's nerves on edge. "I think he would have been disappointed if you hadn't. If he finds you again, he'll certainly kill you, but he was quite proud of you all the same. 'Boy has the family brains,' he told me."

Lev drew in a long breath.

Being reminded of his murderous crime-boss uncle who wanted to kill him was not, honestly, the type of dinner conversation he would term relaxing.

"Well," he said at last, forcing his face into its typical calm. "I'm flattered."

Grigory chuckled again. "He also told me about how you ate a centipede."

Of course he had.

Lev managed to keep from gritting his teeth. "My uncle's ability to bring in specialty dishes is unparalleled, in my experience." He smiled pleasantly as he watched the small barb sink in.

He'd never enjoyed being tested, especially by people who were debating killing him.

Grigory's face darkened slightly, but at last he shook his head. "Well, you'll judge for yourself in a few minutes." He leaned forward on the table. "As I said, Lev, I have heard a great deal about you. But all this can wait until we have food on our plates. Conversation flavoured with salt is much more pleasant, I've always found."

For a few minutes, they made small talk about the ship, and about the view, and about the luxury of the gambling hall and dining room.

"I hear," Grigory said, "that your friend the pilot is enjoying the gambling hall. Perhaps too much. I might mention that to her, if I were you. There are people on this ship who it's best not to get on the bad side of. I've asked them not to kill her outright, if possible, but it would be bad for morale if I let it go."

"I will certainly bring it up," Lev murmured.

Of course, bringing it up would only make Jez more determined to cheat more deadly mafia killers out of their money, but

He sighed. This was something Masha would have to deal with, if "dealing with" was a term you could use in relation to Jez.

The food arrived, and, to Lev's relief, it seemed to contain a noticeable lack of centipede. He took a tentative bite.

It was surprisingly good, the flavours complex and developed, the profile rich and savoury and slightly smokey. He raised his eyebrows.

"There," said Grigory. "You think my food is as good as your uncle's?"

"It's delicious," said Lev, with complete honesty. Grigory smiled at the compliment, and took a bite of his own food.

"I hire chefs here who have proved outstanding planet-side," he said as he chewed. "I find that even the most home-loving chef is eager to come along once I've explained to her what she might expect out here in deep space." He paused a moment. "And, of course, if they don't?" He shrugged. "I had to kill a chef once. It was a pity—he was a man of many talents. But you see, in the business I'm in, you must act decisively. You may think it petty of me. You may think, there are so many chefs. If one chooses not to come, surely it's no trouble to find another?" He paused a moment, watching Lev. "But you see, as soon as one person can say no to me —as soon as one person thinks they can get away with telling me what they will do or will not do, which orders they will follow and which they will not—then—" he spread his hands. "Then I'm a lost man. I'm a man waiting to be taken down by some young person rising in the ranks, who's not afraid to kill a chef. So—" he shrugged again. "So, I killed the chef. And now I have whoever I choose come work for me here on my ship, and the food that you order is the very best of the best."

They ate without speaking for a few moments.

Lev studied the man surreptitiously as they ate.

Grigory was enjoying his meal, seeming entirely comfortable with the silence.

"Lev," he said at last, looking up from his plate. "We aren't all that different, you and I. Both of us grew up poor. Both of us had only our wits to get ahead. And yet, here we are." He gestured around him expansively. "You know, I asked you all here because I wanted to speak with Masha. But—" he paused, shaking his head. "The more I looked into the people she was traveling with, the more I realized what kind of a genius she was. She's not always going to be the smartest person in the room, Masha. But she will always be the person who knows the smartest person in the room. Her skills are getting the best of the best together. But you—you are the best of the best. You, Lev, have always been the smartest person in the room, I imagine."

Lev gave a self-deprecating shrug, and Grigory smiled, leaning forward on the table.

"Lev. My boy. You could do well here. Most of the people here have worked their way up from the bottom, but someone like you?

We could do business, you and I."

"Perhaps," said Lev, keeping his tone carefully neutral.

The secret was, of course, to keep him talking. Grigory clearly was trying to woo him over, but for what, he wasn't sure. But give a person enough space, and enough time to say their piece and enough encouragement to keep them going but not quite enough to make them certain of you—well, there was almost no one he'd met who could withstand that.

Grigory placed both hands on the table, palms open. "I don't want to keep secrets from you, you know. I'm willing to be an open book."

"And I am more than willing to listen," said Lev, voice still neutral. "But I have very little information to go on, other than what Masha told me. And—" he shrugged. "You know Masha."

It was a calculated gamble—Masha may have been playing the crew off as completely united. But he somehow doubted it. And besides, with Tae's unhappy scowl clearly visible on the cameras that had been placed in their rooms, it would be obvious to the most casual observer that they were not as united as might be hoped.

There was a gleam of interest in Grigory's eyes. "I do know Masha," he said, "but not, perhaps, as well as you do."

Lev shrugged again. "I'm not sure any of us really knows Masha. She can be close-mouthed about details."

"Ah." Grigory nodded and leaned back slightly, and there was just a hint of satisfaction in his expression. "I can see that. From what I've heard, Masha has always been one to play her tokens from a closed hand."

"You might say that," Lev murmured, letting just a hint of wryness bleed through his tone.

"So. What do I want from you, Lev? That is a fair question."

Grigory paused a moment. "You and your friend Masha burned bridges I spent years building. And Olyessa Janovik's people—they had some powerful members in that prison you broke out. And now they're back at the table, and they're bringing credits, and they have a solid hand of tokens. There are people in the government who were once on my payroll who've been thinking about how to use this to get ahead."

He smiled. "None of that worries me too much. But this impasse with the government? Masha told me something about the government's plan. Perhaps you could confirm it's correct?"

Lev raised an eyebrow. "I assume you're talking about the Vyernist Protocol? The program to hack into the brains of every person in the system and be able to eliminate them at will? If that's what you're referring to, then yes. I can confirm that that is correct." He rubbed a spot at the base of his skull ruefully. "I can also confirm that it will be the death of me and of every other member of my crew if we don't find a solution."

It was possible that Masha hadn't informed Grigory of the extent of their interest in taking down the Protocol. Still, this was a calculated gamble. If Grigory didn't already know he and the rest of the crew had been infected, he'd find out soon, and when dealing with a man like Grigory it was always better to defuse the inevitable revelation upfront.

Grigory raised an eyebrow, although Lev was fairly certain nothing he'd said had surprised the man.

"I see. So to say you're motivated to find a solution to that would be correct."

Lev gave a measured nod. "Of course. I have no doubt we'll find a solution, but time is always a factor. More of it would be useful."

"It would be a loss indeed for people as talented as your crew to be killed."

"Of course. Besides the admittedly personal reasons I have to regret that outcome," said Lev dryly.

Grigory chuckled. "I like you, Lev. Your uncle was right. He told me I would."

Lev suppressed a sigh. Of course. His murderous uncle would speak with perhaps the only person in the system more murderous than himself and give Lev a character recommendation. And it would prove to be true.

He wasn't certain this was a form of flattery he appreciated.

"So. We're after the same thing," said the mafia boss. "You want to stop this program from going forward. I don't want my rivals in the government to have that type of power—I would be a begging dog at their table, just like every other begging dog, asking for scraps in return for favours. But, Lev, I think we can solve all of our problems with one solution. As I told Masha, I'm putting on a conference. Through a friend, of course, a friend who has contacts. We can talk business, the officials who attend and I. My plans wouldn't affect you, of course—I'm only looking to take things back to the way they were before Masha planted her explosives. And, since she's so kindly agreed to help, I invite your government friend who's over that program. Her top assistants. And then—" He spread his hands. "There's an accident. You're safe, and I'm safe, and things are back to what they were before this misunderstanding with Vitali started in the first place."

Lev sat back in his chair and watched Grigory.

Things back to where they were.

He knew very well what 'back to where they were' meant—it meant Evka, experimenting on street kids in the university while everyone turned a blind eye. It meant poor families like his dying of hunger and exposure every single winter. It meant Tae's friend Ivan, and the professor he'd met in prison, locked up for reading the wrong books or saying the wrong things, it meant Lena's ilk preying on the edges of the system like deep-space scavengers, killing off the weak and the old and anyone, like his family, who was one cargo run gone wrong, one theft, away from starvation. It meant the mafia's fingers all through the government, pinching and prodding and sucking out the money that had been in turn sucked from the pockets of desperate dirt-eater farmers on remote outer-rim planets.

Perhaps it said something about what had happened a few weeks ago that 'back to where they were' sounded almost appealing.

Still …

He smiled slightly.

Still, he could use this.

Possibly.

This was the most delicate part of the conversation.

"It appears you have things well in hand," he said. "As you said, stopping this program is as important to you as it is to me. I'm not certain what benefits I could add to you, after Masha's already offered to help. Or—" he paused delicately. "What benefits you'd offer me in return."

The words landed heavily. Grigory's expression darkened, his brows pulling lower over his piercing eyes, the simmering rage surfacing in his face for the briefest moment. And for just that moment, Lev wondered if he'd made a miscalculation.

But at last Grigory shook his head and gave a small, forced chuckle. "Lev. I do like you. Not one to mince your words. That is a trait I can admire." His tone under the words he spoke, though, said something different.

Grigory would kill him without a second thought.

They were hunting alongside a harobeast, and if it turned on them, it would tear them to shreds. There was no loyalty, no mercy, nothing but cold self-interest. They were alive because they were useful.

But then, Grigory could be useful as well.

"What I want you to do, Lev, is help me to plan this. It needs to go off perfectly. If what your uncle tells me is correct, planning is a talent of yours."

Lev didn't let the wryness creep into his smile.

He was pretty sure that since he'd met Masha, there hadn't been a single incident he'd planned that had gone off 'perfectly.'

Still—

"As for what I could do for you?" Grigory smiled, but there was an unmistakable menace behind it. "Well, Lev, I could keep you alive." He paused a moment, deliberately. "From the government, of course," he added. "Because, as you said, an error in timing is something you can't afford at the moment."

Lev kept his smile cool and bland, tried not to show how quickly his pulse was racing.

Grigory wasn't telling him everything. That much was obvious. Still, as long as the man could do what he promised, any other consideration was hardly relevant.

And, of course, there was something else, too. The reason he'd agreed so readily to dinner with Grigory in the first place. Perhaps killing the minister would give him a couple months, but there was a way to stop the program completely.

Grigory was perhaps the only person in the system with the connections and resources to get to Evka.

He blinked at the familiar lightheaded rush, the blend of regret and anger and fondness and hate the thought of her flooded through his brain.

Jez, lying on his lap, blinking sleepily up at him …

"I must admit, I'm intrigued," he said at last, slowly. "However—" he stopped, and spread his hands.

"What do you want, Lev?" asked Grigory, leaning forward. There was a tension in his posture that spoke of anger, controlled, but there.

Lev gave a deprecating shake of his head. "What's talk of a price between people with a common goal?"

"But, I insist. If you are willing to work with me, I want to make it worth your while." There was an edge of menace, and an equal edge of wryness, to his tone.

Lev paused again, as if considering. "I had a professor, once," he said slowly. "She's the mind behind this Vyernist Protocol. I don't think we dare even risk inviting her to your conference—she's brilliant, and she's far too canny to be caught like this. But after this job is done? With your resources and your people …" he trailed off delicately.

Grigory smiled, a genuine smile this time. "Ah. Yes, that is something I could do for you, Lev. And I would do it happily. And furthermore—" he spread his hands. "If this goes well, I would give you an invitation to continue to work with me. I may be able to offer you a position here. Perhaps your friends as well. I think we could work well together. And I'm not an unappreciative friend."

Lev raised his eyebrows. "That is a generous offer." He paused a moment, taking a bite of his almost-cold food and chewing it carefully. He swallowed, and took another bite, aware of Grigory's eyes on him.

He was probably as close now as he'd ever been in his life to being shot, but somehow the knowledge didn't frighten him as much as it might have.

Because this was his kind of game, and he knew how to play.

At last, he looked up. "Your offer is kind. More than kind. And I accept. I'll help you plan your conference with pleasure."

"And in return, if all goes well, I will help you track down this canny professor of yours, and I will offer you a place in my leadership," said Grigory, a smile spreading across his face. "The word of two free citizens." He reached out his hand across the table, and Lev reached out to take it.

From outside the door, there was the unmistakable staticky hiss of a heat-blast, and the limp body of the server tumbled through the curtains. The dish he'd been carrying shattered on the floor, the bright red sauce of one of the dishes spreading across the dark carpet like blood.

Grigory jumped to his feet, and the bodyguards threw themselves in front of him as three masked figures ripped aside the curtain and stepped through. They were holding laser guns along with their heat pistols, and one of the bodyguards fell almost immediately, a bright line burned through her body armour, her strangled scream cut off almost before it began. Grigory jerked the platter from the dinner table up in front of him, and a blast bounced off it. Lev had to dive to one side to avoid it as it ricocheted across the room, burning a long black stain across the skylights. The bodyguards were already shooting, and the heat-armour on the guards' chests and the attackers' chests glowed and sparked as it disbursed the heat. Grigory fumbled in his pocket, and a moment later he pulled out a small pistol that Lev recognized instantly from months of being in close proximity to Ysbel. He threw himself under the table as the weapon went off, and for a moment his vision was nothing but white light, and he could hear nothing but the low reverberations of the gun.

When his vision cleared again, all three attackers were down, along with another of the bodyguards.

Grigory calmly holstered his pistol. "Are you alright, Lev?" he asked, raising his voice slightly.

Lev pushed himself to his feet. His hands were shaking slightly, but he managed to still them.

You'd think, after all this time, he'd get used to being shot at. He'd been friends with plaguing Jez for long enough that it was becoming par for the course.

"Yes," he said, lifting his chair back up and resuming his seat. "I'm fine, thank you."

Grigory walked around the table and stared down at their attackers. Then he bent and pulled the mask sharply from the face of the first of them.

"Olyessa's people," he said, and there was a tone in his voice that told Lev that he hadn't always been a high-brow mafia boss. Before he'd risen to the position he was in now, he had been something else —a man who killed with his own hands, and who had been good at it.

Had enjoyed it.

He looked up at Lev, that cultured, vicious smile spreading over his face again. "I apologize. This is Olyessa's doing. She's been trying to kill me for some time now. If I had known, I wouldn't have put you in danger. But—" he shrugged. "For a man of my position, going about my day-to-day life is danger enough. We must work with what we have." He pushed himself heavily to his feet. "Well, Lev. I am glad you survived that unhurt."

"The assassins?" asked one of the bodyguards.

Grigory made an impatient gesture. "Get someone in here to clean them up. I think one of them is still alive. Keep him alive. I'd like to talk with him for a while before I deal with him."

The guard nodded and slipped out the door. Another bodyguard knelt beside one of her fallen comrades.

"She's still alive," the woman said after a moment, looking up at Grigory.

"Good, good," said Grigory. "When they come for the bodies, get her taken into the med bay. She's a good soldier, and she'll be rewarded. You can put together a gift for her family, put it on my desk to approve."

The guard nodded and straightened. Grigory turned back to the table and smiled at Lev, but there was something predatory under his smile.

But predatory, Lev could use.

He shoved aside the cold that had worked its way into his stomach and managed a smile in return.

"Now, my boy," said Grigory jovially. "There is still plenty of food on our plates, and I believe the server was coming to offer us dessert. I hope this hasn't spoiled your appetite."

7

"I've been told you do beautiful work, Ysbel."

Ysbel raised an eyebrow, scanning the room she'd been brought to with interest. It was not quite as well-insulated as the weapons room she'd put together on the *Ungovernable*, but what it lacked in insulation, it made up for in the sheer quality of the materials and tools.

"Well, that depends on what you consider beautiful. But—" She shrugged. "I am very good at blowing things up, and I understand that's what Grigory wants. So—"

The woman nodded, a small, unreadable smile on her face. "As the krestnaya told you, he wants an explosive. How you make it is up to you, but he wants something powerful, like in the specs he asked me to send through to your com. He wants to see what you can do. I assume you've looked at the specs?"

She raised one eyebrow. "Of course."

"And can you make what he wants you to make?"

Ysbel gave her a flat look. "As long as you've given me the correct materials, I can make whatever I choose to."

She tried to push the morning's conversation with Tanya to the back of her mind.

"Ysi. What are you agreeing to?" Tanya's face still bore that unfamiliar hardness. The children had left the room earlier and were playing in the main suite, with Tae keeping an eye on them. It seemed like a very long time since she and Tanya had been alone.

"I'm doing what I have to to keep you and the children safe," said Ysbel, keeping her words steady. Trying not to let her voice tremble.

"That's not enough, Ysbel!" Tanya turned away abruptly. "You have not even asked what they want this for. You showed me the specs he gave you. You're making something that could kill hundreds of people, and you're making it for the mafia. And you don't even care enough to ask."

"I care, Tanya!" Ysbel snapped, and the harshness in her own tone surprised her. She took a deep breath, and softened her words slightly. "Tanya, I care very much. But what I care about is you. You, and Olya, and Misko. If this will keep you safe, then you're right. What he uses it for is not something I will concern myself with."

Tanya didn't turn at her words, but there was a stiffness to her posture, and Ysbel could see the rise and fall of her breath, far too quick.

She closed her eyes for a moment.

"Tanya," she said at last, her voice choking slightly. "Please understand. I can't lose you again. I can't let the government hurt you, or my babies. I can't watch—" She swallowed hard, unable to continue.

For a moment, she thought Tanya might turn towards her. But instead, she dropped her head.

"Ysbel," she said quietly, still without turning around. "You are not the only one who was hurt when those people came and took you. You are not the only one who cares for our children. Once, you trusted me just as much as you asked me to trust you. I don't know what happened to you."

"I'll tell you what happened," said Ysbel finally, standing. She crossed over to where Tanya stood, but there was something about her wife's posture that stopped her from putting an arm around her shoulders. "I lost you. I watched you die, you *and the children. And I will give up anything in the world to make sure that doesn't happen again."*

"Anything?" asked Tanya. "Even me?" This time she did turn, and her eyes found Ysbel's.

There was a sadness there, a quiet vulnerability, that made Ysbel's throat tighten.

"Tanya," she whispered, and after a moment's hesitation, Tanya stepped forward into her embrace.

Ysbel held her gently, her eyes closed.

She hadn't answered the question.

Because—well, because the truth was, as much as she loved Tanya, as much as she needed her, like the very blood in her veins—if giving up Tanya was what it took to keep Tanya safe, perhaps she'd be willing to do even that.

"You should have everything you need," said the woman. She paused a moment. "I assume you're as committed to helping Grigory as you've said you were."

Ysbel frowned slightly. "I am exactly as committed as I need to be," she said. "Masha and Grigory agreed on something. I'm willing to perform my part of the transaction. That's all."

The woman raised her eyebrows. "Of course. I'll leave you to your devices, then."

There was the slightest hint of smugness under her words, and a calculating look in her eyes that made Ysbel glance quickly around the room again.

Only one exit. Useful if you were testing explosives, because doors were much harder to protect from a blast. The walls were padded with non-reactive material, and the floor and ceiling were painted with non-reactive coating. It would almost certainly withstand an explosion, even one from one of her explosives.

Also useful if you were planning an ambush.

And as an added bonus, one she was almost certain the woman had thought of before bringing her down here—it was virtually sound-proof. No one to hear you scream, or beg for mercy.

Of course, she thought reflectively, that advantage could go two ways.

She smiled slightly to herself.

If they really wanted to try to ambush her here, in the middle of a room full of explosives—well, that was their choice.

She bent to her work as the woman stepped out of the room, but every muscle in her body was on alert.

It was almost fifteen minutes before she heard the soft, almost imperceptible *click* of the door being carefully opened.

She didn't turn. Not yet.

Let them all get inside first.

It wasn't until the door clicked shut again that she straightened and turned to face the people who had gathered.

There were five of them. All of them looked like people who weren't squeamish about violence.

She gave a slightly nostalgic smile.

It had been a long time, really, since someone had so blatantly tried to hurt her.

She'd almost missed it.

"Ysbel," said a man she didn't recognize. His voice was cold. "I understand you're here because you're helping your friend Masha. But I wonder if you might need some convincing as to your loyalties to Grigory."

Ysbel raised an eyebrow. "I'm sure you're very frightening," she said, making no effort to disguise the humour in her tone. "However, there is no need to convince me of anything at the present. I'm doing what your boss asked me to do. I believe that's all that was required."

"Maybe that's what you understood," said the woman who seemed to be the leader of the small group. There was a threat, poorly hidden, in her tone. "But I'm afraid that's not how we do business on this ship. I'd like to hear you tell me about your loyalty to Grigory before we leave here."

Ysbel was studying her. "No," she said at last. "I don't think I will. Because what you're asking is stupid, and I don't like to talk to stupid people." She made as if to turn away.

"You'll answer the question," the woman snapped.

Ysbel gave her a long look, letting the emotion drain from her face.

A hint of uncertainty began to form in the woman's expression.

"It was very brave of you, bringing your family on board Grigory's ship," said the man who'd first addressed her, stepping forward and putting a hand on her arm. There was a smile on his face, but it wasn't a friendly one. "Your wife is a lovely woman, you know. And your children—"

She grabbed him, gave a short twist of her arm, and suddenly he was bent forward, whimpering, his arm twisted up behind his back. She pulled him around so he formed a barrier between her and the others with their heat guns.

"You see," she said, in a reasonable voice. "This is an example. You come close to someone like that, someone you don't actually know, and you try to grab them by the arm? Like I said. Stupid."

She twisted harder, and he whimpered again.

"And you talk like that about my family?" she said, even softer. "That is very, very stupid." She paused a moment. "I could break your arm, but then, that's not a very big problem for you, is it? A few weeks, some boneset, and it's healed. So no, on balance, I don't think

I want to break your arm." She hauled him up. He bent over, rising awkwardly on his toes to take the pressure off his shoulder.

"I could break your shoulder, of course, but again, that's hardly the sort of permanent solution I prefer."

There was a look in his face, something that might have been pitiful if he hadn't been so obviously used to pushing people weaker than him around.

And he'd mentioned Tanya, and the children.

No, she didn't feel any pity at all for this man.

The woman had drawn a heat-gun, but she didn't have a clear shot. Ysbel smiled.

From the corner of her eye, she caught a glimpse of a third man, who had sidled along the wall until he was almost in position to shoot her without hitting his companion. She yanked a heat-gun out of her pocket with her free hand and pointed it at him.

He froze.

"It's funny, you know," she mused. "I've listened to you all talking in the hallways. You think you're very tough. You brag that you don't keep track of how many people you kill." She twisted the arm just a little bit farther, right to the point where he'd feel like his shoulder was about to snap in two, but where it wouldn't actually be in danger of doing so.

Yet.

"But I do. At least, all the ones I remember."

The three mafia thugs were all frozen, staring at her, and she smiled nostalgically. "You might want to ask around. I'm certain you had some friends we broke out of prison a couple months ago. In the mean time—" She paused a moment, and bent forward, so her mouth was close enough to her erstwhile attacker's ear that she could practically whisper. "In the mean time, if I wanted to, I could take the limbs from your body one by one. If I felt like it. And that, you know, wouldn't count as a murder. Because you'd still be alive when I was finished." She paused a moment. "Well, for a few minutes, anyway," she amended. "Now. Do you understand me?"

He nodded frantically.

"Good. So. What is going to happen is, I'm going to let you go in just a minute here. And your friend, who thought it was such a good idea to try to get behind me with his heat gun, is going to move back to where he started, so I can keep an eye on all five of you. And then —" she smiled slightly. "And then, we can talk about my family, if you like, and why I felt safe enough to bring them here."

She could almost feel him shaking in terror. She smiled to herself, then, with a quick jerk, yanked his arm up just a fraction more, let go, and shoved him forward. He staggered away from her, tears of pain in his eyes, and before the woman in front of her could re-calibrate her aim, Ysbel pointed her modded gun at the ceiling and pulled the trigger.

There was a blinding flash of light that left white balls of fire ricocheting across her vision, even though she'd known what was coming and closed her eyes, and the skin on her face felt stretched and raw from the blow-by heat.

For a few moments, there was no sound at all in the room, except for the slow 'drip … drip …" of melted non-reactive coating puddling on the floor, and the high-pitched 'ting' and 'crack' of overheated material cooling.

When she could see again, she noticed, with satisfaction, that the five mafia boyeviki were huddled together in the corner, staring at her with what could only be described as terror.

The woman spoke frantically into her com, her voice low, and a moment later, the door burst open, and boyeviki flooded in. They were brandishing a mix of heat pistols and brass knuckles that were probably supposed to be frightening.

The posture of the woman in the corner relaxed, and a small smile spread across her face.

"Alright, Ysbel," she said, when the boyeviki had assembled themselves around her. "You've shown me your toy pistol is impressive. But I'm not sure that's enough to—" She frowned. "What are you—"

"As I told you. I care about my family very, very much. But do you honestly think I would have brought two small children onto Grigory Korzhikov's ship if I didn't think that this was the safest place in the system for them? And perhaps you want to know why I think that." She paused. "It's because if anyone even thought about touching them, that person would die in a very messy way. And then no one else would think about touching them, for as long as I was on this ship."

There was dawning worry on the faces of the gathered mafia, but before they could react, Ysbel had ripped the top off a packet of her gel explosive and squeezed a cold spray of sharp, acrid-smelling liquid across the group of them.

They froze.

"I could," she said, in a conversational tone, "blow you into a crater that would take out the shell of the ship. If I wanted to." She paused for a long, long moment, watching the visible swallowing.

"But," she said at last, "I don't believe I will at this moment." She paused, and turned to the woman. "I think, perhaps, before you decide it's a good idea to threaten guests, you should maybe look a little closer into their backgrounds. I'm a mass murderer. Perhaps you know that. And that was five and a half years ago. Five and a half years that I've been improving my explosives. So." She paused again. "I think, perhaps, we should come to an agreement. You will agree to stay very, very far away from my family. You will tell all of your friends the same thing. And, because I'm feeling generous at the moment, I won't blow you up."

There was a long exhalation from the gathered boyeviki.

"Now," she said, her voice almost friendly. "I would suggest you all go shower off, and that you make sure you wash well, and you make sure that all the waste water is vented outside the ship. Because it would be a pity if I were to accidentally bump the controller. It would cause a mess, and I don't think Grigory is the kind of person who likes a mess on his ship. Am I correct?"

There were a smattering of timid nods.

"Good. Well then, off you go." She waived a shooing hand at them.

There was a moment of terrified stillness, and then, one by one, they slipped out the door.

Beneath the fear in their eyes, she saw a hint of respect.

She smiled to herself in satisfaction. Unless she missed her guess, Grigory's ship would be running low on warm bathing water over the next hour or so.

When they were all gone except the woman in the corner, Ysbel gave her a small smile.

"I assume that is a sufficient demonstration? Because I can demonstrate further if you want me to."

The woman glanced involuntarily down at her soaked shirt and shook her head, in a shell-shocked sort of way.

"Good," said Ysbel. "Then I think I will go back to my work. And you can tell Grigory whatever you would like about my loyalties. Now. Off you go."

The woman glared at her, but she turned and followed the others out the door.

Ysbel smiled grimly to herself.

Perhaps she'd made enemies. But still, she'd always found that enemies who were very, very convinced that you could kill them without a second thought weren't enemies she was particularly worried about.

She drew in a long breath, and turned back to her work.

Perhaps Tanya didn't agree with what she was doing. But if it kept her and the children safe—well, perhaps that didn't matter, in the end.

8

Tae stepped out the door to their quarters, looking around him quickly.

The hallway was empty, but for some reason that didn't stop the shiver that ran down his back.

He tapped something into his com.

He couldn't spoof all the cameras on the ship without making them suspicious, but at the very least, he could make it so they'd have to track him with visuals. So he let himself show up on the cameras when he couldn't avoid it, and kept his com untraceable, and made very, very certain that the way the blocker on his com was set, there was no way they could overhear anything he said.

He tried to force his shoulders to relax as he walked down the hallway.

It said something that it was easier to avoid being watched in prison than on this opulent ship. Then again, as between here and prison, the chance that he'd be murdered in a hallway was a lot higher here.

Whatever Masha had told Grigory seemed to have worked. Most of the others had already been co-opted in to help—except for Tanya, who they clearly viewed as Ysbel's child-care, and probably

Jez, who mostly seemed to be intent on making enemies out of every single person on the ship—but to his surprise, he'd been left alone.

It wasn't going to last, he was almost certain. But in the mean time—in the mean time, he couldn't handle sitting on his hands in the suite of rooms they'd been given for one moment longer.

Grigory wasn't telling them everything. Masha wasn't telling them everything. And yes, he wasn't some genius like Lev, and yes, the chances of him somehow figuring out what was going on by wandering around the ship were slim to none, but—well, at least he could tell himself he was doing something.

The hallway he was walking down joined another that connected to the kitchens, and at the intersection he stood back for a moment, hesitant to be swept into the flood of humanity, servers hurrying back and forth, boyeviki coming and going, kitchen staff shouting down the hall for supplies. He took a deep breath and was on the point of turning around, when he frowned suddenly.

There was something familiar about one of the servers. He was facing away from Tae, but it was something about the way he was walking, the shape of his silhouette.

He couldn't place it, but he'd swear he knew the man from somewhere.

There shouldn't be anyone on this ship he knew, other than the crew.

He frowned and stepped into the hallway, trying to keep the man in sight.

Whoever it was walked quickly, and Tae dodged around servers and boyeviki, and got sworn at at least half a dozen times, before he saw the man disappear through the swinging doors into the kitchen.

He glanced around quickly.

No one was looking at him, at least not in particular.

He pushed through the doors and stepped inside.

Stepping through, he almost bumped directly into a server who was sweeping past with two large trays of expensive-looking drinks. She shot him a withering glare, and he flattened himself against the wall and looked around quickly, taking in his surroundings.

This must be the kitchen behind the bar in the gambling hall. It was small and crowded, packed with servers coming and going, all dressed in the dark blue-black trimmed with gold that seemed to be the uniform here. It was clearly a busy time of day, and trays of drinks and food were being whisked past him at a speed that almost made his head spin. There was a low buzz of chatter, interspersed here and there with a raised voice, calling for an order, shouting at an underling.

And then he heard a voice raised in anger, and glanced over, and almost forgot to breathe.

The man he'd followed down the hallway, dressed in a server's uniform and holding a full tray of drinks balanced on one hand, stood in front of an hard-eyed woman who appeared to be a supervisor. His face was turned away, his voice low and intense, but for just a moment he'd glanced over in Tae's direction, and Tae was almost certain …

Through some fluke, the noise of the kitchen faded for an instant, and in that moment, he heard the man's voice.

"No," he said quietly.

Tae felt suddenly dizzy.

He knew that voice.

"You can't send him out there. You've seen those people. He's just a kid."

"He's going out, and he's going right now," the woman snapped. "They requested a young server."

"No. I'll go."

"You know who this is. She won't hesitate to shoot you."

"And you'd send a kid into that? I'm going." The man turned in frustration, and Tae glimpsed his face again. Despite the short beard and the unfamiliar clothing, the man's pleasant features, his cultured air and tall, slender form, the good-humoured smile-lines around his eyes and mouth that were apparent even now, when he was scowling, were unmistakable.

He hadn't been dreaming it.

It was Ivan.

What the hell was Ivan doing here? Because Tae was pretty sure that the last time he'd seen the man, after they'd broken him out of prison, he'd been climbing onto one of the ships Tae had resurrected, and, if Tae remembered correctly, planning to go find some old friends where he could lay low until the government wasn't actively trying to recapture him anymore.

Ivan swung around, headed out the door to the gambling hall, and Tae recognized the determined set to his shoulders.

Damn.

Whatever was about to happen, it was probably going to mean trouble.

He took a deep breath and shoved his way as quickly as he could through surprised servers and angry supervisors, ignoring the shouted questions behind him, and burst out the door after Ivan.

The room he'd stepped into practically dripped wealth, the sort of careless opulence that managed to convey that whoever stayed there had so many credits that they could drown in them, so many that the weight of that much wealth hung around them like gravity, and they didn't care that the rest of the system knew about it. The gold gleamed from the walls and pillars like reflected sunlight, sharpening the contrast between the brilliant, elegant glow of the artificial lights, and the dark, whisper-soft carpet and walls, the smooth, expensive sheen of the stone of the tables. He blinked for a moment, too dazzled to see what he was looking for.

And then he heard a voice raised sharply, and he turned instinctively towards it.

"I asked for a young server. That kid I saw in the back. What are you, almost thirty? I won't be insulted like this." The voice was sharp and hard, and a moment later he saw the woman it belonged to. She was dressed in the rich style of every other person in this room, wide-legged trousers of some rich, embroidered material, soft, knee-high boots, a shirt the colour of ivory, and a small golden vest that accentuated the richness of the embroidery on the front of the shirt. Her face was hard, and she'd grabbed Ivan by the front of his uniform. Tae felt a momentary jolt of terror.

"I'm sorry," said Ivan, his voice mild, but with a note of steel under it. He still had the tray of drinks balanced in one hand. "I'm taking his place for this evening, and I'll be happy to help you."

The woman snatched a drink off the table and dashed it into Ivan's face, shoving him backwards. There was a *crash* as the tray dropped to the ground, and then Ivan was grabbed from behind by two people who must have been bodyguards. His face was grim, and there was that familiar set to his jaw that Tae recognized from prison.

Damn it to hell.

Tae snatched a glass off the tray of a passing server and sprinted across the room. He reached them as one of the bodyguards planted a heavy fist in the centre of Ivan's stomach. Ivan doubled over, gasping for breath, and Tae flung the contents of the drink in the face of one of the guards and smashed the empty glass across the bridge of the other's nose. Then he shoved the sputtering first guard backward, wrenched Ivan's arm from his grasp, and pushed him out of the way.

Ivan stared at him in open-mouthed astonishment.

"Come on!" Tae grabbed him by the arm and yanked him forward, and Ivan blinked, and started after him at a run.

"Where are we going?" Ivan hissed as they ran.

"I have no plaguing idea!"

The eye-watering califaction of a heat-gun blast distorted the air over their heads, and Tae pulled Ivan down into a half-crouch.

"Alright. Out into the hallway and turn left," Ivan panted as they shoved through the doors, shouts and running footsteps following them.

Tae didn't bother to question, just ran, and a moment later, Ivan dragged him down a small side corridor and shoved him into what appeared to be a supplies closet. He pulled the door shut behind them, and for a moment they sat there in the dark, breathing heavily.

Running footsteps passed in the outer corridor, and they could hear the sound of muffled shouting and swearing through the thick door.

When the last of the clamour had finally passed, Ivan hit his com light, and in its dim blue glow, he stared at Tae.

He had a short-cropped beard now, and his black hair, tousled from their mad escape, fell in dark curls across his forehead now that it wasn't cut prison-short. But he had the same warm, sensitive face, the same cultured look as he'd had when Tae had known him, and even in the dim light the good humour in his mouth and eyes was easily visible. But where in prison he'd had an air of weariness and hopelessness, now his dark eyes twinkled with repressed amusement, and a smile danced around the edges of his mouth, no matter how grim he was clearly trying to look. And Tae found he was smiling in relief at the sight of him.

"Tae?" asked Ivan after a moment. The disbelief in his voice, combined with the strain of the last few minutes, was enough to make Tae have to bite back a laugh. "What—I'm sorry, but what in the actual hell are you doing here?"

Tae drew in a deep breath, still fighting the irrational urge to laugh, and shook his head. "I was about to ask you the exact same thing."

They looked at each other for a long moment, and at last Ivan blew out a breath and shook his head. "Since you just saved me from probably getting a heat-blast in the gut, I guess I owe you one." He paused a moment, gathering his thoughts. "I'm here because—well, after you and your friends broke me out of prison, I went back to some cousins of mine to lie low for a while. But—" He let out a quick, frustrated breath. "I told you my family's been in government forever. My sister has a position as an under-minister. And they told me Grigory's people have been trying to meet with her for months now. She hasn't agreed, but then a few weeks back, they stopped. Everything stopped." He shook his head tightly. "I'm worried about her. I think something's going to happen. She's been hearing rumours about something big going down in the mafia, and—" He shrugged, with a small, self-deprecating smile. "I suppose I thought maybe I could find out something, maybe keep her safe. Grigory's ship stays in ungoverned space. A perfect place for a former convict to apply for work. I hired on as a server two weeks ago, and I've been trying to figure out what's going on."

Tae was still staring at him. "I—I thought you'd—I don't know, try to stay alive for a few months, at least?"

Ivan gave a slightly-rueful laugh. "If you recall, I was thrown in prison in the first place for protesting against the government. I—suppose I was never really the smart type." He frowned suddenly. "But why in the system are you here? Did the mafia capture you? What's going on?"

Tae shook his head and sighed. "It's—a long story."

Ivan gave a low laugh. "Honestly, Tae, with what I know about you and your friends, I'd be shocked if it wasn't." He glanced around quickly. "I want to hear all of it, but we'll probably need to move. That woman I insulted is notorious here. Her bodyguards will do a lot more than a cursory glance-through to find me for her." He gave a rueful smile. "And I suppose I should thank you, again. It seems like every time I meet you, you're pulling me out of the way of someone's fist."

"And every time I meet you, you're trying to stick up for some stupid, helpless kid who's got himself into trouble," Tae muttered, grinning despite himself.

Ivan laughed again. "Well, in my defence, you were never actually either stupid, or helpless." He pushed himself to his feet. "Come on."

Tae stood as well. "Where did you want to go?"

Ivan shrugged. "I don't know. Another closet, probably. If we can stay out of sight for long enough that she takes her pique out on someone else, I'll sneak back into the kitchens later."

Tae stood as well, with a decisive shake of his head. "No. I have a better idea. I'll take you back to our rooms." He glanced at his com. "Masha will be gone, most likely, and most of the others, and you can sit tight there until it's safe to come out."

Ivan gave him a worried glance. "You can't take me back there. You'll end up in more trouble than you're already in."

"Give me a minute," said Tae. He glanced around quickly, slipped out of the cupboard, and walked casually down the hall between two of the cameras. Once he'd passed, he tapped his com and fed the video image into the spoof. Then he sprinted back down the hall and yanked the closet door open.

"We've got to hurry," he said. "This will only work as long as there's no one else in the corridor. Let's go."

Ivan stared at him for a moment. "What—"

"I spoofed the cameras," he said through his teeth. "Let's go."

Ivan shook his head, chuckling. "I'd almost forgotten what it's like to work with you, Tae. Alright, let's get out of here."

They ran down the corridors as silently as they could manage, and when they reached the door, they were both panting. Tae waved his com in front of the lock, and the lock clicked. He pushed the door open, shoved Ivan inside, pulled it closed again, then tapped something into his com. He took a deep breath as the spoof disengaged, and glanced behind him down the corridor.

No one.

Nothing odd about him strolling casually down the corridor on camera, pausing in front of the door, and opening it.

He slipped inside, pushed the door shut, and leaned against it, releasing the breath he'd been holding.

Ivan smiled at him from a seat in the corner. He glanced around the small room and raised a questioning eyebrow. "So. Time for your long story, I think."

9

Jez frowned at the muffled voices from the room outside. It was Tae, but she was pretty sure the other voice wasn't Lev.

She stood, putting her hand to her heat-pistol. Kid hadn't got himself in trouble, had he? From the way he'd been skulking around, she wouldn't put it past him.

Carefully, she nudged her door open just a crack.

She stared for a moment. Then she shoved the door all the way open, grinning in delighted disbelief. "Ivan?"

Ivan turned and saw her, his face forming a look of mingled happiness and wariness.

"Jez?" he asked cautiously.

"Yep." She came over and dropped down into a seat beside him, still grinning broadly. "What the hell are you doing here, you sly bastard?"

"Last time I saw you, you looked closer to dead than alive," said Ivan, his expression bemused and still slightly cautious.

Jez laughed loudly. "Can't get rid of me that easily. Anyways, it's been like two months. I got over it."

"That—isn't very long, for some people," murmured Ivan. "Although I'm beginning to suspect that for you—" He shook his head. "So, I assume you've been keeping busy, then."

She shrugged. "Well, since then basically Lena tried to blow us up
—"

"The smuggler boss?" asked Ivan in a sort of fascinated horror, turning to Tae. Tae nodded.

"And then the government tried to blow us up, and some police officers tried to blow me up, and then some assassin tried to blow me up, except tech-head here disarmed the bomb—" she paused a moment. "OK, the assassin might have been government too. Anyways, and then Lev's old university professor tried to blow me up, and then we breathed in a bunch of crap that supposedly is going to let the government kill us all as soon as they figure their way around whatever Lev and Ysbel and tech-head did to mess with their system, and then the mafia kidnapped Tae's friend, and then—" she paused again, considering. "Nope, guess that's all."

Ivan stared at her for a moment, then stared back at Tae.

"I—what—I—Is she telling the truth?"

Tae sighed heavily, and nodded. "Unfortunately, yes."

Jez leaned back and enjoyed the look on Ivan's face. "Hey," she said, when it became apparent that he wasn't going to say anything unless someone stepped in. "Didn't peg you as the type to join the mafia."

Tae glared at her. "He didn't join the mafia. He's here because there's something going on, and he's trying to figure out what it is."

She raised an eyebrow. "Yeah? What is it, then?"

Ivan turned back to her, his expression concerned. "I wish I knew." He sighed. "I haven't been able to learn much. I've only been here two weeks or so, to be honest. But he's moving his people around, and there are weapons and credits flowing in here like he's calling in all his favours. Whatever it is—" he broke off, shaking his head. "I don't know if you've ever had a run-in with the mafia, either of you, but if they end up with more power—well, you think the system is bad with the Central Committee in charge." His voice took on a hint of wryness. "It is bad, I know—I spent four years in prison proving it. But this would be worse. Much worse. These people are brutal. They make the government enforcers look like damn saints."

Jez watched him, a faint unease stirring in her stomach.

To be honest, she'd felt uneasy since the moment they'd set foot on this ship, but she'd managed to push it aside until now, managed to convince herself it was because of that idiot Lev and because she was stir-crazy, and because she wanted to be back on the *Ungovernable*.

But it wasn't.

She'd worked with Lena, for years. Lena had been working with what she had, and what she had was a small crew and a few beater ships, and just enough more ruthlessness than the other smuggling bosses to take jobs that no one else would.

But Grigory, working with what he had?

She shivered.

Still ... Jez knew what had happened to Masha's family, at least some of it. And she was pretty damn sure that Masha wouldn't work with these bastards unless she had a very, very good reason to. And so far, Masha hadn't actually betrayed any of them, at least not yet. Even when she probably could have.

"So," she said at last, "what do we do?"

Ivan raised an eyebrow at her. "Well, I was actually hoping that Tae would explain to me what you're all doing here. I mean, besides apparently almost getting killed."

Tech-head's expression was back to its customary mixture of

worry and frustration. She sighed and leaned forward. "I'll tell you," she said quietly.

Tae shot her a grateful look.

"We didn't plan on coming here, exactly," she said. "Except they kidnapped one of Tae's street-kid friends, and told Masha to show up here if we wanted her back. And—" she shrugged. "I guess after everything, we didn't really want Masha to go alone. So we came with."

Ivan turned to Tae, his mild face creased in concern. "Are they still holding your friend?"

Tae shook his head mutely.

"But here's the thing," said Jez. "I wasn't joking about the crap the government's doing, with the gas that gets inside your brain. When we were at Lev's old university, we found out about it. But we weren't quite in time to stop it. And now there's a thing in our heads, all of us, and basically everyone in Prasvishoni, and Tae's friends and everybody. And Lev and Ysbel and Tae screwed up the government's system, and it's going to take them a while to fix it, but once they do?" She shrugged. "We're dead. All of us. And a whole lot more people too, and there's nothing to stop the government from using it on every damn planet in the system."

Ivan turned back to Tae, frowning.

"It's a metal alloy," Tae said, his tone short with worry. "It's highly soluble, and it's highly susceptible to electricity, and they can program it. And if you breathe it in, or it gets in your water or food—once it's in your bloodstream, it's programmed to congregate in your brainstem. And once there's enough of it built up—You remember the chips they implanted in your head in prison?"

Ivan's hand came up, with a movement that looked almost involuntarily, to touch the scar on his temple.

Tanya had a matching scar, and Olya, and Misko.

"They'd be able to kill you," Ivan said softly. "They'd be able to send a charge and kill you."

Tae nodded.

Ivan shook his head, and the expression on his face reminded Jez of how she'd felt the first time she'd heard about the program. Of the sick, empty, horrified hole that had opened up in her chest when they were standing on the steel walkway, gas hissing around them, and she'd held her breath until she thought she was going to pass out, and then, because she didn't have any choice, she'd breathed in the thing that would kill her.

"What does that have to do with the mafia?" Ivan asked at last, turning back to her.

She shrugged wearily. "It doesn't. Except apparently he's planning on getting a bunch of low-life scum-sucking bureaucrats onto his ship to agree to lick his boots in exchange for credits, and Masha's convinced him to invite the minister over the program to come along. And then he's going to shoot her."

Ivan's frown was deepening. "And in exchange you're working with Grigory? All of you?" There was a tone in his voice that was something between worry and concern and horror, and Tae wasn't meeting his eye, which was stupid, because of all of them, Tae was the only one who'd actually not agreed to this.

"Well," she said, "Masha is, and Ysbel and Lev. And I'm with them, I mean, even though I've basically just been cheating as many of the bastards as I can out of their credits." She paused a moment, grinning reminiscently. "But Tae didn't. Isn't. He's here because he's too damn stupid to leave the rest of us to whatever it is we deserve, and too smart for us to be able to get along without him. So he said he'd stay to make sure we didn't get into trouble we couldn't get out of, basically."

Ivan glanced over at Tae again.

"I—" Tae sighed. "Look, Lev thinks this is the only way to fix this."

"And do you?" asked Ivan at last, quietly.

Tae shook his head, looking away. "I don't know. Maybe. But I—" he looked up again, his habitual scowl back on his face. "I don't believe working with Grigory is the answer. I know how the mafia works. I know what they do, and—" he broke off. Ivan was still watching him, one eyebrow raised.

"Well," Ivan said at last, but the worry was clear in his tone, "I'll be honest, I'm with Tae." he paused a moment. "There's something going on. Whatever it is Grigory's planning, I can promise you it's more than corrupting a few government ministers. And if he has someone like Lev working with him? Or Ysbel? I've seen what you people can do. He's using you for something, and it's probably nothing good."

The unease from earlier had grown, and it coiled in her stomach.

"OK," she said finally. "You're trying to figure out what Grigory is up to. Whatever it is you think he's using us for. But you don't know what it is yet, right?"

Ivan nodded.

Tae was looking at her, frowning.

She shot him a grin, which didn't seem to reassure him at all. "Well, turns out, you lucky bastard, you just might have caught a break. Because I bet you could find out things a lot more easily if you had a bit of a distraction. Keep the mafia bastards busy, let you poke around a bit."

There was a look of dawning realization on Ivan's face, and dawning horror on Tae's.

"Jez—" Tae began. "You're not going to—"

She grinned wider.

"What are you—"

She rolled her eyes. "Relax, tech-head. It's basically not even dangerous."

"Why do I not believe you even a little bit?" he said through gritted teeth.

She shrugged. "Maybe you have trust issues. Anyways, I've been gambling with those mafia bastards, and—"

"You've been—" Ivan started.

"And thing is, they all want to know how I'm cheating them, it's basically driving Fyoder crazy, so they keep agreeing to gamble with me. And anyways, I figure I can keep at least some of them focused on something other than a couple idiots who want to play spy, at least a few days." She stood, with a sigh of happiness.

She damn well needed something to keep her mind off … well, off everything.

"You've been cheating—" Ivan said.

"Jez, you can't just—" Tae began at the same time. She gave both of them a tight grin.

"Look. I can. And I have. And here's the thing, if I'm stuck on this damn ship for one more day without doing something I'm going to start getting into fights, and then I figure they're going to eventually get sick of me and try to kill me, so—" she shrugged. "So figure this is doing me a favour too."

Tae sighed. "Jez."

"It's a good idea, tech-head. I was going to do it anyways. You may as well take advantage."

"You were going to do what, exactly?" asked Ivan cautiously. Tae turned to him in exasperation.

"She was going to go into a mafia-run gambling hall and cheat the highest-ranking mafia officers she can talk into playing with her out of everything they own, is what she was going to do."

Ivan raised an eyebrow. "That sounds—about what I would have expected, to be honest."

"Yep," she said cheerily. "Anyways, I have an appointment down in the gambling hall in about ten minutes. I was just getting ready to head down there when you two showed up. So—" She shot them a jaunty grin. "Gotta run."

Tae had dropped his head into his hands. She rolled her eyes at him.

"Tech-head. Relax. They're not going to kill me until they figure out how I'm cheating them."

"How … exactly are you—" began Ivan.

She winked, sauntered to the door, and pulled it open. "Good to see you, Ivan."

"Be careful," he called after her. "There are people down there who— "

She didn't hear the rest of the sentence, because the door swung shut behind her.

She stood in the passageway for a moment, bouncing on her toes. The unease from earlier was still twisting in her stomach, and it mixed with the vague sense of wrongness she'd had ever since she set foot on this ship, and with the tight wad of something in the back of her head, that she wouldn't let herself think about, and that tried to crack open every time she looked at Lev, and it set her fingers drumming restlessly against her thigh and her heel tapping against the carpet if she stood still for even one second.

She took a deep breath.

It was fine, and she was fine. It would all be fine, she just needed to get into the gambling hall, and maybe tonight would be a good night to get drunk.

No.

She squeezed her eyes shut.

Ivan was here, and he wouldn't be here if there wasn't something wrong. And maybe he was right, maybe Grigory was using Lev and Masha and the others for something, and they had no idea.

Or maybe—

Masha wasn't telling them everything. Masha never told them everything. And maybe, just maybe—well, after however many months, she had actually begun to like Masha. She'd actually begun, just a little, to trust her. But Masha knew a hell of a lot more than she was letting on.

And the look on Masha's face when she'd first seen Grigory, that had been gone so quickly that Jez almost thought she might have imagined it—

Well. Let Ivan and tech-head figure that out. Right now, she had an appointment to keep.

She wasn't more than half-way to the gambling hall before a voice from behind her stopped her dead.

"Solokov."

The voice was unfamiliar, but there was a purring menace in it that told her whoever it was either knew her, or knew of her.

She turned slowly.

Five boyeviki stood there casually, blocking the hallway.

None of them looked like they were here to make friends.

She grinned at them. "That's me. Who's looking?"

The man stepped forward. "We are. We're here to teach you some manners before you go down to the gambling hall tonight."

She felt her grin widen. "Yeah? Well, sorry to disappoint you, Fyodor already did that. So figure you all can—"

"Fyodor asked us to finish what he started," said the man.

Jez dived out of the way as one of the women, who'd been edging her way along the side of the corridor, leapt for her.

She rolled, jumped to her feet, and took off at a dead run, heart pounding.

No time to call for help, and honestly, calling for help would probably only get more people hurt.

Someone grabbed her by the arm, and as her momentum swung her around, she caught a fist in her stomach that knocked the breath from her. She doubled over, gasping, and caught another fist in the ribcage.

Damn.

She grimaced, pretending to go limp, and when the grip on her arm loosened she straightened abruptly, jerking her arm from her attacker's grasp and bringing up her elbow to connect with his jaw. He staggered, and Jez ducked another fist, driving the top of her head into the woman's sternum. The woman fell back, gasping for breath, and someone else grabbed Jez from behind. She stamped down hard on the toe of a soft boot, and its owner howled in pain. Jez spun, her back against the wall, and yanked out Ysbel's modded pistol.

"You think—" one of the men growled.

She squeezed the trigger.

All five of her attackers dropped, stunned, to the ground.

Jez looked around at them in satisfaction, then tapped her com to the private line. "Hey Ysbel. Got the right gun this time."

"What trouble are you getting into now, you lunatic?" grumbled Ysbel though the com.

Jez shrugged. "Me? None at all. The idiots who tried to attack me, though—"

Ysbel sighed heavily. "Well. I'm glad you picked up the right pistol this time."

Jez shoved the gun back into her pocket, wincing slightly at what was probably going to be a pretty impressive bruise across her ribcage. "Me too, actually."

She tapped off the com and surveyed the unconscious boyeviki for a moment before she headed down to the gambling hall.

Wouldn't Fyoder be in for a surprise.

She glanced around quickly at the gambling hall entrance. Her marks were already waiting, a man and a woman she didn't recognize.

She paused abruptly.

And one man she did—Fyodor himself.

For half a moment, she considered ducking back out the door. But if he wanted to try to either kill her or beat the hell out of her again, she'd rather it happen in the gambling hall, in full damn view.

He looked up and saw her, and for a moment surprise and fury chased themselves across his face.

She gave him a wink and sauntered across the room. Her heart pounded, every muscle in her body tight.

"Hey there, you bastard," she said, sliding into a chair across from him. "Surprised to see me? Your friends here must have told you I'd be coming. Thought I'd get into an accident on the way over?"

He narrowed his eyes. "Jez. I'm glad to see you alive and well."

She cocked an eyebrow. "Really? Because that's not what I would have guessed. Considering you damn well had me ambushed in the corridor on the way here."

The other two glanced at Fyodor, but he didn't take his eyes of

Jez's face. "Don't overestimate your importance, Solokov," he said grimly. "They were there to do something I couldn't—teach you manners. And if you killed them—"

She grinned breezily. "Nope. 'Course not. Because I'm not a rotten plaguer like you are. They're alive. Might wish they weren't when they wake up, but—" she shrugged. Then she leaned forwards on the table. "But, be a shame if word got out that when you can't win at tokens, your next step is murder. I mean, I'm sure everyone in this hall knows you're a damn murdering scum-eater, but you want them to know you're a bad loser as well? That'd be a bit of a mark on your reputation."

The fury in his face was now completely unmixed with any other emotion. "Listen, Solokov—" he began through his teeth.

She leaned back. "Here's the thing, though. It's your lucky day. Told your friends here I'd play nice and slow tonight, give them a chance to figure out what I was doing. Since you all seem to be so damn convinced I'm cheating somehow. You can watch. You figure it out, guess you can kill me without any issues. Because hell, who cares if you kill a cheater? So—" She shrugged again.

He glowered at her for a moment, the hatred emanating from him thick enough she could almost reach out and touch it.

"Fine," he snapped. "I'll watch tonight. And I'll watch you every damn night, until I can prove what you're doing. And then—" he broke off, with a small, unpleasant smile. "Well. Grigory needs me, but he doesn't actually need a pilot."

She leaned back in her chair. The adrenalin pounding through her brain was as good as alcohol, and her whole body was light with it. "Guess we'd better get started, then."

She held out her com to the gambling chip in the centre of the table and let the credits click over. The woman she was playing against did the same. Then Fyodor pulled out a bag of gambling tokens and dumped them on the table, spreading them out between the players and turning them over, one by one.

"There. You can see these are regular tokens. I brought them myself, in case you fixed the tokens at the table."

She put on a slightly-offended look.

As if she was that much of an amateur.

"Jez," he said, still watching her with narrowed eyes. "Here's the thing. I respect Grigory. The people who work for me, they respect me. And when they respect me, I take care of them. I make sure they don't have problems. I make their lives run just a little easier. And when I need a favour from them? Well, what's a favour between friends?" He gave a small shrug. "You're a smart kid, Jez. I want to help you, I really do. But the way you're behaving, I can't. Think about that, alright?"

Jez donned her most innocent smile. "Yep. I see what you're saying." She paused a moment, waiting for the first hint of satisfaction on his face, before she drawled, "And if I ever feel like being respectful, you bastard, you'll be the first one I tell about it."

His expression hardened abruptly. "I think—"

"Hey," she said, spreading her hands. "We playing, or not?"

His eyebrows lowered, but slowly, he flipped the tokens over and spread them, then drew. She took a long, satisfied breath and drew as well, her fingers tingling with adrenalin.

The token she'd palmed was smooth against her hand.

And he hadn't even noticed.

She played three rounds with each of them before the evening was over. She could feel their eyes on her as she scooped up the betting chip. She shot them all a toothy grin.

"Look, better luck next time, OK? I played as slow as I could, figured you'd catch on."

No one said anything, but there was flat death in their stares. She gave them a wink, pocketed the chip, and strolled out of the gambling hall. When she glanced over her shoulder, they were still staring at her.

But she was pretty damn sure they weren't going to kill her now, not until they figured out how she was cheating them. And— She patted the chip in her pocket, a warm satisfaction flowing over her.

And she could probably cheat them out of a hell of a lot more credits before they caught on, honestly.

Really, distracting these idiots for Tae and Ivan looked to be maybe the most enjoyable job she'd had in a very long time.

10

Tae crouched behind a low partition in the small dining hall. It was dark now, the lights extinguished, the busy room empty.

Except for himself and Ivan, of course.

Ivan leaned over to him. "Only time of day when no one's in here. Between 600 standard and about 1200 standard. And since 1100 standard happens to be when the gambling hall opens, with Jez wreaking havoc at the tables, I assume most of the boyeviki's attention will be focused there."

Tae shot him a quick grin, then stood carefully, glancing around the room.

"There. The register," whispered Ivan.

The register stood behind the bar across the room, a long expanse of open space between them and it. And even though he'd spooled the cameras, and even though there was no one in the room, it was clearly visible from the outside hallway.

Cautiously he crept out from behind the partition and edged his way along the wall, keeping in the shadows. He could hear Ivan's soft footsteps behind him.

There were other footsteps, quick and sharp, from outside in the corridor, and he froze, hardly daring to breathe.

They passed, and he moved again, as quickly as possible without making noise.

More footsteps. He froze again.

Again they passed, and again he let out a breath. They were so close to the bar, and if they could just get behind it—

He glanced around again, and made a quick dash across the last of the open space, ducking down behind the bar. A moment later, Ivan joined him.

"We'll have to hurry," Ivan said. His face was tense. "I just got a notice on my com. Sounds like they're opening early today." He turned towards the bar and started pulling open drawers. Tae did the same.

There was nothing in the first drawer he checked, and an old, dusty bottle of alcohol that looked like it probably cost more than a standard long-haul ship in the second. Then—

"Found something," he whispered, scooping up the handful of chips. He dumped then into a pile on the floor, then started feeding them one at a time into his com. "What are we looking for?"

Ivan glanced over his shoulder. He'd found a pile of chips as well, and had them cupped carefully in his hand.

"There would be four columns, all numbers," he said. "Not sure what it would say at the top." His voice was tight with strain.

Tae gave a short nod. The chip he was holding looked to be a list of staff and their work times. Not bad information to have, at any rate, and he set his com to copy it, then pulled it out and tried another.

"Anything you find that might be useful, copy it," he whispered. "I set up a spoof file on your com—as long as you save it there, they'll have a hard time finding it even if they check you."

Ivan shot him a quick, tense grin.

Tae shoved four chips into his com in rapid succession. None of them were what he wanted—lists of supplies, a register for how much alcohol the ship had purchased in the last twenty days, a ledger for the day's purchases, a payroll. He copied all of them, because you never knew what would come in handy, and he certainly couldn't memorize everything at a glance like Lev could.

The thought of Lev made worry once again twist in his stomach, but this was not the time to worry about the mental and emotional wellbeing of his friend, considering one slip-up would end with both he and Ivan dead.

"Got it," Ivan whispered in satisfaction. He tapped his com quickly to copy the file. "I'll send it to your com as soon as we're—"

He froze suddenly, and Tae followed his lead.

The footsteps that had come down the hallway, that he'd heard from the corner of his brain and ignored, had turned into the room now.

He exchanged glances with Ivan. As silently as possible, he scooped up the handful of chips he'd spread out on the floor. Carefully, barely daring to breathe, he pulled open the drawer and carefully, he lowered the chips inside.

Ivan pulled the chip he'd been copying free of his com and started to do the same.

The footsteps were coming closer. They weren't running, and from the slow, steady tread of them, whoever it was hadn't noticed anything wrong. So that, at least, was a relief. But—

The lights in the dark room flooded on, and he and Ivan were suddenly completely illuminated.

They stared at each other, panic on both their faces.

The footsteps resumed their pace towards the bar, and Ivan managed a wry grimace, but Tae could see the fear behind his eyes.

Tae brought up his com, biting his lip, and tapped something in. The holoscreen popped up, and he began typing rapidly.

He'd gotten into the system to spoof the cameras, and he didn't really have time for anything else, but maybe, since he was far enough in already—The footsteps were almost there, and he could almost feel Ivan's tension—There!

The lights in the back corner of the room flickered off.

The footsteps slowed.

"What the hell?" a woman's voice muttered, and the footsteps paused a moment, then started off in the direction of the extinguished lights.

Ivan grabbed his arm and gestured with his head for Tae to follow. Tae nodded, and they crept out from behind the bar, inching their way around the tables towards the exit.

In the back, a short woman dressed in a server's uniform had pulled a chair around and was standing on it under the lights, peering up at them.

Maybe—

He tripped, and his foot bumped one of the chairs. It wasn't a loud noise, but it was enough that the woman turned, just as Ivan pulled him down behind the table. She was frowning, and her eyes scanned the room, and it would be only seconds—Tae pulled up his holoscreen and typed something frantically, and behind her, the extinguished light flickered a couple times.

She turned again to glare at it, and Ivan pulled him to his feet, and they sprinted the last few metres out the door and down the hallway, collapsing against the wall when they were out of sight. Tae hit his com and re-started the light he'd been fiddling with, and then he sank back against the wall in relief, closing his eyes for a moment.

When he opened them, Ivan was grinning at him, and he felt his heart rate slowing at last.

"Not bad, Tae," Ivan said. "You'd think you'd done something like this before."

Tae gave him a reluctant grin in return. "Or maybe just my entire life on the streets trying to get past police."

Ivan was watching him curiously. "I—didn't realize you'd grown up on the streets."

Tae shrugged.

The odd thing was, months ago he would have instantly felt defensive, certain that anyone who wasn't a street kid would use that information to find a way to either hurt him or turn him in.

But for some reason, it wasn't something he particularly worried about anymore. At least not here. There was something about the mild, good-humoured expression on Ivan's face when he wasn't thinking about anything, the intelligence mixed with kindness in his eyes, and—well, and he was a good man. Tae knew him well enough to know that.

"Well," said Ivan at last. "I'm glad you survived it. Not many do, I've heard."

Tae nodded again, suddenly sober.

It was true. And actually, the more he thought about it, the more he realized how sickeningly lucky he was that his kids had survived him being gone, because to have someone live to his age on the streets, to Caz and Peti's ages, was something that was growing increasingly uncommon.

And there were so many street kids. So many dead every winter season, so many fewer on the streets when the weather finally, grudgingly warmed.

The thought had always made him sick. But now, in the middle of the opulence of the mafia ship, he had to choke back the bile in his throat.

"Yeah," he said quietly, without meeting Ivan's eyes. "I was lucky, I guess."

Ivan raised an eyebrow. "I have a feeling it was a lot more than luck, Tae. You forget, I've worked beside you before." He paused a moment. "Lev, last night. He said—" he hesitated a moment. "He said your friends were—safe?"

Tae nodded, and Ivan smiled slightly in relief. "I'm glad."

"So am I."

They smiled at each other for a moment, then Ivan pushed himself to his feet. "Well, we should probably—"

"Tae Bezdomnikov."

Tae started, and spun around.

Behind him stood a tall woman, dressed in the uniform of the mafia boyeviki.

She had a slight smile on her face, and she was looking down at both of them.

Tae scrambled to his feet. His heart was racing, and his hands shook slightly.

"What are you doing here?" she asked quietly, but there was menace under her tone. Tae opened his mouth to reply, even though he wasn't entirely sure what he was going to say, and then from behind him he heard Ivan's voice.

"I'm sorry, Anfisa," he said, in that calm, mild tone of his. "I'm afraid it was my fault."

Tae half-turned in horror. He might be safe, somehow, considering that Grigory still wanted to stay on Masha's good side, but Ivan—

Ivan had gotten to his feet, and was looking down, slightly shame-faced. "I—we met the other day, when I was coming off my shift. I

—he was—I'm sorry, but I've always been a sucker for wavy hair, and—" he smiled sheepishly. "I asked him to meet me here when I was off work."

Anfisa looked at Ivan, her eyes narrowed. "I understood servers were not to flirt with patrons, Ivan Ivanovich."

Tae glanced at Ivan and cleared his throat. "Don't worry. There's no need to protect me," he said quietly. He turned to Anfisa, and gave her a small smile. "It wasn't him. I was the one who asked. I'm sorry if that wasn't permitted."

Anfisa turned to him thoughtfully. "Well," she said at last, "I suppose even in deep space love will find a way." There was an ironic tone to her voice that would have probably been offensive if he hadn't been so deeply relieved. "Well, Tae Bezdominkov. I was wondering if you'd come with me for a moment. If you two can bear to be apart for that long."

Tae shot Ivan a wry glance, and almost smiled at the sparkle of amusement in the man's face.

"I think we can manage," said Tae dryly. "Ivan, I'll see you another time. Time you got your rest anyways."

Ivan nodded, leaned forward, and gave Tae a kiss on the cheek, his short beard brushing Tae's skin. "I'll call you tonight," he whispered, then turned and walked off, and for a moment Tae was too shocked to respond. At last, he shook his head and glanced up. Anfisa was still watching him, her eyebrows raised.

He sighed to himself. First Dmitri in the university, and now this. Apparently, even though he might possibly be the only person on the entire *Ungovernable* crew who had never actually slept with anyone in his entire life—never even kissed anyone until a few weeks ago, although the thought of that still made an empty place ache in his chest—he was destined to be the one with the damn reputation.

"Alright," he said, bracing himself against the amusement in the woman's face. "I'll come. What do you need?"

He might as well get used to it at this point, honestly.

She led him down the narrow hallway and into one of the main corridors. "Masha told us that you'd all agreed to help," she said as they walked. "She mentioned that you didn't have the kind of skills we needed. But I was hoping that she was wrong."

He frowned, his stomach tightening.

Admittedly, Masha couldn't very well have told them that he'd rather walk out the damn airlock than work for the mafia without risking all their lives—but the fact was, it was the truth. Still, better to find out what they wanted.

He recognized the next hallway they turned down, and his stomach clenched tighter.

At the end of the hallway was a door with unmistakable gold trim.

Just before it, they turned aside to another door set into the wall, and Tae wasn't sure whether to be relieved or terrified. His guide tapped on the door, muttering something into her com, and a moment later pushed it open, gesturing Tae inside.

Slowly, his heart beating so fast that he was certain it would be audible, Tae stepped past her into the room.

Even after almost a week on the ship, the sheer opulence of the place still had the power to shock him.

Zhenya was sitting behind a large desk. They—he was pretty sure Zhenya used "they" pronouns—smiled as Tae stepped into the office, and he breathed in, fighting back the panic, and looked them over more carefully.

They were not much taller than he was. They had shoulder-length hair pulled back into a rats tail, similar to Masha's, and lazy, dark eyes. They were slender, probably middle aged—there were lines on their face, and a strand or two of grey in their dark hair—but there was a wiry strength behind their slender build. There was just the dusting of a beard along their jawline, accentuating the lines of their face, and their posture was that of a predator, all lazy confidence and repressed energy.

"Tae Bezdnomikov, Pakhan," said Anfisa, inclining her head respectfully. Zhenya nodded.

"Thank you, Anfisa," they said, and gestured Tae to a seat in front of the desk.

He sat warily.

There were body guards, of course, in the corners of the room, but they were making themselves inconspicuous, which was probably a good thing at this point. He managed to bump his com against his thigh as he sat—not much, but it should at least send his coordinates to the others if he disappeared and was never heard from again.

Anfisa left, closing the door behind her, and for a long, long moment, Zhenya studied him. At last they gave a small, predatory smile.

"Tae. I've been meaning to talk to you for some time." Their voice was light, without the hint of Grigory's outer-rim accent—they sounded like someone born and raised in Prasvishoni.

"Yes?" said Tae warily. "I'm not sure if Masha told you, but I don't—"

They raised their hand, and gave a slight, amused shake of their head. "I've heard what Masha's told me. I haven't got to where I am, though, by relying on what other people tell me." They leaned forward across their desk and studied Tae closely.

"So, Tae," they said at last. "I hear you're a hacker. A techy."

He clenched his teeth. "I thought Masha would have told you—"

Zhenya shook their head, a small smile on their face. "As I said,

Tae, I don't rely solely on what people tell me. I've looked into your background. I've looked into all your backgrounds, believe me. Grigory is a smart man, but he doesn't have time to check everything. That's my job. And I'm very, very good at it." They paused a moment. "You're a hacker and a techy. But not just that, are you?"

"I'm—not sure what you mean," Tae mumbled.

Was this about Vadym Dulik? About his prison sentence? Or—

"You're a street kid," said Zhenya, still watching him with that faint smile.

His blood turned cold.

Whenever someone brought that up, it meant they were going to try to hurt him. Or kill him. Because everyone in the damn system knew that former street kids were disposable.

"I—" His hands were sweating slightly.

The rest of the crew would probably never find him, although honestly, at the rate at which they'd been getting themselves into dangerous situations lately, the only surprising thing was that he'd lasted this long.

At least they'd know he'd been here, and Lev would be able to make the connection, and maybe Ivan would find the others, tell them what had happened. The information they'd needed was on Ivan's com, he was pretty sure—

"I'm honestly impressed," said Zhenya, one eyebrow raised slightly. They were watching Tae, as if gaging his reaction.

Tae stared at them for a moment. "I—You—"

"I'm impressed." Zhenya shrugged. "It's not easy to stay alive on the streets." They paused a moment. "Is there still that fallen down building to shelter under behind the apartments on Reka Street?"

Tae stared at them, frowning. Zhenya's smile broadened. "Did you think you were the only street kid to survive to grow up?”

Tae just stared, unable to speak for a moment.

“I go by Zhenya Novikov these days. We chose our new names on the day we become full boyeviki. But before I joined up with the mafia, I was Zhenya Bezdomikov.”

For a moment, Tae thought he’d somehow forgotten how to breathe. “You—you were a street kid?” he asked at last, his voice slightly choked. Zhenya grinned and leaned forward.

“Yes. I was a street kid.” They glanced around their office. “And now look at me. You know how long it’s been since I’ve been cold, Tae? How long it’s been since I’ve been hungry, and not known where I was going to get my next meal? It’s been a very, very long time.”

They smiled at the look on Tae’s face. “I know. You’d never have dreamed a street kid could grow up to become Grigory’s second in command. The thing is, though, the mafia’s not like the rest of the Svodrani system. Here, you’re judged on what you can do, not where you came from. And here, anyone, even a street kid, can rise in the ranks. Can rise to where I am.” They relaxed slightly, leaning back in their chair, and Tae studied them in disbelief.

Now that Zhenya had told him, he could see it in their posture, that eternal air of caution, of readiness, that slight tightness in their muscles that meant that no matter what the next threat was, they’d be able to fight or run on a moment’s notice. He had it, and Caz and Peti had it, because any street kid who didn’t was probably already dead.

“So,” said Zhenya, still smiling slightly. “Now you know. And what do you think of it?”

“I—” he trailed off, shaking his head slightly.

“I know. A bit of a shock, yes? But then, as soon as I found out you were a street kid, I knew I had to talk to you. Because I knew you'd help us. You'd have to, really. You have friends, don't you? Other street kids? I've heard things are bad back in the city these days. But when you have the kind of pull I have?" they shrugged. "It's not hard to pull some strings, get police to turn a blind eye, get a housing voucher for someone who might not have got it otherwise."

Tae swallowed, still staring.

A year ago, he might have jumped at this offer. A year ago and desperate, watching Mila shivering under her blankets, watching the agonized look on her brother's face, the blind, hopeless trust in his eyes when he glanced at Tae, that desperate faith that Tae would fix it, Tae would have a way to make it better and keep his little sister alive …

But—

He shook his head.

He would have wanted to jump at the offer. Just like something in him, the part of him that remembered that Caz and the others would be dead the moment the government figured out how to solve the bug Lev and Ysbel had planted in the Protocol system, wanted to jump at the offer now.

But he wouldn't. Wouldn't have, even then. Because he knew the price he'd have to pay, and he wasn't willing to pay it.

Of course, saying that out loud right now would be problematic. As in, would lead to his body being dumped from an airlock.

"So, Tae. What do you think?" said Zhenya.

Tae took a deep breath. "I—appreciate your kindness. I—your offer is—but—what would you want me to do? I mean, I'm probably —probably the best hacker on the streets. I could—" He tried to make his voice sound desperate. "Maybe it's not much compared to people who went to school. But I'm a fast learner. I bet I could pick it up quickly."

He caught the slight flash of uncertainty in Zhenya's eyes, and he bit back a quick breath of relief.

Zhenya frowned slightly. "Everything I heard said you were the best there was."

"I—am the best, on the streets," he said, pathetically eager. "Masha always said so. She said that's why she wanted me, instead of those other idiots who went to school."

Masha had better not have said anything about him, or there was a very good chance that both he and she would be killed for this.

Still, he didn't have any other ideas at the moment that didn't leave him either dead or working for the mafia.

"You—don't think you could keep up here?" Zhenya asked at last.

He forced his hands to relax, forced himself to breathe in and out slowly, rather than suck in the panicked breaths he wanted to. "I— I'm sure I could. If you gave me a chance, gave me some time."

Zhenya was still frowning, and their eyes had narrowed slightly. "Masha wanted you with her crew for a reason, yes?"

"Yes," he said finally, bitterly, dropping his head. "She did. She told me—she told me she wanted someone who was disposable. They all know it." He looked up. "But I swear, I'm good! If you just give me a chance to learn—"

Zhenya studied him for a few moments, thoughtfully.

"Alright, then, Tae," they said at last. "I'll give you a chance. I'd like your help with something."

Tae sucked in a quick breath, and Zhenya smiled slightly. "I just want you to hack something for me. I want to see what you can do."

"I—" He shook his head and let the breath out again. "I'll do what I can."

"Good," said Zhenya, raising their eyebrows. "Very good. Then why don't you show me what you can do?" They opened a drawer and pulled out a com that had been inside it.

"The other day, Grigory was attacked. We took this off of one of the dead attackers, but it has a code to it that I haven't been able to figure out. Could you take a look at it?"

They handed it over the table, and slowly, Tae reached out and took it.

"Go ahead," said Zhenya, nodding at him encouragingly.

He turned it over in his hands, then tapped it open and examined the chip. It looked like an internal chip, likely set to erase memory the moment you tried to draw it out.

Still—he turned it over in his hands again, frowning at it.

The solution was almost too simple.

Maybe this was the test, that if he couldn't do this he was obviously faking, because the solution was so obvious, masquerading under something that looked difficult.

He took a deep breath.

Whatever way he played it, he'd only get one chance at it.

He studied it for a few minutes longer, as if trying to figure it out. Zhenya was watching him, their face impassive.

His palms were wet, and he wiped them surreptitiously on his trouser legs. How long could he examine this without looking suspicious?

At last, after he'd taken as long as he thought would be believable, and then a little while longer still, he glanced up at Zhenya. "I— think I might see a way to get this information," he said slowly. "I'm not sure it will work, though."

Zhenya raised an eyebrow, and again, Tae had no idea what they were thinking. "Well," they said at last, gesturing. "Go ahead. Do what you can."

Tae looked back down at the com, his heart beating too quickly.

It was far too simple, and he was taking too much time, and Zhenya would almost certainly suspect him by now.

Gently, he jiggled the back of the com back and forth, loosening the connection. When it was almost apart, but not far enough apart to trigger the defence, he rummaged in his pocket and pulled out a scrap of wire. Gently he fed it in, and then took the other end and touched it to the connecter on his com. He didn't look up as he did it.

Maybe that was the trap, maybe Zhenya wanted a chance to spy through to see what he had on his own com.

But they couldn't have anticipated the mods he'd put on. If there was something set to grab his information the moment he connected, Zhenya would get a copy of the spoof he'd set up—a normal com schematic, with nothing even remotely unusual loaded onto it.

He pulled up his holoscreen and began typing, keeping his keystrokes slow and uncertain. Make it look like even now, he wasn't completely confident in his solution.

This wasn't even hacking, this was just using whatever crap tools you had to force the system.

This was going to look almost ridiculously suspicious. There was no way that Zhenya wouldn't catch on.

But they were still watching him impassively.

Finally, when he thought he could put it off no longer, he typed in the final command.

A holoscreen popped up above the com he'd been working with, and he gave what he hoped was a convincing sigh of relief.

"There," he said. "I did it. See?"

Zhenya looked at the com, then at him, then back at the com.

When they turned back to Tae, they were wearing a broad smile.

"Well, Tae," they said. "I see Masha's been holding out on me. I've never seen someone use a solution like that to retrieve com memory. Maybe you're not a hacker. But you're smart. That's a good thing. I can use that."

For a second, he thought they were joking.

Then, to his horror, he realized they were … serious.

They were honestly impressed.

He bit back a curse.

Zhenya leaned back in their chair, an expression of satisfaction on their face. "Well, Tae," they said. "I'm glad I spoke with you today. I hope that Masha isn't underutilizing your talents."

He had, for a moment, the brief flash of too many memories jumbled together, standing in front of some locked door or security system franticly trying to hack through before someone killed them all.

He'd felt a lot of damn things since he'd joined Masha's crew, but under-utilized had never been one of them.

He managed to paste a smile on his face. "Thank you."

"No," said Zhenya, "thank you. It is always good to meet a fellow street kid." They rose, and held out their hand. Reluctantly, Tae took it.

"You never know, Tae," said Zhenya softly. "There's a long ways to rise in the mafia. If you have the temperament for it, you could do very well here. And you'd always have a friend as long as I'm around."

"I—appreciate it," said Tae, swallowing down the panic in his throat.

Zhenya smiled, and walked around the side of their desk, pulling the door open for him. "I assume you can find your way back?"

He nodded, and stepped outside.

Once he was out of the office and down the hall, he leaned against the wall and shut his eyes and tried to stop his hands from trembling.

His com was buzzing, and he tapped it.

"Tae?" Lev's voice was thick with concern. "Are you alright? Ivan came running in here, and I got your message—"

"I'm fine," Tae said wearily.

There was a moment's pause. "Where are you? What were you doing?"

He took a deep breath. "I'm outside of Zhenya's office. And apparently, I'm making all sorts of damn friends in the mafia."

11

Ysbel frowned down at her work table.

At the very least, they had good equipment here. Possibly the best she'd ever worked with, in all honesty. If having this much funds allowed you to have this caliber of equipment, it was almost no wonder that working for the mafia was such a prized job.

And, unsurprisingly, since the incident in the weapons room a few days back, she'd been left entirely to her own devices.

Apparently there were rumours circulating about her.

Not a bad thing, to tell the truth.

"Ysi?"

She turned quickly.

Tanya stood in the doorway, that strange, hard expression on her face she'd been wearing so often these days.

"Come in," said Ysbel, standing, and Tanya slipped inside. "Do you want to sit?"

Tanya hesitated a moment, then at last pulled up a chair and sat on the edge of it. There was a note of tension in her posture.

"Ysi?" she said again, and Ysbel turned to her, frowning.

"What is it, my love?"

It had been a long time since the two of them had talked. It seemed that every time she came in, Tanya was with the children.

Since the incident in the weapons room, the mafia had left Tanya and the children completely alone. At any rate, they had no reason to be interested in Tanya aside from as a pressure point to use against Ysbel. Tanya had sworn Masha to secrecy about her past, and Masha had agreed. It wasn't as if the information was easy to find. Grigory seemed to believe that Tanya and the children were necessary inconveniences if they wanted Ysbel's help.

But Ysbel hadn't spoken alone with her wife since Tae had revealed, yesterday, that Ivan was on the ship, and why. And Tanya's lips had pinched, but she hadn't said a word, and she hadn't spoken of it since.

"What are you working on?" asked Tanya abruptly. "The explosive still?"

Ysbel hesitated a moment, then nodded.

"Of course." Tanya's voice was bitter.

Ysbel frowned. "Tanya. Please. What's the matter?"

Tanya turned to her, her face cut with worry. "I don't like this, Ysbel. I know how the mafia works. I saw it when I was in university in Prasvishoni, because the government and the internal security department and the mafia work so closely together that it's hard sometimes to distinguish one from the other. And then, when I was in jail. There were mafia there. You know that. But do you know what kinds of things had sent them there? And they were the ones who'd been sacrificed. The ones who planned those massacres, they were always the ones like Grigory, who walked free. I've known Ivan for years, while we were in prison. He's a smart man, and if he thinks there's something going on here that we don't know about, I trust his instincts." She met Ysbel's eyes, finally, and there was that hardness in her expression.

"And you heard, and you hardly seem to care. What has happened to you, Ysbel? I've known you since I was a child, and I suddenly don't know you anymore. Because the woman I married, twelve years ago—she wouldn't have worked for the mafia. She wouldn't have designed weapons that she knew would be used to kill, perhaps, other families like hers, who had the temerity to stand up against criminals. And she certainly wouldn't have done this without even talking to me first."

Ysbel watched her, frowning, and something twisted in her stomach. She reached out gently, and took Tanya's hand. Tanya stiffened, but didn't pull away.

"The woman you married," Ysbel said quietly, "would always have done whatever it took to protect you, and to protect our children. And if this was the only way—"

This time Tanya did pull away. "Then maybe I didn't know the woman I married as well as I thought I did," she said quietly. She stood, glancing over at the holoscreen. "Your work is brilliant, Ysi. As always. This is something Vitali Dobrev would have been proud of."

She turned abruptly and left, and Ysbel looked after her, something aching in her chest.

Tanya was wrong. This time, Tanya was wrong.

Or perhaps she was right, but in the end it couldn't matter.

She'd watched Tanya die twice, once when their cottage burned, and once in prison, when Tanya and the children were dragged bodily from the room by guards to be taken to the sedation chamber.

Both those times, Ysbel had been bound and gagged, unable to do anything but watch.

It had almost killed her. Even the memory was enough to set her pulse racing, panic rising in her throat. She couldn't do it again. She couldn't bear to do it again.

And this time, she wasn't bound and gagged. She wasn't powerless. This time she'd do something if it killed her—because not doing something, sitting back and watching Tanya and her babies die, would kill her anyways.

Perhaps Tanya didn't understand. Perhaps she couldn't.

Perhaps Tanya would never understand, and this wall between them would grow too high and too thick to climb, and perhaps that would kill her too. But she'd have kept them safe.

And that had to be worth it. Didn't it?

But the thought did nothing to dispel the memory of how Tanya had looked at her, before she turned away, or the hollow sickness it left inside her.

If she lost Tanya—however she lost Tanya—she wasn't certain she'd survive it.

12

"Lev. It's so good to see you again." Grigory smiled at him expansively. "Sit. I have something special for you today."

Warily, Lev took a seat across from the krestnaya. As usual, Yana and Zhenya were sitting to either side of him, but they made room for Lev.

"And how is the planning for the event?" Lev asked. "Did you get responses from the invitees?"

Grigory smiled. "Yes. Everyone who I invited was more than happy to attend. As you suggested, I spoke personally to the aide who I've purchased who works for Yegor, and he dropped the idea to Nika. Then my people made it very clear that the best place to have this financial conference was on Vladlena's gambling ship, because it was the only one available—again, as you suggested, we booked the others so it was in fact the only one available. And then we had our man provide her with a list of invitees, and all the invitations came through her. All above-board, nothing suspicious at all. You, Lev, are a treasure."

Lev gave a self-deprecating nod. "Thank you. But the invitees— the ones I asked for specifically?"

"Yes, of course." Grigory pulled up the holoscreen over his com and flipped through the screens, then held it up for Lev to see. On it, there was an invitation for Yulia, Minister of Innovation and Development, with Yefim and Mikhail to accompany her.

All three sections of the invitation were confirmed.

Lev nodded. "Thank you. I'm glad you were able to arrange this." He paused a moment. "I see you invited their families as well?"

Grigory nodded. "Yes. It is customary for families to come along to this type of event. If I hadn't, it would have looked suspicious, and we would never have gotten them."

Lev nodded, but there was the beginnings of a twinge of unease in his stomach.

The fact was, he would do this, whatever it took. He'd decided that long ago.

But—

"Don't worry, Lev. I have every capability of keeping people alive who I wish to keep alive. The family is only a minor inconvenience, and the deaths of the minister and her assistants will look like an accident—nothing suspicious at all, and nothing except to send condolences home with the grieving families."

Lev nodded again, but Grigory's words did nothing to calm the unease in his stomach.

"Thank you," he said.

Ivan was right—Grigory was making plans that he wasn't talking about to Lev, but they certainly had something to do with the 'symposium' that was coming up. And Lev was very, very certain that there would be no grieving families sent back with Grigory's condolences after the minister was killed.

Still—

Still, three families against the lives of every person in Prasvishoni —it could hardly be a contest.

And if he was being honest with himself, three families he didn't know and had never met, against the lives of Jez and the rest of the crew—it was still, unfortunately, no contest. He'd learned from the best, after all. Evka had been his mentor. He could be as coldly self-interested as necessary.

"Anyways," said Grigory, turning back to face the front of the room. "I brought you in here because I thought you might enjoy seeing this. Considering you were here when it all started."

Again, that twist of unease in his stomach.

The door opened, and three bodyguards came in, dragging a figure with a hood pulled over his eyes.

Whoever it was had apparently been badly beaten, because Lev could see dark stains soaking through the tattered clothing, and dark wetness spreading slowly across the hood that obscured the figure's face.

Again, something twisted in Lev's stomach, and again, he pushed it down.

"The man who tried to assassinate us at dinner the first time we spoke," said Grigory in a friendly voice. He turned to Lev, and lowered his voice conspiratorially. "You remember, Lev, how I told you the story about the time I had to kill a chef."

Lev nodded wordlessly.

"This isn't all that different, really," Grigory continued. "I could have just had him killed, you know, it would have been easy. Such an easy, clean death. My people would have made him talk first, of course, but besides that, the death would have been easy. But you see, that's the problem. People would talk, you know. They'd start talking about me, about how Grigory is going soft, about how if you try to kill him and one of his guests at dinner, well, the worst you have to face is a little questioning, and then—" he made a gesture with his hands. "Poof. That's not all that frightening, is it? You think if people talk, well, I'm so big and powerful, it wouldn't matter. But that's where everything starts, Lev. That's where it all begins. I'm powerful because people are afraid of me, and they're afraid of me because people talk about what I do." He shrugged. "Honestly, I'm not a cruel man. I wouldn't do this from choice, but, you know—my hands are tied."

The tone of his voice, the satisfied anticipation in it, belied his words.

In front of them, one of the bodyguards jerked the hood from the figure's face.

The bound man was middle-aged, his face bloodless and terrified. He had a long gash along his forehead that looked like it had been made by a ring on a fist that had hit him, and one side of his face was bruised and swollen almost beyond recognition. When he saw Grigory, his expression turned sick. He tried, clumsily, to drop to his knees, but the bodyguards jerked him up.

"Please," he whispered. "Please. Krestnaya. Boss. Papa. I'll join you, I'll tell you whatever you want me to tell you. I can be useful. Please."

For some reason, even though this man had tried to kill him, it took everything Lev had not to look away from his frantic, pleading face.

"Vlad," said Grigory pleasantly. "I know all about what you can tell me. And I know all about what you can do for me. I do need you, Vlad."

For half a moment, the man's terrified face twisted with an almost painful hope. "I—You do? I'll do anything you need, anything you ask me."

Grigory leaned forward, the pleasant expression never leaving his face. "I need you, Vlad, to be an example to whoever else might think that I'm growing weak in my old age. I need you to show them exactly what they're facing if they decide they want to try to come after me. And don't worry, my friend. You're already doing it, exactly what I need you to do."

Realization spread over the man's expression, and his body sagged, legs giving out beneath him. "Please," he whimpered. "Please, Grigory, Yana, Zhenya."

Grigory sat back and gestured to the bodyguards. "Proceed. Please."

It was almost an hour later when Lev finally left the room.

He walked slowly down the hallway towards their suite. He felt dirty, something he wasn't certain he'd ever be able to wash off, and there was a cold, hard sickness that sat in his stomach like a stone.

He'd managed a polite smile at Grigory as he left, though, and had exchanged pleasantries with him as if the sights of the last hour wouldn't be burned into his mind forever, as if he'd be able to sleep without hearing the screaming echoing through his dreams.

This was what he'd decided to work with. This was what he was agreeing to.

And still—still, he wasn't sure he could bring himself to regret it.

When he reached the door at the end of the hallway that led to their room, he stood in front of it for a long moment.

It was early afternoon, and the others were probably out doing whatever it was they did to keep themselves entertained. At the very least, he hoped they were.

He stared at the door handle for a few moments before it registered in his brain that he needed to do something to open it, if he wanted to go inside. He reached out, tapping his com against the handle, and the lock clicked.

He noticed, vacantly, that there was a small splash of blood on the cuff of his shirt.

Unsurprising, really, although they had managed to be uncommonly clean about the entire business.

He pushed the door open and stepped inside, closing it after him.

As he'd suspected, the room was empty.

He stood for a moment, directionless, then made his way over to the table and sat down, letting himself slump forward, his elbows on his knees, his head in his hands.

He sat there for a while, thinking of nothing, trying to keep his mind blank, because he knew that the moment he didn't, the images would come oozing back in, and he wasn't sure he could examine those images right now and not go mad.

So. This was what he had turned into.

No, this was what he'd have to turn into. This is what he'd have to become, if not by action, at least by complicity, if he wanted Grigory to give him a chance to save everyone else.

And once he'd saved them, then what?

But if he saved them, did it really matter?

At last he raised his head, and stared sightlessly at the table.

Then he frowned. There was a chip there, and a paper with his name scrawled on it in Tae's hurried writing.

He picked it up, turning it over in his hands, then slipped it into his com.

His holoscreen popped up, and on it, columns of data, names and amounts and dates.

He scrolled through them, frowning. Tae had said he and Ivan were going to be looking for the ledger of the event, and it looked like they'd found it.

And it looked nothing at all like the ledger Grigory had shown him earlier.

His frown deepened as he scrolled down.

The names wouldn't have meant anything to Tae. Possibly something to Ivan, but he'd been in prison so long that even if he knew who was who in the government, his information would be years out of date.

But—

Something cold clutched at his chest as he scrolled through the names.

These weren't the low-level diplomats that Grigory had told them he was bringing in to corrupt. In fact, Lev was relatively certain that at least half of the names he was reading wouldn't be corruptible, at least not without much more money than Grigroy had allocated.

But they were all placed in strategic positions in the government. No one too high up, no one so big they'd draw suspicion, or refuse to come to a conference like this, even if invited by Minister Nika. But exactly the right combination that—

He sucked in a breath and slapped his hand over the com, shutting off the holoscreen.

He sat for a moment, staring ahead sightlessly, his mind grappling with the magnitude of the realization.

Finally, he tapped his com again. "Tae?" he whispered.

"Lev?" Tae answered immediately. "Where are you? Is everything alright?"

"I'm in our room on the ship. I got the chip you left for me." He paused. "I—need to talk to you. Ivan. Everyone."

There was a pause from the other end of the com. "I'll be there in a minute," said Tae, worry clear in his voice.

Whatever it was Tae did, it took him less than half an hour to gather everyone in the main room, around the table. When he'd come into the room and seen the look on Lev's face, he hadn't even asked questions, and Lev was honestly ridiculously grateful, because he wasn't sure he'd be able to hold his voice steady for long enough to string together a sentence at this point.

Jez sat across from him, and there was thick concern in her face, but he focused on Masha as he pulled up the holoscreen on his com.

"Masha," he said, in a voice that somehow came out steady. "This is a ledger that Ivan and Tae were able to find. It has the complete list of invitees." He scrolled down to the list of names.

"As you and I suspected, Grigory is not telling us everything. The names he gave us are indeed on the list. But," he scrolled down farther. "So are these."

She frowned at the names, glanced up at him, and looked at the names again.

He waited for the realization to dawn on her face, and when it did, he saw, for just an instant, the shock that he'd felt when he'd finally put the pieces together.

"He's not trying to put things back to where they were," he said softly, covering the com gently with his hand. The holoscreen flickered and disappeared, and they were all staring at him.

"No," said Masha quietly. "No, it appears he's not."

"Well?" asked Ysbel irritably. "What is he doing then?"

Masha turned to her with that bland, pleasant smile she always wore, but Lev could see the strain behind it.

"It appears, Ysbel, that he is planning a coup. Those people on the list were chosen very carefully. One of them would hardly make a difference. But all of them, combined? The government would be paralyzed. It would cease to function entirely, and Grigory could take complete control. There would be nothing to stop him."

"But—wait," said Jez. "Take a hell of a lot of money to corrupt that many of the bastards, even though it wouldn't surprise me if they're all for sale."

"It would," said Lev softly. "It would take a great deal of money, probably more than Grigory can access at the moment. If you recall, I do have some insight on his current financial position."

"So—" Jez began, and then she stopped abruptly.

A quick glance around the table told Lev that everyone had come to the same realization.

"He never intended to corrupt all of them," he said, his voice somehow light. "A few, certainly. But the rest?" He shrugged, and turned to Ivan. "You said that he'd paid the ship's owner an obscene amount for the use of her ship, correct? Enough to buy it outright, I think is what you said."

Ivan nodded slowly, a horrified expression on his face. "It's because he did buy it, isn't it?" he asked softly. "But there's no need to get supply chains going for a ship that's he's only going to own for a few weeks."

"And no point in temporary contracts for servers, when it's the last job they'll ever have," said Tae, his voice sick. Ivan shot him a quick, sympathetic look.

"He's going to blow it up, isn't he?" Tae said, turning back to Lev. "Kill everyone on board."

Lev nodded. "That's what it seems. All of them dead, and the families too, I imagine."

"I—thought you said he was going to corrupt some of them," said Jez, sounding slightly dazed. "Kinda hard to do that if they're dead, I'm guessing."

"I imagine," murmured Masha, "that he'll have a way of separating off the ones he wants killed from the ones he wants to own."

Lev tapped his com and pulled up the holoscreen, scanning rapidly through the specs on the gambling ship. Then he expanded the screen and pulled it over to the centre of the table.

The others peered at it.

"There," Ivan said. "There's a partition between the two sections of the gambling hall. Blast doors?"

Lev glanced at the diagram and nodded.

"Well," said Masha. "Then I imagine he will find a way to gather the individuals he's marked for murder on one side of the blast doors. It would be a simple matter to seal them off, and the explosion would take care of the rest."

There was something odd in her voice, and Lev turned to look at her, frowning slightly.

He could swear she'd been surprised by the news.

But—not horrified. Not like Tae and Jez and Ivan and the others had been horrified.

Almost—satisfied.

That question, that had never quite stopped nagging in the back of his head—what game was Masha playing?

And he still had no idea.

"We'll likely need more information," Masha murmured. She glanced around the table. "We'll have to discuss how to get it."

"And report it to you?" he asked quietly, turning to her. "Do you have information we should know, Masha?"

She watched him for a moment, her expression inscrutable. "I am learning what I can," she said at last. "And no, I suspect it would be best if everyone reported what they find to you. I have found myself extraordinarily busy these last few days, and I would hate for you to be waiting on me. If there is information I find I need, I will be certain to ask." She stood, and gave them all that bland smile. "And now, if you'll excuse me, I'll leave you to your discussions."

She turned, and a moment later the door to her room closed firmly behind her.

They looked at each other for a long moment.

"Lev?" asked Tae at last. There was something grim in his expression.

"I—" he began. He felt as if someone had punched him in the stomach, and he hadn't quite caught his breath.

He should, he imagined, be horrified by what Grigory was planning. And if he were being honest, he was.

But the thing that was tearing at him from the inside was the sickening calculation he had to make—deciding which was worse: stopping Grigory, and saving the government, and the minister surviving, and the time before Evka killed them all measured in weeks? Or letting Grigory take over the Svodrani system government, but killing the people who held the crew's life in their hands, first the minister, then Evka? And, of course, killing hundreds of innocent people with them.

He'd decided he'd do anything to save the rest of the crew. He needed to be able to do anything.

But—

But right now, with Vlad's bruised, terrified face painted fresh on his memory, he couldn't seem to think clearly enough to make the decision.

"Lev, we can't," said Tae quietly. "You know that. There will be hundreds of people there. Innocent people—families, children, servers. We'd be killing them. Even if you don't think—" he broke off. "It wouldn't be better, Lev," he said, finally. "If Grigory took over the system, it wouldn't be better. We have to find a way to save them."

Lev closed his eyes a moment.

Maybe Tae was right. It had been a long day, and he couldn't seem to wrap his mind around the enormity of what was happening. Had happened.

And until he could, until he could figure out how this new information factored in, perhaps this was for the best.

"Well then," he said at last, looking up and trying to smile. "I suppose we put a stop to it."

13

Jez glanced over at the table, where Lev, Tae, and Ivan were huddled around Lev's holoscreen.

"That's not going to work," said Lev, and there was annoyance in his voice.

"Well, maybe you can come up with something better," Tae snapped. Ivan glanced between them, then over at her with a wry look on his face.

She grinned at him.

"You two eggheads look like you're having fun over there."

Tae and Lev both looked up, glaring at her.

"Jez," said Tae, and she could hear the familiar exasperation in his tone. "If you don't have something helpful to add—"

"Hey," she said, grinning. "I have all sorts of helpful things to add, probably. What are you doing?"

Lev took a deep breath and pinched the bridge of his nose. "The same thing we've been doing for the last twenty-four damn hours, Jez," he said through his teeth. "And we're no closer to a solution, as far as I can see."

She sauntered over to the table and leaned in, glancing at the holoscreen. "OK, but to be fair, I wasn't actually paying attention to whatever you said you were going to be figuring out last night."

There was something mildly gratifying in the way Lev sucked in his breath between his teeth.

She was standing close to him, and she suddenly realized that, but if she shifted away from him it would feel too much like admitting how shaky her muscles went when she was close to him, which, now she thought about it, she was starting to feel a little shaky right now. Which was completely stupid, honestly. So she took a deep breath instead, and turned to grin at him.

Which maybe wasn't the best move, all things considered, because the way his eyes caught hers, and his expression went suddenly unfocused—

She turned quickly back to Tae, who was watching both of them with an expression of completely undisguised exasperation.

"We're trying, Jez," he said through his teeth, "to figure out how the hell we're going to stop Grigory from taking down the entire Svodrani system government."

"Yeah, but I though *we* were trying to take down the entire—"

"Jez. Can you please focus for three seconds? Yes, we want to take down the government. But replacing it with Grigory isn't going to make things any better, and will probably make them a hell of a lot worse."

She grinned. "OK, fair enough." Honestly, if she would admit it, she was harassing him because it was the only way she could think of to get rid of the tight ball of worry that was sitting in the pit of her stomach.

Because she'd known people who'd worked for the mafia. She'd flown with them, when she was a kid and flying for Lena.

And she knew, maybe better than Tae did, what a system run by those damn bastards would look like.

Honestly, this whole time she'd been running with Masha, she'd been more worried about whatever the hell it was they were dealing with at the moment than Masha's grand plan to take down the entire system government. Because she'd somehow, horrifyingly, realized that there were people in the system that she really wanted to keep alive, and trying to keep them alive—and to keep herself alive at the same time—seemed to take up most of her available attention at any given moment.

But this? This was serious.

And she knew damn well she didn't want this Grigory bastard running anything bigger than this ship.

"Anyways, I'm going back down to the gambling hall," she said, straightening.

Tae sat up abruptly. "We have about three days, Jez. Do you really think going down to the gambling hall—"

She shot him an easy grin. "Not doing it just for fun this time. And anyways, you seemed happy enough about it when I was distracting all those bastards so that you could sneak in and get that ledger. Masha said she wanted to get some information, which, by the way, pretty sure you wanted too, so I told her I'd get it."

"And how are you going to get this information?" asked Lev warily, straightening as well.

She was almost close enough to touch him right now, which was definitely not a good thing, because the problem with that was, she wasn't totally sure she'd be able to stop herself from touching him if he looked at her again that way he had, and—

"Jez?" said Tae with a sigh.

"I got the guy she thought might have the information to come gambling with me." She straightened, and enjoyed the sight of Lev obviously trying very, very hard not to say anything.

"Jez," said Ivan, frowning in concern. "I'm not sure that's the best —"

She shrugged. "Hey. You get information your way, I get it my way."

Tae scowled. "Jez—"

She winked at him, and sauntered out the door. "Good luck with your figuring crap out," she called over her shoulder as the door swung shut behind her.

When it was closed, she paused for a moment, glancing around. She'd have to be down in the gambling hall pretty soon, but she still had a few minutes.

If she was being honest with herself, she'd left early more because she couldn't stand sitting still for one damn second longer. Yes, this wasn't as bad as prison. But if she had to sit still too long, it started to feel pretty damn close.

She started briskly off down the hall towards the main deck. Probably find something interesting happening there, be easy to kill a few minutes before she showed up to the gambling hall.

When she stepped into the main deck, at least three of the boyeviki sitting there turned to glare at her.

"What are you doing here, Solokov?" one of the women grumbled, her hand going to her pocket, where Jez could see the unmistakable bulge of a heat pistol.

Jez shrugged and dropped into a seat. "Just walking around, seeing the sights and whatever," she said innocently.

The woman scowled at her. "You're going to wind up in a corridor with your insides cooked one of these days," she said through her teeth.

Jez shot her an easy grin. "Guess you could always try. But then you'd never win back what you lost at tokens, would you? That'd be a pity."

"I think that's a chance I'm willing to take," said the woman, shoving her chair back.

Jez's muscles tightened with anticipation, a pleasant rush of adrenalin washing through her. She leaned back in her chair and put her hands behind her head. "Well, you bastard, that assumes you could out-draw me. I'm willing to take a chance on that." She raised her eyebrows suggestively.

The woman's brows lowered. "No, it doesn't," she spat. "It only assumes there are enough of us to take your sorry carcass. And judging from the people I've talked with in the last few days, there are more than enough for that."

"Yeah?" Jez drawled. "Well, you never know. Guess if you don't think you can handle me, killing me's got to be the best option, right? I mean, you certainly can't damn well handle me on the gambling floor."

The woman took a few steps closer, her gaze icy. "Believe me, Jez, I've been watching you. You can handle gambling tokens, if you cheat. You can handle a fight, if you fight dirty. But you're not the only one who can fight dirty."

Jez gave her an easy smile, heart beating more quickly.

Looked like her life could get a hell of a lot more interesting in the next few days.

She glanced quickly at her com, and swore. "Sorry kids," she said, pushing herself to her feet. "Got places to go and things to do."

"I'm not finished, Solokov—" the woman started.

Jez glanced over her shoulder and winked. "Get in line. Probably a waiting list to kill me, at this point."

She strolled out of the room and headed for the gambling hall.

Nikoli was sitting at a table, looking decidedly impatient, when she entered the room. She could see him right away, seeing as there was no one else who'd dared to sit within two tables of him.

She grinned to herself.

A couple threats to her life, a gambling partner who looked like he drank credits for breakfast—so far, this was shaping up to be good evening.

"Hey," she said, pulling up the chair across from him and dropping into it. "Guess you're ready to throw some tokens."

He gave her a cold look. Behind his chair, his two bodyguards were giving her identical hard stares.

"I've been ready for the last ten minutes, Jez Solokov," he said, his words cold.

She shrugged easily. "Sorry. Time got away from me. I was listening to one of your boyevik friends tell me about all the different ways she wanted to kill me."

He stared at her for a moment, then raised an eyebrow. "You know, most people would be at least somewhat disturbed by that."

She shot him a cocky grin. "Yeah, well guess I'm not most people. Anyways, I was watching the plaguer. Bet her hands shake when she shoots, so see, I'm not too worried."

"Who was it?"

"Inna, I think."

He looked at her, frowning slightly. "They do, actually," he said, after a moment. "Her hands, I mean. They do shake just a bit when she shoots. How did you know?"

She shrugged again. "Been in enough fights, I guess. Live longer when you figure out crap like that."

He sat back, watching her, eyebrows raised. "Well," he said at last. "And here I was expecting someone who was only good at gambling. You're surprisingly perceptive."

"Nah. Just lucky," she drawled.

Nikoli leaned forward slightly against the table. "Lucky, you say. I'd heard differently. In fact, I'd heard you were quite the grifter."

She gave him her most innocent look.

He sighed. "I'm not stupid, Jez. Believe me, I wouldn't have survived to get where I am if I were stupid."

She kept her innocent smile.

He gritted his teeth. "I'm beginning to wonder how you survived to get where you are," he said quietly. "I think at least half the people on this ship at the moment want to kill you."

She raised an eyebrow. "None of them have yet, though."

He watched her for a moment, narrowing his eyes. "Alright," he said at last. "You asked me to come here. And I agreed. I'm one of Grigory's top avtoritete. Believe me, I have plenty of better things to do with my time than gamble with some low-life cheating smuggler pilot. So, Jez. Do you know why I agreed?"

"'Cause I'm so damn hot?" she suggested, grinning.

His eyes narrowed further. "No. I'll tell you why. Because, Jez Solokov, I understand you've been promising to teach some of my people your tricks, and ended up cheating them out of everything they owned."

Jez gave him a reminiscent smile.

"So here's what we're going to do—you are going to tell me how you're doing it. Because it turns out that what you do could come in handy."

He didn't bother to state what would happen if she refused, and she'd been around long enough to know exactly what that meant.

She studied him for a moment.

She had him. She had his interest, which hell, was probably the most important part. And OK, she still had to get the information out of him, and judging by his narrowed eyes and suspicious expression, it might not be as easy as she'd imagined.

Still, not like she hadn't come here with a plan. Despite what those idiots Lev and Tae seemed to think, which was actually a little insulting now that she thought about it, she was damn good at coming up with plans.

"Well, here's the thing," she drawled. "The only reason I'm probably still alive here is that there's a hell of a lot of people on this ship asking themselves the same question you're asking me, and they aren't going to kill me until they figure it out. So I figure, just telling you straight out isn't going to do me much good."

He frowned and opened his mouth, and she shot him a quick wink. "But see, I like you. Seem like a pretty decent person. So here's my deal." She glanced around quickly. "You send your bodyguards away."

His frown deepened. "I'm not going to send away my guards."

She shrugged. "Not like they have to go far. Couple tables down is fine, just don't want them to hear what we talk about."

He glared at her for a few moments, then at last he gave a slow nod. "And if I agree to that?"

She smiled at him. "Then I'll give you the same offer I gave everyone else. You pick the game. I'll play slow. And if you can catch what I'm doing—" she quirked an eyebrow. "You win. Or, maybe it's just beginners luck, and there's nothing to catch."

He glared at her again, rubbing his chin thoughtfully. "And if we play and I don't catch what you've done, and I still win?"

She grinned wider. "Then you win, and I tell you. Easy peasy. Can't say I don't play fair."

"I think everyone who's played against you would disagree with that."

She tried to hide a smirk. "So. We have a deal?"

For a moment he was silent, looking at her. At last he nodded, a quick jerk of his head. "Fine. We have a deal." He gestured with his chin, and the guards withdrew to a table that was just far enough to be out of earshot, but close enough that the wouldn't even have to aim to cook her insides to well-done.

She grinned at him. "Guess we can do business. Figured you might be the type."

He watched her carefully. "We'll see," he said, and there was a hint of coldness in his voice.

She gave a luxurious sigh and leaned back. "Alright then, we can get started. What's your game?"

He pulled out a bag of gambling tokens. "My own tokens. I assume you want to inspect them?"

"May as well," she said, taking the proffered bag. Her fingers tingled with adrenalin, and the grin on her face was widening, because she honestly couldn't help it.

She looked up after a moment, dropping the bag of tokens on the table and glancing around. "Not very courteous of you, honestly," she said as he took the bag, checking it carefully, probably to see if she'd tampered with it.

"What do you mean?" he glanced up.

She raised an eyebrow. "Well, bit of a shame to invite someone to play, and then not provide the refreshment."

He gave her a wry glance, but beckoned a server over.

The woman approached. "The usual, sir?"

He nodded. "Please. A bottle, and two glasses. And bring some massandra as well, please."

She nodded and moved off, and returned a moment later with a bottle of something that looked very, very expensive, and very, very strong, and another bottle that looked just as expensive, and much less strong.

Jez gave a dreamy grin. "See, you bastard? I knew I liked you."

He leaned forward on the table. "The game, Jez, is fool's tokens. I'm not stupid enough to think you'd have offered to let me chose the game if you hadn't figured out how to cheat at all of them. But from a purely academic standpoint, if I'm going to catch you, I'd like it to be at the game that's impossible to cheat at."

He pulled out the two glasses, and lifted the bottle that honestly probably couldn't even get Tae drunk.

She winked at him. "Nah. I'll have what you're having."

He gave her an appraising glance. "I'm not sure that's a good idea. This is pretty strong stuff, and you don't weigh much."

She shrugged, still grinning. "Well," she drawled, "guess it will be pretty easy for you to win at tokens if I'm falling-down drunk. So don't see that there's a downside for you."

He raised an eyebrow, but uncorked the bottle and poured a small splash into the bottom of each of their glasses.

She took a sip, and frowned. "You don't have anything stronger than this?"

He gave her another long look, but she could see the annoyance under his neutral expression.

She'd got him.

"Alright," he said, standing. "It's your funeral." He beckoned the server over and said something in a low voice. She slipped away, and as Jez watched, she pulled down another bottle from the bar, covered with dust, its contents a dark amber. She placed it on the table, and Nikoli nodded his thanks.

When he pulled out the stopper, the sharp fumes of alcohol wafting from it was enough to make people three tables down from them cough and blink back tears.

"That's more like it," said Jez, grinning broadly. He raised an eyebrow, and she splashed a generous measure into each of their glasses. She raised hers, the alcohol vapour burning her sinuses delightfully.

Not too often you could do exactly what that bastard Masha asked you to do and also enjoy yourself at the same time.

"Well, you plaguer, let's see how you do at fool's tokens."

14

Lev looked up from his holoscreen at the loud 'thump' on the door.

Then he noticed the time, and his chest clenched with sudden worry.

Jez wasn't back yet. She should have been back by now.

"What—" Tae began, frowning.

Ysbel stood, pushing back her chair, and crossed quickly to the door, one hand on her heat pistol. "Stay back, please," she said over her shoulder.

The 'thump' came again, and cautiously, she cracked the door open. Then she swung it wide, cursing.

Jez stood there, swaying slightly, and for one panicked moment Lev's mind flashed back to that night in the jail on a remote prison planet, where Jez, swaying and bloody, had somehow managed to get the key they needed to escape, and almost died herself in the process.

He jumped to his feet, crossing to the door in a few quick strides. His eyes scanned Jez's rumpled clothing—no blood, at least none that he could see, no visible burn marks, nothing visibly broken—

And then the overpowering scent of alcohol hit him, strong enough that he almost staggered back.

"Is she—" Tae was standing as well, his voice worried.

Jez turned and gave Lev a drunken grin. "Hey genius," she slurred.

"Jez—" he began, voice tight with a fear that was rapidly turning to irritation.

"Yep," she said, obviously over-enunciating her syllables. "'M not hurt at all. Just—just drunk. Really damn drunk."

He stared at her for a moment in utter disbelief, then he grabbed her arm as she swayed alarmingly. The panic from a few seconds ago was still sloshing through his veins, and he found his hand on her arm was shaking.

"Jez," he said through his teeth. "You could have been killed. What were you thinking? Getting drunk on Grigory's ship, which happens to be filled with people who want to actually kill you—"

"Come on, get inside, you idiot," Ysbel grunted, taking Jez's other arm.

It seemed to take Jez a moment to remember how to move her legs, then she staggered inside, leaning against them heavily.

He closed his eyes for a moment, trying to convince his heart to stop trying to pound its way out of his chest, and his breathing to slow down enough that he could actually think.

"What exactly do you think you were doing, you lunatic?" Ysbel ground out once she'd closed the door behind them. "I thought you were planning on actually being useful. I'm sure Lev told you before you left that we only have a few days, and we don't have time for people to get drunk."

Jez blinked up at Ysbel dreamily for a moment, eyes unfocused. "Tell you what, though, if you're going to get smashed, he had some pretty damn good stuff to get smashed on. Tell you that."

Ysbel narrowed her eyes and propped Jez up against the wall.

Jez promptly collapsed.

Tae had come over and was standing beside them, a look of utter exasperation on his face. "I thought, Jez," he said, speaking as slowly and clearly as he could, "that you were planning on going to get some information for us."

She gave him a very self-satisfied look from where she'd somehow managed to prop herself up against the wall. "Well, figure I did."

Lev let out a long breath and crouched beside her. His heart was still hammering wildly, which did nothing to assuage his irritation. "Information on something other than what you'd prefer to get drunk on, Jez."

She grinned up at him. "What? Think I'm … I'm stupid or something? Because …" she trailed off, staring into the distance with a vacant grin on her face.

"Honestly, Jez, I'm currently wondering," said Lev grimly.

She glanced up at him. "I ever tell you you're damn hot for a—for a scholar boy? 'Cause I'll tell you, scholar boys aren't usually my thing. But you're—you're—pretty damn hot, actually. Anyways, here's the thing. Told you I'd get information. Told Masha I would. Her fault, honestly, because I just did exactly what—what—" she waived her hand. "Whatever the hell her name is told me to do."

"Masha?" said Lev through his teeth, trying very hard to ignore her words.

She was, as she'd put it, really damn drunk.

"'T's the one." She grinned at him vacantly.

"So," said Tae, clearly trying to control his complete exasperation, "You're telling me that Masha told you she wanted you to go get so smashed that honestly I'm actually wondering how you're conscious right now?"

She shook her head, and almost fell over. "Nope. Told me to get information. And thing is, Nikoli doesn't like giving out—giving—telling people crap when he's sober, you know? So figured—figured the best plan—" She trailed off again, blinking.

Lev closed his eyes and drew in a long breath. "Come on, Ysbel," he said. "Let's get her to bed."

"Nope," Jez muttered, jerking her head upright. "Gotta—gotta listen to me first. Because hell, you think I'm drunk, you should see the bastard I was talking to. Nik—Niki—whatever the hell his name is. Mafia avtoritet. That one."

Now they were all staring at her. "You—got Nikoli drunk?" Lev asked at last.

Nikoli had a reputation for being able to hold his alcohol.

"Yep," said Jez with relish. "He's sleeping it off right now on the damn gambling—thing. Table."

"You drank Nikoli under the table," said Ysbel flatly.

Jez gave her a drunken grin. "Over the table, actually," she slurred. "Anyways, he got pretty talky last few drinks. Told me some things. Figured you'd want to—want to—" she waved a hand vaguely, and barely caught herself again before she fell over.

Tae, Lev, Ivan, and Ysbel exchanged glances. Then Lev turned back to where Jez was slumped against the wall.

She was going to actually kill herself one of these days. She was going to get herself killed, and there wasn't a damn thing he could do about it, because of course she wouldn't listen to a damn thing he said.

He took another deep breath.

"Jez," he said carefully. "You're saying you got important information from Nikoli."

"Yep."

He shook his head. "Alright. Let's get you to bed, you can tell us in the morning."

She laughed drunkenly. "Thought you were—a genius or something. Guess you don't—don't go out much, you bastard. Not going to remember a damn thing in the morning, probably. Better tell you now." She tried to get up, and completely overbalanced. He caught her before she toppled over, and looked helplessly up at the rest of them. Ysbel shook her head grimly.

"The idiot is probably right. Let's get everything we can before she passes out."

Lev set his jaw grimly and put an arm around Jez, hoisting her laboriously to her feet. She was doing absolutely nothing to help, which was probably just as well at this point. Ysbel leaned down and took her other arm, and between them they got her into a chair. Her head was starting to nod.

"Jez," Ysbel snapped, and Jez jerked her head up.

"Yeah?"

"You had something to tell us."

Jez looked at her, trying very hard to focus her eyes. "Something— Dunno what you're talking about. Anyways, genius boy is pretty damn hot. Did I say that? Because he is. And he's a damn good— he's a damn good kisser, too, by the way. But maybe—"

Lev gritted his teeth, his cheeks heating.

She was bloody off her head drunk.

"Something about Nikoli," Ysbel said in a flat voice.

Jez blinked at her for a moment, furrowing her brow. Then she grinned. "Oh. Yeah. Nikoli. Crafty old bastard. But I'll tell you what, he knows how to get good alcohol, tell you that." She paused a moment. "Niki told me stuff, y'know. How they're going to—going to get everyone split up. They've rigged the—the—thing, with the tokens. Gonna have a tournament, and make sure—make sure—"

she trailed off, looking around blearily.

Lev frowned at her for a moment. "They're … going to rig the gambling tournament," he said slowly, looking up at the others. "That must be it. The one Grigory's set up for the evening's entertainment. He could do it so as the players move up or down the tables, whoever he wants to kill ends up in the right part of the ship."

Tae gave a thoughtful nod. "That—makes sense, I suppose."

"Yeah, that's it. What he said," Jez slurred. She was still grinning broadly, and looking extremely pleased with herself. "Gonna rig the —what he said. Said no one—no one's supposed to know 'bout it, but we were friends, see, so he said, said he'd tell me stuff, you know. Figured you'd want to hear about it." She subsided, still grinning.

Ysbel stared at her for a moment, then up at the others. "This was her plan," she said in a flat voice. "This was her plan—go on a drinking binge with Nikoli, and eventually they'd both be so drunk he'd tell her whatever she asked him, because neither of them would be in any state to remember it the next morning."

Ivan was also staring at Jez. At last he raised his head, expression slightly awed. "Well," he said, shaking his head, "I—suppose if you can pull it off—"

Lev took a deep breath, and let it out again through his teeth.

She could have been killed. There were about a hundred ways she could have been killed, and he needed to stop thinking about them right now or he was going to lose his mind.

"Alright," he said. "Alright. Jez got Nikoli completely off his head passing-out drunk, and somehow convinced him to tell her what we needed to know. And somehow, for some insane reason, it worked. And somehow, I'm still not certain how, Jez isn't dead from alcohol poisoning, although if I have to breath the fumes coming off her any longer, I'm afraid I might be." He shook his head.

Jez's head was starting to droop again. "Not even tired," she muttered, blinking hard. "Don't know why you plaguers—" She swayed, and Ysbel caught her before she could fall off her chair.

"Is that all, you idiot," she asked, giving Jez a shake.

Jez blinked, then looked up at her with a vacant grin. "'S what all?" she slurred. "Mean, guess I could tell you 'bout—his family, didn't like his mom, he said. Told me all about it. But figure that's probably—don't really care much 'bout his mom, I guess." She giggled. "He didn't either. Care 'bout—'bout—" she subsided again, head starting to nod.

"I'm not sure whether to be horrified or impressed," said Ivan, still staring at her.

"Honestly, it won't make the smallest bit of difference," said Lev, still talking through his teeth. He met Ysbel's eyes. "We'd better get her to bed, before she passes out at the table."

"And you'd better get her something to puke into," Ysbel called after him as he levered the boneless, swaying Jez to her feet. "I'm pretty sure she's going to need it."

Somehow he managed to get the half-conscious Jez into her cot, gently deflected her drunken kiss, propped her up on pillows, and left a bucket for her to vomit into. He stood watching her for a few moments, worry and panic and irritation and something heavy and heart-stopping that he refused to think about struggling inside him. Finally he sighed, and, grim-faced, turned back to the main room.

"I can't believe her," he muttered as he sat down. "I can't believe she thought—" He broke off, shaking his head.

"Well," said Ivan, "In fairness, it worked."

Lev glared at him. "Don't ever tell her that. Because if she gets one word of encouragement—"

Ysbel raised an eyebrow. "You honestly think it would make any difference?"

He sighed. "Fine. Look, we have the information, but we need to figure out how—"

He broke off abruptly, staring at Tae. "Wait. Tae. We can't get into the database with the invitations, correct?"

Tae nodded slowly. "I could, eventually. But they have a fence around the system that shows any sign of tampering, and to get through without triggering it would probably take me at least a few days, which we don't have."

Lev nodded slowly. "Alright. And there's no way we could warn them."

"Not that we've figured out yet," said Ivan. "And if I recall, Masha said warning them would end with all of you being killed, which, I believe, isn't the preferred outcome at this point."

Lev nodded. He was biting the inside of his cheek, his fingers unconsciously smoothing the surface of the table. "What if," he said slowly, "we weren't trying to stop them from coming in the first place?"

Tae glanced up at him, frowning.

"What if, instead, we made it impossible for Grigory to carry out the plan? We rig the rigged games, so he can't separate off the people he wants to keep alive?" He turned to Ivan. "He wouldn't blow it up if the people he bought would be killed as well, would he?"

Ivan shook his head slowly, eyes beginning to sparkle. "I—don't think he would. He's invested far too much in them at this point. He wouldn't want to have to start from fresh. The way he's organized the coup, he'd need people in key positions for the transfer of power, people with institutional knowledge. If he lost all of them, it would make the transition far too messy. Olyessa's people, or any splinter group with enough weapons power, could come in and take it from him before he had time to get settled." He was still shaking his head. "No, I don't think he would."

"And Jez," said Tae, still frowning. "I can hack into the gambling algorithms if I need to, but I couldn't possibly write something that would fool the dealers. If we're going to fix it, we'd need someone who knows how to cheat so well it's almost undetectable. And—" he glanced towards the door to Jez's room. "And, assuming she survives her hangover, I think we actually have that."

Ysbel took a deep breath, and chuckled softly. "Well," she said. "I'm glad we figured this out. But I'm not certain that Masha knew exactly what she was getting into when she asked Jez to get information. In fact, I think Masha—"

The lock clicked, and the door swung open. "Masha what?" came Masha's mild voice, a hint of sharpness underneath it. "And may I ask who has been drinking something in here that's so strong I can smell it from the hallway? I thought Jez was out gathering information tonight."

They exchanged glances.

"You—might want to sit down, Masha," said Lev at last, pulling out a chair. "We—may have found a solution."

Masha took a seat, eyebrows raised slightly. "I—see. And dare I ask where Jez—"

From Jez's room came the unmistakable sound of someone being violently sick into a bucket.

"I—don't think you'd better," said Ivan carefully, shaking his head.

Ysbel looked up with amusement when Jez finally staggered out of her room, late in the afternoon. The pilot looked like she'd been dragged along the concrete behind a skybike for a few kilometres.

"Hello, you idiot," Ysbel said. "I was wondering if you were still alive."

Jez gave a faint groan and collapsed onto the couch, wincing at the movement. "Not sure I want to be," she muttered.

Ysbel pushed herself to her feet. "Here," she said, crossing over to the couch. She dropped two pain tablets into the pilot's hand. "I thought you might want these."

"Not sure they'll be enough," Jez muttered. She popped them into her mouth and swallowed them dry.

"You know," Ysbel said, shaking her head in amusement. "It's easier not to get hangovers if you don't get drunk."

Jez groaned something weakly that might have been a swear word.

"Jez." Lev came over and knelt beside the couch, a mixture of concern and irritation on his face. "Drink some water. It'll help."

Jez opened her eyes a crack and glared at him.

He sighed. "Come on. Here." He handed her a glass of water. She managed a long drink, then dropped back onto the couch, pressing the heels of her hands into her eyes. "You could talk a little softer, you plaguer," she muttered.

"We could," said Ysbel, not bothering to lower her voice, "but then, the rest of us don't seem to mind."

Jez winced, and glared at her.

Ysbel grinned.

By the time Tae and Ivan had gathered, Jez was sitting up, still scowling and blinking.

Masha hadn't come. She didn't seem to be available to come these days, and Ysbel had seen the concern on Lev's face when she'd politely refused.

Still, there wasn't much they could do about Masha at this point.

Tanya slipped out of their room and glanced around the table. For a moment she looked unsure of where to sit, and Ysbel's heart squeezed in her chest.

And then she gave Ysbel a small smile, and slid into the seat next to her, and Ysbel tried not to let her sudden sick panic show on her face.

Were they really as far apart as all that?

Just long enough to get this done, and then things could go back to how they had been.

But something inside her whispered that how things had been might have been an illusion all this time. Something was broken, and it went much deeper than just a disagreement.

And she didn't know, anymore, how to fix it, and keep her family safe at the same time.

She took a deep breath. "Alright," she said gruffly as the others took their seats. "Lev, I assume you have a plan?"

Lev glanced around the table. "Yes. I may have something that will work, based off what we talked about last night."

Jez blinked up at him painfully. "Hey. Genius. You want to tell the rest of us what we talked about last night?"

He sighed. "Jez. You were the one who was doing the talking."

She managed a self-satisfied look. "Yeah? Well, figure it wouldn't have been a very good night if I could remember any of it."

He sighed again. "Alright. Fine. I'll go through it again for those of us—" he shot her a flat look, "who were so smashed that they have zero recollection of anything that happened in the past twenty-four hours."

Jez managed a smirk. "I remember some things. Like, I'm pretty damn sure I cheated Nikoli out of a hell of a lot of credits." She got a slightly dreamy look on her face. "Not sure I remember a whole lot after that, to be honest, but that was some good stuff he bought us.

Should ask him the name of it sometime."

Tae rolled his eyes, and Ysbel let out a long breath.

To be perfectly honest, she wasn't sure how the pilot was upright, after how she'd looked last night.

But—she shook her head grudgingly. In fairness, Ivan was right. She'd actually managed to pull it off, despite the fact that "it" was something so absolutely ridiculous that no one other than Jez would have considered it.

"Jez. You told us that Grigory planned to rig the gambling, so that as the rounds progressed, the people he wanted to get rid of would end up in the side of the casino ship that he plans to blow up."

Jez looked mildly impressed. "I said all that? While I was that drunk?"

"No," said Lev resignedly. "You didn't. We had to put a lot of slurred rambling together to get there."

Jez gave another self-satisfied smirk. "Alright, so now we know that, what's the plan?"

"That's what Ysbel just asked," said Lev patiently. He looked up at the rest of them. "Alright. So, we need to somehow mess with how they're going to rig the game." He paused, as if bracing himself. "Jez," he said flatly. "I don't suppose you have any idea about how they're going to do it?"

She frowned, then winced. "Maybe when my damn head stops feeling like someone's pounding on it with a damn mallet," she muttered. "But it's probably going to be something they do from inside the gambling hall. I'd guess rigged tokens, but—" She shrugged, and winced again. "And you could talk a little softer, you damn plaguer."

Lev rolled his eyes, but lowered his voice. "Alright. So we'll have to figure that out. The point is, between what Tae and Ivan have found,

I should be able to figure out where we need to change things to wreck their system. And then all we'll have to do is send someone in who can beat their game."

Everyone turned to look at Jez.

She grinned, winced, and leaned back, shoving the heels of her hands against her eyes. "OK, but here's the thing," she groaned. "I'm not totally sure I'm going to be alive after today, to be honest with you."

"You'll be fine," said Ysbel heartlessly. "I'm very, very sure you'll be fine."

Jez lifted one hand and glared at her, then sank back into her seat.

Lev was shaking his head resignedly. "Alright. But the thing is, everyone on this ship knows Jez. So we can't just send her in there to play—there's no way they'd let her in, first of all, and second, they'll know immediately that whatever she does, it's going to mess with their system."

"So, what do you suggest?" asked Ivan.

Lev smiled. "I suggest this—we find a way to get Jez in the room, but hidden somewhere. We send Tanya and Olya in as well, and Jez tells them what they need to do to rig the games. I assume you could do that, Jez?"

Ysbel sucked in a quick breath, but Tanya put a hand on her arm.

Jez lifted the hand off her other eye and glared at him as well, then nodded sullenly.

"And knowing Tanya and Olya, I don't think we need to worry about putting Jez's instructions into effect."

"Lev," began Ysbel, her voice grim.

Tanya shot her a quick glance, then turned back to Lev. "We'll do it," she said quietly. She paused a moment. "Even if this means I tell my daughter to take instructions from Jez," she added, looking at the hungover pilot with some distaste.

Ysbel's heart was beating a little too quickly, but she bit her tongue.

This was a conversation she and Tanya could have afterwards.

"Thank you, Tanya," said Lev. "In the meantime, I'm going to go over the information Tae and Ivan brought me, and I'll try to figure out which games we'll have to rig in order to change the outcome. We don't want to attract attention, so the fewer things we have to mess with, the better."

Ysbel sat up, avoiding Tanya's eyes. "And Lev," she said quietly. "If I agree to this plan, I need to know that the Minister for Innovation and Development will be killed. You'll have to find a way to make that happen."

Lev looked grim. "I'll work on it as best as I can."

"Ysbel," said Tanya quietly, turning to her. "I think we need to talk about this." There was something in her voice and in her face that made Ysbel's chest hurt, just a little.

"Well anyways, I'm going back to my room, because you damn plaguers don't know what talking softly actually means," Jez grumbled, pushing herself gingerly to her feet. She swayed, grabbed for the back of her chair, and missed, and Lev jumped to his feet in time to grab her as she almost overbalanced.

He caught her awkwardly, one hand on her arm, the other on her waist, and both of them froze. For a moment they stood like that, not seeming to notice that everyone around the table was watching them, and neither of them seemed to be able to take their eyes off the other's face.

Even sitting half a metre away, Ysbel could almost feel the tension sparking between them.

And then, finally, Lev took his hand from Jez's waist and

swallowed. "Are—" He cleared his throat and tried again. "Are you alright, Jez?"

"Yeah," she muttered, her voice catching slightly. "I'm—fine." She turned, and almost overbalanced again. Lev grabbed her elbow to steady her, and she stiffened as if she'd been jolted with a shock-stick. Then she pulled her elbow from his hand, and made her unsteady way from the room.

Lev stood looking after her for a long, long moment, and there was a look on his face that held so much undisguised longing that Ysbel was very, very glad that the children weren't there to ask questions.

And then he gave a sharp shake of his head and turned back.

Everyone around the table dropped their gazes simultaneously, but she noticed Ivan fighting back an amused grin.

"Alright," Lev said. He was clearly pretending not to notice, but there was a touch of irritation in his tone. "The rest of us had better get to work then. Tae, could you please send whatever you and Ivan have found over to my com?"

Tae glanced up at him. "Why don't Ivan and I come with you? We may have some insights. Anyways, it will probably involve me hacking something at some point, since I'm not sure that we've ever come up with a plan, in the entire time we've been working together, that didn't involve me hacking into something."

Lev nodded, and the three of them stood and made their way back to Lev's room.

"It's just as well Tae and Ivan went with him," Tanya whispered, a hint of humour in her tone. "I'm not sure he would have made it to the right room otherwise."

Ysbel smiled, and for a moment, it was like it used to be.

And then Tanya dropped her eyes again. "We should talk, Ysbel," she said quietly, and Ysbel nodded.

They walked back to their room, and Tanya closed the door after them. Then she turned and faced Ysbel.

"Tanya," said Ysbel. "I don't like that Olya's doing this."

Tanya looked at her searchingly. "Ysi," she said, finally. "Olya is perfectly capable. You know that as well as I do. I don't believe that is what you're worried about, is it? You are more worried about the Minister being killed than you are about keeping Grigory from staging a coup to take over the entire system." There was a hardness in her voice that Ysbel hardly recognized.

She shook her head stubbornly. "Listen to me, Tanya—"

"No," said Tanya sharply. "You listen to me. We are doing this. You can choose, Ysbel. But I am doing this. My children will not grow up in a system that is run by the mafia."

"Our children might not grow up at all if I don't—" Ysbel began.

Tanya narrowed her eyes. "You will have to make your choice, then," she said quietly. "But if you choose not to stop this—I don't know if we know each other well enough anymore, Ysbel."

She turned away abruptly, and there was a long, long silence. Ysbel stared at her wife's slender shoulders, the tense muscles of her neck and back, the tension that ran through her posture, and for one aching moment she wanted nothing more than to pull Tanya into her arms, kiss her until the hardness melted from her face and the tension melted from her body.

But she couldn't.

For half a moment, she thought maybe she understood the look that Lev had sent after Jez.

She was losing Tanya.

And … well, as much as she hated to admit it, perhaps this time, Tanya was right. Ysbel had known her long enough to know that nothing she could say or do would stop Tanya once Tanya had made up her mind. Perhaps for the moment, this may be the only way to keep her safe.

At last she sighed. "Tanya. My love. Listen to me. You, and the children, you are everything to me." She paused for a moment. "For you, then, my love, for now, I will agree to this. I'll work with Lev to stop this thing."

Slowly, Tanya turned towards her, and Ysbel was shocked, suddenly, at the weariness on her face. "Ysbel," she said at last. "I—"

And this time Ysbel did gather her into her arms, and Tanya sagged against her, and Ysbel held her, stroking her hand down the tense muscles in her back.

"It will be alright," she whispered.

But the tension in Tanya's shoulders remained, no matter how tightly Ysbel held her, and Ysbel wasn't entirely sure that that it would be alright.

15

Tae looked up at a tap on the door, and blinked at the contrast in light.

He'd been staring at his holoscreen for so many hours now he'd lost count, and it took him a moment to re-focus his eyes. When he did, he saw Ivan slip through the door.

Ivan's face was drawn from lack of sleep, his dark hair disheveled, barely-disguised circles under his eyes. He'd been working night shifts in the kitchen, and spending the days helping them with their plans, and he looked somewhere beyond exhausted. But he smiled slightly when he saw Tae.

"Tae," he said, and there was worry in his voice. "Someone's coming this way. Best put that away." He glanced around. "And I'd best get back to the kitchens, our deception notwithstanding. I'm technically off-shift, but they said they might need me if it got busy." He shot Tae a wry grin, and Tae grinned back despite himself. Since the day in the corridor the rumours had spread, and now it seemed no one questioned Ivan's frequent visits to their rooms.

He shook his head ruefully as Ivan slipped back out into the hallway.

Once, just once, it would be nice to have a reputation that he'd actually deserved.

Someone knocked on the door a moment later, and he stood to open it.

A boyevik stood there, with a folded invitation made of actual paper. Tae took it and broke the seal, opening it carefully.

Tae, it read. *Grant me the pleasure of your company this afternoon in the dining room. 1400 Standard. I will be looking forward to it.*

It was signed, *Zhenya.*

Tae glanced down at the folded paper for a long moment, worry churning in his stomach.

What could they possibly want with him?

Then again, what options did he have?

"Tell Zhenya I'm honoured," he said, looking up at the boyevik and trying not to let his feelings show on his face. "I'll be there shortly."

"Tae," said Zhenya, as Tae ducked through the heavy curtain into the private dining room. "I'm so happy you could join me." They gestured to a seat, and Tae sat warily.

"I'm—flattered you asked me here," he said, trying to keep the nerves from his voice. "But I'm not certain—"

"Tae." Zhenya was smiling, a self-satisfied smile that made Tae's stomach tighten with worry. "You worked very hard last time we met to convince me that you were a mediocre hacker at best."

"I—don't know what—"

Zhenya held up a hand. "You were very convincing, don't worry. I'm not attempting to cast aspersions on what you did. But something didn't sit quite right with me. Because as I told you, I know Masha. She's not the kind of person to work with a mediocre hacker."

"I told you, I'm not——"

Zhenya shook their head. "Please. Tae. Let me finish." They paused a moment as Tae subsided. Then they smiled. "Of course, I couldn't be completely sure that I was correct. Were you really what you said you were, a clever, over-eager street kid who managed to pull a con on Masha, and then make himself useful enough that she wouldn't get rid of him? Or did you have hidden depths? I couldn't tell." They leaned forward. "But I love a puzzle. And the boyevik who brought you to my office last time told me an amusing story about you and a server. And eventually, I believed I had a solution. Which is when I called for you."

Tae's heart was beating faster now, a feeling of dread creeping up his throat.

"So I thought we'd play a little game," Zhenya continued. They tapped their com.

"Yes, Pakhan, what do you need?" someone answered immediately.

Zhenya smiled at Tae as they spoke. "I'd like you to send up some blini for myself and my friend. I want them fresh—we don't mind waiting." They paused a moment. "Oh, and send my friend's friend, Ivan Ivanovich, as a server, please. It would be a nice touch."

The sick, formless worry had solidified, knotting itself around Tae's chest at the mention of Ivan's name.

Zhenya tapped off their com and leaned back in their chair. "So, Tae. It usually takes our esteemed chef about ten minutes to prepare a plateful of fresh blini. Maybe another minute for your friend Ivan to bring them up." They glanced at their com, and tapped a button. "And—yes. I've just armed the device I had my people plant here earlier. When Ivan walks through the door, it will go off, and he will be blown into pieces. Unless, of course—" they shrugged delicately.

"Unless someone were to hack through and disarm it."

Tae swore softly, feeling the blood drain from his face.

Ten damn minutes, and he'd have to choose between keeping his hacking abilities secret and Ivan's life.

It wasn't even a contest, although it probably should have been. He tapped his com, pulling up the holoscreen, and did a quick scan, ignoring Zhenya's eyes on him.

A simple laser tripwire. The moment the curtain brushed it, it would go off.

He could set it off early, perhaps—no. It wasn't just a tripwire. There was a pressure plate behind it, so it would only go off if there were someone standing there.

Damn, damn, damn.

He shook his com to reset it and did a second scan, a little more slowly.

The trap must have been set into the room's security system.

He hadn't tried hacking into the security systems yet, staying at the relatively shallow level of cameras and audio, because he'd wanted to keep what he could do a secret. And it was damn well not a secret any longer, because he wasn't going to watch his friend blown to bloody fragments in front of him.

He started typing rapidly. The system was complicated, more complicated than anything he'd hacked into recently, which only made sense, really—Grigory probably had people trying to kill him on a regular basis—but he was pretty sure he could do it. It would just take time ...

Which was exactly what he didn't have.

He scowled at his screen, biting the inside of his cheek.

It was complicated, but not impossible. If he could just manage to find a way in, he was pretty sure he could figure it out—

He worked quickly, trying to force his fingers not to tremble, trying to focus on each successive keystroke rather than the seconds ticking away, the panic rising in his chest.

There! He was in. Now all he had to do was find where exactly the trap had been set into the system. And then disarm it, of course.

In the background, he heard voices over Zhenya's com, but he ignored them, because he had to get this done, he absolutely had to, there wasn't another option.

He was close, though, and it had only taken him five or six minutes so far, he should have plenty of time …

"Tae."

He jerked his head up. Zhenya was smiling at him.

"Good news, Tae. Our chef has outdone herself. Ivan is on his way as we speak."

Tae felt the chill through to his bones as he turned frantically back to the screen.

Damn.

He was never going to find it in time, there was no way—how long would it take for Ivan to get from the kitchen to their private dining room?

For one frantic moment, he wondered if he could hit the com button, warn Ivan, and Zhenya would probably shoot Tae, but maybe—

"Don't bother," said Zhenya, still smiling. "There's another server behind him with a heat gun. If he makes one move, he'll be shot in the back."

Tae squeezed his eyes shut for a moment.

Think. Where would Zhenya have hooked it in? This was a test, sure, but you could only hook something like this into the system so many ways—

His eyes snapped open, and he began typing desperately. He was pretty sure—yes! There it was, and once he'd found it, disarming it was just a matter of a simple command.

There were footsteps in the hallway outside.

Holding his breath, he typed something into the system, fingers shaking, and hit enter.

And then the curtains pulled back, and he jerked his head up, not wanting to watch but needing to see, because if he'd failed, if he hadn't figured it out, this would be the last time he saw Ivan alive …

Ivan ducked through the curtain, and when he caught sight of Tae he gave him a friendly smile. Then he frowned, and Tae realized he must look awful. He must look like he was about to faint, because he honestly felt like he was about to faint, whether from the gut-wrenching terror or the sick relief he wasn't sure.

"Your blinis, Pakhan," Ivan murmured, casting a worried glance at Tae.

"Thank you," said Zhenya. "That's all, I think, Ivan."

Ivan bowed slightly, but as he turned to go, he mouthed, "You OK?" to Tae.

Tae managed a weak smile and gave a small nod, and Ivan, still frowning, ducked out the curtain.

When he was gone, Tae sat for a few moments, not certain if he could move even if he wanted to. Every single muscle in his body seemed to have turned to water.

"Well done," said Zhenya. Their voice was smug, but under the smugness was honest admiration. "I've never seen anyone hack like that."

Tae took a long breath and turned to Zhenya. "I did what you asked," he said quietly, but his voice was hard. "I showed you what I could do. But I swear to you, I will die right here before I ever help you. I survived on the streets for twenty years, and it took everything I had to stay alive. But I will cut my own damn throat first."

The words were probably stupid, but he didn't actually care at this point.

Zhenya watched him calculatingly for a long time. At last they gave a pleasant smile. "Tae. Don't worry. I know enough about you to know that threatening to kill your … friend would not endear me to you. But then, you never had any intention of helping us, did you? So really, what was there to lose?"

"And what did you hope to gain?" Tae asked, his tone still hard.

Zhenya shrugged. "Nothing, really. But as I said, I look into everyone here. That's my job, and I'm good at it. And yes, I need to know everything about who Grigory is working with. But it's also my job to know everything about who Grigory may be working against." They gave Tae an insincere smile. "Here. Have a blini before you go. You worked hard enough for them."

Tae shoved back his chair and stalked out of the room, not bothering to respond.

When he reached the room, Ivan was waiting for him. He looked exhausted, but he stood quickly when Tae entered.

"Tae. Are you alright? What—"

"I'm fine," said Tae wearily. "I—they know what I can do now."

"How did they—" began Ivan, and then he stopped, and Tae could see the exact moment when Ivan finally figured out what had happened. He sank back into the chair, shaking his head, face slightly pale.

"You saved my life, didn't you?"

"I damn well put it in danger in the first place," Tae snapped. He dropped down into a chair and closed his eyes for a moment. "I—guess I'd better call Lev. This may put a kink in our plans. I won't be able to do any hacking, other than something that's relatively undetectable, like into the coms and vid feeds. Otherwise they'll know exactly who it was."

"Tae," said Ivan softly. "I'm—sorry."

"No. It was my fault," said Tae. "If I'd—"

"'If you'd' nothing," said Ivan, standing abruptly. "Cut it out, Tae. You need to stop feeling guilty for existing. Zhenya is brilliant, that's the only way they survived as long as they did on the streets, and the only reason they've survived this long in the mafia. And they chose to do this, and there was nothing, aside from letting them kill me, that you could have done to stop it. It's their fault, not yours."

Tae stared up at him for a moment, and finally managed a weak smile. "Yeah," he said at last. "I guess so."

Ivan smiled back, then dropped back into his chair, rubbing his eyes. "Oof. I don't know how you did this in prison, but I'm going to be honest, this never sleeping thing is getting to me. As terrible as it sounds, I'm happy Grigory's conference will be over and done in three more days. I'm not sure how much longer I'll last."

Tae chuckled, and didn't let himself think of how close they'd come to Ivan not lasting out the end of today, didn't let himself think of what Zhenya knew or wonder what they'd do with that knowledge.

Because Ivan was right—at this point, there was absolutely nothing he could do about it.

16

Lev took a deep breath, and stared out of the floor-to-ceiling glass that was the only thing separating the inside of Grigory's luxurious observation room from the vastness of deep space, outside.

They were moving fast, especially for a ship this size, and he knew it because Grigory had shown him, once, the controls, had asked the pilot to demonstrate the speeds she was able to travel.

But with the endless expanse surrounding them, it was difficult to tell.

The conference started in less than twenty-four standard hours. And they were on their way to join it.

He couldn't shake the tension from his muscles.

He and Tae and Ivan had sat up long into the night, trying to figure out what exactly needed to happen with their crazy, cobbled-together, last-minute plan.

And he still wasn't certain he'd made the right decision when he'd agreed to help the others stop this. Because it was likely that if Grigory's scheme failed, he wouldn't bother to kill the minister. And it was certain that he wouldn't help Lev go after Evka.

Lev still could see, behind his eyelids, what Grigory had done to his would-be assassin. He'd said it was something he was forced to do

196

to stay alive, and maybe that was correct.

But—he'd enjoyed it. Lev had watched him, from the corner of his eyes.

Grigory had enjoyed every moment of it.

He was born to this.

No. He wasn't born to this, any more than any person was born to it. He'd grown into it. He'd become what he needed to be, day in and day out, until now, that day, he had become a person who enjoyed watching that type of torture, enjoyed watching the screams of pain, the horror and the fear on the man's face.

And—

And the problem was, the worst part of that whole thing was, that, watching it, Lev was very, very certain that he could, one day, if he chose, become the kind of person who could do something similar. Maybe he'd never enjoy it the way Grigory did. But he could be, he'd been suddenly, sickeningly sure, the kind of person who could watch it with dispassionate interest.

Hadn't he, just minutes before it had begun, agreed with a plan which he knew, without doubt, would end in the death of not only the three people who were holding his and the rest of the crew's lives in their hands, but their families as well? Their husbands, wives, partners. Their children.

Because one of those families, he was almost certain, had children. Young children.

And he'd nodded blandly, knowing, as he did so, that those children would be killed, and he'd been willing to sacrifice them to keep Olya alive, and Tae and Ysbel and Masha, and Jez—

Jez.

He shut his eyes briefly and shook his head.

He'd been willing—

He opened his eyes again, staring sightlessly at the blackness surrounding him.

And he still wasn't sure he'd made the right choice.

He wasn't sure there was a right choice.

The ship they were approaching loomed ahead of them in the distance. It was big enough that it hardly looked like a ship, the bulk of it rising up to one side of them, blocking off the stars behind it, making it a hulking dark, thicker and more substantial than the surrounding blackness.

They'd be there in a matter of minutes. The government ships, some of them, were probably already there.

He didn't move from his vantage point until he felt the slight jolt of the ships joining, the smaller jolt, then the steadying, of the airlock connecting.

They were hooked on.

He closed his eyes again for a moment and took a deep breath.

Tomorrow.

If they were going to stop this, this ridiculous, cobbled-together plan they'd come up with would have to work, because they had no more time.

He turned and walked slowly towards the airlock. Best to scout out what they were working with now, so he'd have some idea, maybe be able to give Jez—

He broke off the thought, because he needed a clear head, damn it, and now wasn't the time to think about the way she'd looked at him the afternoon before, hungover and unsteady, the way her eyes had widened, the way her body had softened under his fingers, the way she'd leaned, unconsciously, towards him—

He gritted his teeth.

They were bloody well friends. Crewmates and friends. And he bloody well had to get a handle on himself right about now.

He'd reached the airlock without noticing. He shook his head and glanced around.

There were guards Grigory had posted at the door, but it appeared that they were more interested in keeping unauthorized people off of Grigory's ship than they were from preventing people from getting onto the casino ship. They barely glanced at him as he stepped past them into the narrow airlock passage.

If Grigory's ship had been nothing but class, the dark blue-black of space reflected in the carpets and pillars, trimmed with gold—this was something else entirely. It still had an air of opulence, the thick, cloying scent of far too many credits hanging in the air like a perfume, but there was nothing understated about this place. The carpets here were a rich red, the walls plastered with gold, the servers dressed in outfits that accentuated both their bodies and the opulence of their uniforms. He blinked, and then gave a faint, reminiscent smile.

Not a place, certainly, that Jez would have appreciated yesterday, when she'd come stumbling out of her room.

Already, this early in the afternoon, he could hear the *click* of gambling tokens, the rise and fall of voices, the clink of glasses, smell the mingled alcohol and rich cologne from the gambling rooms.

This was a ship that wouldn't keep track of standard time. This was a ship where any hour of the day or night, there would be a place to find alcohol and tokens and a game to play them in.

He wandered along the halls toward the sounds, looking around him at the richness of the walls and furnishings.

If he hadn't just watched Grigory's ship approach, felt the jolt as they hooked in, he would hardly have guessed they were in space.

He reached the gambling hall and stepped inside, standing back against the walls to observe. The tables were already crowded with people, and it was readily apparent that both the tokens and the alcohol were flowing freely.

It was a large room, and despite its open appearance at first glance, as he looked closer he noticed how the tables were set up, the pillars and half-walls and low stairways that somehow, without seeming to, broke the room up into several distinct segments.

That was good to know.

It might make it more difficult for Jez to see what was going on, but it would certainly make it easier for Tanya and Olya to go unnoticed.

Jez too, if it was even possible for her to go unnoticed.

He shook his head slightly, and started back down the hallway to Grigory's ship.

"Lev!"

He looked up quickly.

A woman was standing half-way down the room, dressed in a government uniform, a holoscreen pulled up over her wrist that she'd clearly been studying a moment earlier.

"Ljubika?" he said in disbelief, staring at her.

She smiled, and crossed over to him. "Lev! I never thought I'd see you here." She put a familiar hand on his arm, and he smiled back despite himself.

She'd been one of his first friends when he'd moved over into government. His first lover there, certainly. They'd both been young and ambitious and smart, and he'd actually liked her very much. It had only been three or four months before they'd both been transferred into different departments, but—well, but she'd been a friend when he'd badly needed one.

"What are you doing here?" he asked.

She raised a teasing eyebrow. "The same thing you are, I imagine. Something this big, they decided they needed someone to keep track of things. So that's what I'm doing, I suppose. I'm technically under-minister to the Minister of Finance, but I'm good at logistics, so here I am." She paused. "Last time we met, they were going to move you over into the internal security department. You still there?"

"I'm—not in the exact same department," he murmured. "I'm—working on internal matters with a special team. We tend to work on programs that run a little under the radar." It took him a moment to get his tongue around the magnitude of the deception.

She gave him a curious look, then glanced back at her holoscreen and cursed quietly. "Sorry, I've got to go. I'm on a mid-day to midnight Standard shift." She turned, then glanced back at him.

"Give me a call sometime. For old time's sake. I've actually missed you, you know." She tapped her com quickly against his. "You have my number now. But I really have to run."

"Good to see you, Ljubika," he called as she strode off.

He looked after her for a moment, a hard, cold knot in the pit of his stomach.

Ljubika was here, keeping track of logistics. They weren't together anymore, but she had been—probably still was—a decent person. Not a hero, not a saint, but—well, just a person. A person he was fond of, a person who didn't deserve to die.

How many other decent people were in here, refreshing themselves in their rooms on the deck above, standing in chatting clusters around the gambling floor? How many other people who had friends who liked them, lovers who missed them, children who couldn't wait for them to get back home?

And when the hell had he stopped thinking about that?

No. Perhaps the better question was, when had he started thinking about that again?

He remembered Grigory, the look on his face as he watched the man in front of him die, and shuddered.

How far was he, really, from that?

It didn't matter, not at the moment. He'd told Tae he'd help save these people, and even though he had no idea if that was the right decision, he could parse the morality of it when this was all over.

For now, best to get back to planning. Now that he had some idea of the structure of the gambling hall, he'd be able, hopefully, to put together what Grigory had told him and make the plan a little more firm. He was sending Jez, along with an eight-year-old, into the middle of the mafia. And he certainly did not intend to do so unless he was very, very certain that he could work out a way to keep them safe.

He passed the guards, who waved him though, and headed down the corridor to their rooms, frowning in thought.

He almost didn't notice the movement in the corridor that intersected with his, the muffled sound of running footsteps, until he'd almost reached the intersection. He jerked his head up, and then someone grabbed him by the arm and shoved him backwards down the corridor. Before he could make a sound, the figure put a finger to her lips and made a fierce gesture for him to be quiet. He looked up, and sucked in a quick breath.

"Jez?" he hissed. She gave a sharp shake of her head, then she shoved him back against the wall, snatched the heat pistol from her pocket, and cracked off a shot down the corridor. She dropped as a laser beam burnt a hole in the wall behind where she'd been standing, and he noticed, suddenly, the blood staining the sleeve of her jacket, and something cold and panicky gripped his chest. She jumped to her feet, but her heat pistol had been knocked to the ground when she dived, and she glanced around for it frantically. He grabbed his own and shoved it into her hand, and she gave him a quick, tight grin, leaned out around the corner, and fired again. There was a staticky crackle and a muffled grunt.

"Think I got him," she whispered, grinning at Lev. He grabbed her by the arm.

"Jez! What happened? Are you—"

She shook her head again. "Talk later."

He nodded, and they sprinted down the corridor, bent low. He hit the key button on his com as they reached the door, she wrenched it open, and they practically fell inside, both of them panting. Lev slammed the door shut behind them, hit the lock, and grabbed Jez by the shoulder, pulling her around to face him. He scanned her quickly, his heart hammering in his chest, the panic bleeding through him like a wash of ice water. She had a black eye, and a long, shallow cut along her forehead, and there was blood soaking through the sleeve of her jacket, and there was blood on his shirt as well where he'd stumbled up against her as they were running.

"Jez—" he said through his teeth, grabbing her jacket and pulling it gently off her shoulders. "What happened? Where are you hurt? What—"

"Genius. Relax," she said, giving him a tired grin. "Ran into some people I'd met in the gambling hall, and they weren't happy to see me, that's all. I'm fine. Just—" She winced as he peeled the blood-soaked jacket sleeve gingerly from her arm.

"This doesn't look fine," he said, still speaking through his teeth. His heart was pounding far, far too quickly as he pulled her sleeve gently up to reveal a long, deep gash that looked like it had been done by a knife. He looked at it, then up at her.

"See," she said, "Just a cut. No big deal."

"We need to get this taken care of," he said shortly. "Stay there." He strode over to the corner cupboard, where the first aid kit was stored, and yanked it down. He pulled it open, pulled out disinfectant and a sealing bandage, and stalked back over to her.

She didn't say anything as he mopped up the blood, sprayed on disinfectant, and sealed the bandage carefully over the wound, pulling the edges of the cut together as he set the bandage.

By the time he was finished, his hands were bloody. He looked around for a moment, helplessly, then wiped them on his trousers.

She was still looking at him, not moving.

When his hands were no longer wet, he looked her over one more time, briefly, to make sure he hadn't missed any other places where she was bleeding, or broken, or … He sucked in a deep breath, fighting off the sudden dizziness. Damn it to hell—

He placed his hands on her shoulders again, gently. "Jez," he asked, his voice rough with strain. "What the hell happened? Are you alright? Are you hurt? Are—"

He broke off suddenly.

She was still looking at him, and her eyes caught his and held them, and he suddenly realized that they were standing very, very close.

She took a small step towards him, her eyes never leaving his, and there was something in her expression, something that twisted his stomach into knots and tightened around his chest so he was suddenly unsure if he would still be able to breathe if she took one step closer.

His hands were still on her shoulders, and he was still holding her like he was afraid she'd disappear if he let go, and his heart, which had been racing in panic, was still racing, but with something else now.

He tried to swallow, but his throat was so dry he couldn't quite manage it.

"Lev," she whispered.

He'd somehow taken a step closer as well, and their bodies were almost touching. Her breath came fast and shallow, like it had when she'd been running, and she was still staring into his eyes, and he couldn't seem to look away either. They were close enough that he could feel her breath on his skin, and something like electricity was jolting through him, from where his hands were touching her shoulders, all the way through his body.

She was—she was just a crewmate, they were only crewmates, they'd had this discussion and they'd both agreed—

She leaned forward slightly, and her lips were so close to his that he could almost taste her, and damn it to hell, this wasn't supposed to happen, they'd both decided this wasn't—

He wasn't actually sure which one of them leaned in those last remaining millimetres, all he knew was her lips brushed against his for just an instant, and then they were kissing, hungrily, desperately. Her hands wound into the back of his shirt, and he pulled her up against him, and her body pressed into his until he wasn't completely sure where she left off and he began. Her lips caught his, deepening the kiss, and he slid his hand up, cupping the back of her head, holding her against him. He tightened his fingers into her hair, and she moaned into his lips, her body melting into him, and the only thought in his brain was that this, here, was what he had been waiting for his whole life, searching for even when he hadn't realized he was searching for anything.

She stiffened abruptly, pushing away from him and stumbling backwards a few steps, and they stood there for a moment, panting, staring at each other. Her eyes were wide and panicked.

"Jez," he said finally, his voice hoarse. "I'm—I'm sorry. I—"

She shook her head. "No." She swallowed hard. "No, it's—it wasn't you. I—" She broke off. Her breath was still coming too quickly, and her face was bloodless. She glanced around, and almost fell into the hard chair beside her, and for a long moment, neither of them spoke.

He closed his eyes and took a long breath, trying to slow his racing heart. "Jez," he said at last, and his voice was so thick with longing he could hardly get the words out. "Jez. I—I can't do this anymore, OK? I can't. I—I need you, Jez. I can't—" He broke off, running a hand helplessly through his hair.

Jez was still watching him, but there was something in her face, something frightened and vulnerable and hurt.

"Lev," she said, her voice barely more than a whisper. "Lev, I— look, I thought—I mean, you said—"

"I know what I said," he was talking through his teeth. He could hardly focus on the words he was saying, because all he could focus on right now was the fact that she was here, sitting just across from him, and he hadn't realized until now how much he needed her, he couldn't pinpoint the moment when his entire self had begun to revolve around her like a damn planet around a sun, but it had and he couldn't seem to stop it. "I—when Evka tried to kill you, it terrified me. It scared me more than anything has ever scared me before. I—I couldn't handle the thought of losing you, Jez. I couldn't —" For a moment, the familiar panic welled up in his chest, choking off his words. He took a deep breath. "I—I thought maybe that would protect you. That you not being with me would protect you. But—" He stopped, shaking his head helplessly. "I can't protect you, Jez. I've never been able to. Because you're you, and you do what you want to do, and I don't have any right to tell you not to. And you're still getting hurt, look at you, and—Jez, I can't do this anymore." His voice choked, and he stopped speaking for a moment.

She was still watching him, something unbearably sad in her eyes.

"Yeah," she said at last, her voice soft. "I—figured maybe it was something like that. And you're right, it's a pretty stupid reason. But —" She swallowed hard, seeming to brace herself. "But look, Lev. When you said that, I didn't argue with you, because—because—" she closed her eyes for a moment.

"Because," she said softly, "I—I love you, Lev. I guess I love you. And the thing is—I can't do relationships. I'm crap at them, and there's no way I don't screw them up. Like this, right now. I've already screwed crap up, I—I kissed you, after I said—I said I wasn't going to, and—" she gestured helplessly. "I can't do that to you. I am who I am, and I get scared and run away, and I'd hurt you, and I can't. I just—I can't." There were tears forming in her eyes. She brushed them away quickly. "It's just who I am. I can't change it, I don't know how to change it. And if I tried, if I tried to make it work, I'd panic. And maybe I could make myself stay, I don't know, but it'd be like trying to hold my head underwater, and I couldn't breathe, and maybe I'd die. But I'd have to either do that or hurt you, and maybe I'd die from that, too." She swallowed hard, turning away from him.

There was something sick in his stomach. He took a step towards her, knelt so he was looking her in the eye, put a hand on her arm. "Jez," he said, and he could hear the roughness in his tone. "Listen to me, Jez. I know who you are, and I'd never ask you to do something that would hurt you, and I'd never ask you to change, for me or for anyone else. I understand, you hate being trapped. But Jez —" he swallowed back the pleading in his voice. "The thing is, Jez, I don't care. I honestly don't care. I'd take you for however long you'd want to stay, if that's a year or a month or a day or one damn night, I don't even care. I'll take it. I'd give up every single one of my tomorrows, happily, for one damn night with you."

There was a long silence. He could feel her body trembling under his hand, and his hand was trembling too.

At last she looked up, and gave him a small, sad smile. "Maybe you don't care," she said, not meeting his eyes. "But here's the thing, genius. I do. I'm not going to let you screw up your life. I'm not going to screw up your life, OK?"

She pushed herself up and stood, and looking at her, at the longing in her posture, the set of her body, leaned in slightly towards him, he knew she wanted him as badly as he wanted her, and hell, he'd known that since he'd bloody well told her that they needed some space, and—

She reached out and rested her hand on his chest, and his whole body sparked at her touch, and for a moment he wasn't sure if she was going to grab his shirt and pull him in towards her, or shove him away.

But at last, she let her fingers slide down his chest and drop to her side, and she turned away. "I'm sorry, genius," she whispered. And then she slipped into her own room and closed the door behind her.

He stared blankly at her closed door for a long time, and the adrenalin pumping through him made his muscles shaky.

Finally, he turned, pulling open the door, and stepped blindly out into the corridor. He didn't know where he was going, and to be honest, he didn't really care, he just needed to move, before he lost his mind.

He walked the corridors of the ship for a long time.

His com buzzed a couple times, but he ignored it. If they needed him badly enough, they could tap something out in pilot's code.

Finally, when he'd walked for long enough that he thought maybe, somehow, he could manage to be in the same room as someone else again, he made his slow way back to their suite.

When he stepped inside, Tae and Ivan looked up from the table, and Tae frowned in concern at the look on his face.

"Lev?" he asked. "What's the matter? Ivan and I have been trying to call you, we were going to—"

Lev managed a small smile. "Sorry, Tae," he said. "I have the layout to the gambling hall. I can send it through to your com. But —" He gave a small shrug. "I don't think I'll be much help tonight. Long day."

Tae studied him, still frowning, but at last he nodded. "That's fine. I think you already gave us the schedule of the games with the ones marked off that we decided would be the best to rig. If you send through the schematics, Ivan and I can try to put it together."

"Thanks, Tae," he said, with a small, wry smile. "I appreciate it. I'm sorry for dropping it on you like this."

"It's fine," said Tae, still watching him, concern in his face. "It's not a big deal. Listen, Lev, are you sure—"

"I'm fine," he said. "I think I just need some sleep."

Tae nodded, expression still cut with concern. "Alright. Get some sleep then."

Lev managed one last smile, and crossed over to his room.

When he'd closed the door behind him, he leaned against it, letting the smile fade from his face.

No, there were still things to do. He pulled up his com, scrolled through to where he'd made his notes and done a quick diagram scan of the gambling room, and tapped the button to send them over to Tae's and Ivan's coms.

Then he let himself sink back against the door.

This was ridiculous. Nothing had bloody well changed since that morning, it was exactly the same as it had always been, and anyways, Jez had the right to decide whether or not she wanted to be in a relationship.

He was being ridiculously stupid.

Something on the top of the dresser caught his eye. He frowned, and crossed over to it.

There was a bottle of sump, and underneath it, a note, scrawled in messy, unmistakable handwriting.

"Hey, genius," it read. "Sorry. Thought you might want this."

He stared at the note for a long time. Then he crumpled it in his fist and threw it across the room. He closed his eyes for a moment, breathing heavily, then he snatched the bottle off the dresser and crossed over to his bed.

He dropped down onto his cot and leaned back against the wall, staring up at the ceiling.

Maybe Jez was damn well right, for once.

It had been a long plaguing time since he'd last gotten drunk. But tonight sounded like a good time to remedy that.

He pulled the cap off the bottle and put it to his lips, tipping his head back, and tried not to think about the look on Jez's face when she'd told him she loved him, and then turned away.

"Lev."

He looked up, squinting against the light, into Ysbel's face.

He knew he looked awful, but probably not quite as awful as he felt. At least, he hoped not. On the bright side, the pounding headache and the uneasy nausea lurching in his stomach made it at least easier not to think about Jez. When he could hardly form a coherent thought, it was slightly more difficult to picture her face, the sick finality in it, remember how she felt in his arms, the way his whole body ached with needing her, the warmth of her lips on his, the electricity jolting though his body wherever she touched him … He dropped his head into his hands.

Apparently even a hangover wasn't enough.

"Lev," said Ysbel again, and he raised his head.

"Yes, Ysbel?" He still, somehow, managed to keep his voice calm.

She was staring at him, her expression flat and forbidding. "What the *hell*," she leaned into the emphasis on the word, "is wrong with you?"

He shook his head, and bit back a wince. "I'm sorry."

She was still watching him. "Listen," she said at last. "I get it. You want to sleep with Jez, and Jez wants to sleep with you, and for some stupid reason you've both decided that you're not going to do that, and so she's sulking in her room and you're hungover. I get it." She narrowed her eyes. "But we're trying to save the lives of every member of this crew and about three hundred people besides right now, and prevent a coup by the mafia of the entire Svodrani system, and now would be a very good time to stop acting like a complete damn idiot. Do you understand me?"

He squeezed his eyes shut for a moment, fighting back the nausea. At last he blew out a steadying breath.

She was right, honestly. He needed to pull himself together, because right now they had fewer than twelve standard hours before Grigory's symposium officially kicked off.

"Yes, Ysbel," he said, opening his eyes. "I'm sorry."

She was still giving him that flat look. "I hope you are. And I hope your head hurts badly enough that you won't try that again for a very long time."

"I'm—not sure if it's possible for it to hurt badly enough," he murmured wryly.

She frowned slightly, still studying him. At last she shook her head. "I'm sorry," she said, her voice a little more gentle. "Do you want to talk about it?"

He shook his head gingerly, then winced at the movement. "I'm— not sure I do."

She watched him for a moment more, one eyebrow raised. At last she nodded. "Alright. Well then, if you don't want to talk about it, let's talk about how we're going to keep Jez and my wife and my children from being shot tonight, yes?"

17

"Aunty Jez?"

Jez glanced over to where Olya crouched.

They were sitting at a table in the far corner, hidden from view by a staircase and a large artificial vine, which, to be honest, vines still gave Jez the creeps after that damn incident with Vitali, but what the hell. She figured it was about time for one of them to be useful.

Tanya sat across from her, face tense, and Olya was crouched just under the table, out of view of any passing server.

"Alright," said Lev's voice in her earpiece. She stiffened unconsciously, then forced herself to relax.

She could deal with all the crap about Lev and what had happened last night later.

Or maybe not. Maybe she'd die or something first, if she was lucky, maybe someone would shoot her or maybe they'd calculate wrong and she'd get blown up. Honestly, she wasn't sure which scared her more.

No, she knew damn well which scared her more, and it wasn't getting shot.

She managed a grin, the sick feeling in her stomach mingling with the tight knot of adrenalin to make it almost impossible for her to sit

213

still.

"From where you're sitting, the games we need to rig are the ones at the table on the far right side of where you're facing, the large table in the centre, and the table three tables to the left of you, up the stairs."

"On it," she whispered. "Who needs to win?"

"On the right table, the short woman in the deep blue jacket."

She glanced over and gave a short nod. "Got it."

"The centre table, the man with long hair and pale skin."

"Got it."

"The table to your left, it's the woman in the red, with short black hair."

"Got it." She glanced down at Olya. "You hear that, Olya?"

"Yes, Aunty Jez," said Olya, with a long-suffering sigh.

"Be polite please, Olya," Tanya murmured.

"OK. So here's what we're going to do." Jez pulled out a bag of tokens that Tanya had stolen from the casino the evening before, and dropped them below the table top. "Tae's hacking into their vid and audio feed, so he can keep an eye on the games. And now," she grinned down at Olya, "we're going to work on those gambling skills I taught you this morning."

Olya gave her a superior look. "I'm pretty damn good at gambling, Aunty Jez."

Tanya glared at Jez, then at her daughter. "Olya," she whispered, "Where did you—"

Jez raised an eyebrow. "Come on, Tanya, not like she's wrong."

Tanya glowered, and Jez grinned.

"Alright," she said quietly, shaking the tokens out of her bag. "And you need to pay attention, Olya, because this is important—this isn't the best way to cheat. There's way better ways. But this is the easiest one, and the mafia's already expecting the games to be rigged, so we should be just fine to go ahead. So." She flipped quickly through the tokens, pulled out a handful, and poured them into Olya's hands. "Those ones with the X mark in the top left corner, those are the big-credit tokens."

"I know, Aunty," said Olya wearily. "You told me that this morning."

"Just making sure. Now, you're gong to want to make sure that," she glanced up at the table, "the lady in the blue jacket gets about —" she squinted one eye, calculating.

A little harder to cheat, honestly, if you couldn't see the tokens, and the person you were helping to cheat didn't realize they were supposed to be cheating.

"About four of them into her draw pile, alright? And then you want to take her partner's draw-pile, and add two of them there. The other set of partners playing against them, you want to slip them each one of these." She held up a token with a circle stamped into the top corner. "Got it?"

Olya glanced at the tokens in her hand, and then up at Jez. "So," she said, "You want to give her enough points to win, and her partner enough points to play off her, and then you want to use one of these to handicap the people who aren't on her team because when they see the circle, they'll play that instead of however many squares they have, because it's worth more points. But the X will trump them if she has at least two. Right?"

Jez raised her eyebrows, and glanced up at Tanya. "I'm impressed. Kid's a natural."

Tanya was still giving her that look that usually meant she was imagining creative ways to kill her.

"You got it, kid," she said in a low voice, turning back to Olya.

"But here's the thing—"

"You need me to slip the other side's X-tokens out, I know," said Olya, rolling her eyes. "I'm actually pretty smart, Aunty."

"Olya," warned Tanya, almost automatically.

"Yep," said Jez, grinning. "Figure you are. Off you go then."

Olya looked up at her, and for a moment her excitement flickered through the bored look she'd affected up to this point. Jez gave her a wink, and Olya slipped away.

"Your turn now, Tanya," said Jez, still grinning. "They're playing three blind beggars at the centre table, so you're going to want these." She slipped a handful of tokens into Tanya's hand, and, after a brief explanation, Tanya slipped off as well.

Jez leaned back, surveying the scene with satisfaction through the leafy curtain of the vine. She tapped her com. "Got a visual yet, Tae?" she whispered.

"Give me a sec." Tae's voice was strained, but then hell, Tae's voice was always strained. Kid worried way too much.

"Got it," he whispered at last. "Pushing it through to your com."

She tapped her com, bringing up her holoscreen, and a moment later, three separate feeds appeared. She expanded the screen slightly, grinning.

Olya was almost impossible to spot, which was honestly impressive —Jez was pretty damn sure they didn't usually let kids in these places.

Although, after the way Olya had picked up on the theory of cheating at tokens, maybe that was just for self-preservation.

But somehow the kid managed to look both innocent and slightly lost as she made her unerring way towards the indicated table. She disappeared behind it, and Jez expanded the feed with two fingers.

She grinned at the shock, hastily disguised, on the woman's face, and then at the brief flicker of satisfaction on the face of her opponent as he turned over a token from his pile.

He'd have found the circle.

For an enjoyable few minutes, she watched the game play out exactly as she'd planned it, and then Olya tapped her on the elbow. She jumped, and swore.

"Damn it, kid, I thought I told you to stop sneaking up on me."

Olya raised an eyebrow. "I thought that was the whole reason we brought me here."

"No, we brought you here so you could cheat the damn pants off those idiots at the gambling tables. C'mon, I'll walk you through the next one."

Once the girl had gone, Jez tapped her com again. "Hey. Genius. Got it. Give me the specs on the next games."

From one side of the room, one of the players at the blue-jacketed woman's table swore loudly and started shouting for a server.

Across the room, a fight broke out at the centre table.

"Done," said Tanya, slipping back into her chair, an expression on her face that told Jez she was enjoying this, no matter how hard she'd deny it.

"Good," said Jez. "Lev gave me another three games. Figure it's going to start getting interesting in here in about twenty minutes."

Tae glared down at his holoscreen, biting his lip.

They were in their suite on Grigory's ship, which was the most explainable place for them to be, but it also meant that he was limited to visuals he could hack from the casino-room cameras.

Jez was doing—well, whatever the hell Jez did, and judging from the fact that so far, five outright brawls had broken out in the gambling hall, it was effective. And Olya and Tanya were slipping back and forth between the tables, and—he scrolled down on his screen.

And so far, it looked like it was working.

He glanced over at Lev, who was seated at the table, a holoscreen in front of him. There were still traces of a headache on his face, and there was a grim set to his jaw as he stared at the numbers.

Tae pushed the heels of his hands into his eyes and let his head drop back against his chair for a moment.

"Lev," he hissed. Lev jerked his head up.

"Yes?" he asked, after a moment.

Tae gritted his teeth. "Lev, for the Lady's sake, bloody well pay attention."

Lev took a deep breath. "What do you need, Tae?"

"How are we doing?"

Lev glanced back at the screen, and Tae shook his head.

He hadn't been paying attention. And OK, fair enough, Tae knew what it was like to feel like you were going to break into a hundred pieces if you couldn't be around someone, but this was getting ridiculous.

"We're alright," Lev said shortly, after a moment. "So far. If we keep it up, we should be able to pull this off, at least for tonight." He glanced over to the tall man sprawled out half-asleep on the couch. "Ivan?"

Ivan jerked awake, blinking. "I—sorry," he muttered, sitting up and shaking his head. "What did you ask?"

"How many can he afford to lose?" Lev asked. "I think—" he squinted down at the screen. "I think we have five of his people in the chamber that's set to explode. What's the smallest number we'll be safe with?"

Ivan blinked again and squeezed his eyes shut, and Tae watched him in concern.

He was pretty sure that Ivan hadn't slept more than about thirty minutes running since they figured out what Grigory was doing, and from the looks of him, Tae wasn't entirely sure they could count on him not to actually pass out.

This was maybe the most delicate operation they'd done since they'd started out, and all he had to work with was an exhausted Ivan, who looked perpetually on the verge of collapse, and a still-partially-hungover Lev, who looked like at least half of his attention span at any given time was distracted by images of Jez.

"I'd say—" Ivan closed his eyes for a moment, then blinked. "Sorry. I'd say if we can get ten or twelve in there, that's going to be more than he can afford to lose. Any less, and he might decide to cut his losses."

Lev nodded, looking, finally, like he was actually listening to a damn thing someone else was saying to him. And then Jez's voice came over the com.

"Hey genius. Need another table and the specs." A pause. "Also, Olya is a natural-born gambler. Be a shame to put that kind of talent to waste."

"Thank you, Jez, but—" Tae began.

"Also," she continued, "I figured out the name of that stuff I got drunk off the other night. Golden murder, it's called."

Tae dropped his head against the back of the chair.

No. He wasn't just dealing with an exhausted prison escapee and a hungover lovesick idiot. He was also dealing with a lunatic who seemed to believe this entire situation had been engineered solely for her personal enjoyment.

"Jez—" he said through gritted teeth.

She laughed through the com, and at her laughter, Lev's eyes went slightly hazy.

Tae swore.

"Don't worry, tech-head, not going to get drunk." She paused. "At least, not planning on it at present. There's still enough crap going on to keep me interested." She paused again. "Although if genius-boy doesn't get me the next specs pretty quick, things are going to start to get boring in here, and I can't make any promises after that —"

"I will make you a very solemn promise," came Tanya's voice through the com. She sounded like she was talking through her teeth. "And that promise, Jez Solokov, is if you touch one drop of alcohol of any kind, you won't have time to get hungover, because you'll be waking up tomorrow morning with a headache big enough that you couldn't possibly drink enough to earn it. Do you understand me?"

"Hey now, Tanya, don't underestimate me," Jez drawled. "Don't think you realize how big of a damn hangover I can earn."

Over the com, Tanya sucked in a long breath.

Tae squeezed his eyes shut and tried to fight back a headache.

It was damn well unfair that it was starting to look like he was the only person on this damn crew who wasn't either recovering from a hangover or planning for one, and he hadn't been able to get rid of his headache from the moment they'd set foot on Grigory's ship.

"Lev," he said through gritted teeth. "Get Jez the damn specs for the next damn table."

Lev glanced over at him, startled out of his reverie. "Of course. I'm sorry. Jez, table in the corner furthest from you. I don't care who wins, but the man in—" he squinted, and expanded the screen. "The dark suit, white hair, expensive boots. He needs to lose."

"On it, genius." Tae could almost hear the smirk though the com, and Lev must have too, because his eyes went hazy again for a moment.

"What are they playing?" Jez asked.

Tae glanced at Lev, then gave up and hit his own com. "They're playing lady in the park," he growled.

"Hey, no need to snap at me," Jez shot back. "Figure we're doing pretty damn well in here, aren't we, you bastard?"

"Jez." Tanya's voice was flat. "Olya is—"

"Mamochka, I know what a bastard is," said Olya, in a slightly superior voice. "It just means when a person has a baby—"

"Thank you, Olya," said Tanya. She sounded almost as grim as Tae felt. "We will talk about this when we are back in our rooms. And Jez, you and I will also talk about—"

"Hey, got a job to do here, Tanya. I mean, I know I'm hot and all, but if you're going to get distracted every time I—"

Tae hit his com off for just a moment and groaned.

"Tae. Are you alright?"

He blinked and looked up. Ivan had pulled up a chair next to him, and his voice was warm and amused.

"I—" Tae glanced around helplessly.

Ivan gave him a wry smile. "And I'm not helping, am I?" He chuckled softly. "I can't decide whether I'm jealous of you running with a crew like this, who can pull off something so ridiculous under such—" he glanced at Lev. "Unconventional circumstances, or to feel sorry for you."

"Definitely feel sorry for," Tae grumbled, shaking his head and smiling a little, despite himself.

"Sorry. I'll try to stay awake, I promise," said Ivan, fighting a yawn.

"Tae." Ysbel's voice over his earpiece was tense. "There's

someone coming up the hall."

"Can you—" he glanced around frantically, slapping off his holoscreen. "Lev, Ivan. Grigory's sent someone to check on us."

Lev glanced up, frowning, and Tae swore, jumped to his feet, and slapped his palm across Lev's com. His holoscreen flickered and disappeared.

"Ivan, get—" Tae began hurriedly.

There was a knock on the door, then the lock clicked, and the door began to swing open.

Damn.

There, in full view, on a chair that had been shoved half-way across the room, the ledger chip that he and Ivan had stolen three days ago. It was marked with Grigory's marking, and even just a cursory glance—

Ivan followed his gaze and turned to stare at him, panic on his face, and Lev met their gaze as well, for once looking like he'd finally damn well figured out what was happening.

The door swung farther, and someone was stepping through—

"Sorry Tae," Ivan muttered, and before Tae could react, Ivan grabbed him and pulled him onto the couch. Tae landed cradled in Ivan's lap, Ivan's arms around him. He was too shocked to do anything more than blink as Ivan tilted him back against the arm of the couch and leaned in, his hand tracing the line of Tae's jaw and sending shivers through Tae's entire body.

From the corner of his eye, he saw one of the boyeviki step in. She glanced quickly around the room, and then her eye caught Tae and Ivan and a small smile formed on her mouth.

"I'm sorry to interrupt," she said, her voice amused. Ivan gave Tae a quick wink, then sat up quickly, as if startled.

"I—hello," he said, his voice faintly embarrassed. Tae just sat there, stunned and completely speechless. He was leaning back in Ivan's arms, settled firmly into Ivan's lap, and for a moment he couldn't seem to form a complete thought.

He blinked at the woman, unable to even formulate a reaction.

"Ivan Ivanovich, isn't it?" asked the woman in amusement. "It looks like you and Tae are getting along quite well."

Ivan cleared his throat. "I—I'm sorry. I wasn't expecting anyone —"

From the corner of his eye, Tae noticed Lev half stand, reach surreptitiously over, and slide the chip into his pocket, and even in his stunned state, he managed a quick breath of relief.

"Just wanted to check on you all. Now that things are moving," she said. "Grigory wanted to be sure you weren't forgotten in all the excitement. You have everything you need?" She raised her eyebrows meaningfully.

Tae cleared his throat. "We're—fine. Thank you."

"Yes," she said, with a knowing, slightly amused look. "It looks like you're fine." She turned, and glanced at Lev, who was now frowning down at a sheet on his holoscreen that seemed to contain nothing but a dense treatise on intra-governmental relationships.

"And you?"

He glanced up. "Yes?"

"Is there anything you need?"

Lev frowned and looked around. "No. I—don't believe there is. Although, if the kitchens are open, I would be delighted to know when dinner will be prepared."

She glanced at her com. "In about half a standard hour, I believe. And—" She glanced around the room, frowning slightly. "And where are the rest of—"

"Sorry, Tae," Ivan whispered again, a rueful look on his face. And even though he had a split second to realize what was about to happen, the feel of Ivan's lips on his somehow shoved every other thought out of his brain.

He'd never actually kissed anyone except Dmitri, but Ivan seemed to know exactly what he was doing. And for some reason, even though he knew that the only reason this was happening was the fact that they desperately needed a distraction, Tae found himself leaning into the kiss, his arms sliding around Ivan's back almost without his conscious thought. Ivan shifted, pressing Tae against the the couch, his hand curling into Tae's hair, pulling him closer, and Tae suddenly couldn't remember anything at all except the fact that Ivan was kissing him—

"I—think they're trying to find somewhere else to be at the moment." Lev's wry voice was somehow hazy and distant. "I would as well, but I promised Grigory—"

Distantly, he heard the woman laugh. "I understand. I'll suggest to Grigory that he find the two of them a private suite—" There was a suggestive tone in her voice that probably would have embarrassed Tae if he was in any state at all to feel embarrassed at the moment, but everything had gone slightly hazy, and he was having a hard time thinking about anything at all except Ivan's lips on his, Ivan's strong hands on his back and tangled in his hair, the muscles of Ivan's lean body under his thin shirt, and Lady and Consort, Ivan must have done this before, because the way his mouth moved against Tae's—

In the back of his mind he heard retreating footsteps and the door swinging shut, but he couldn't actually pay attention to that right now, because the only thing he was aware of was Ivan, and Lady and Consort and all the damn saints, the way Ivan was kissing him he wasn't sure he'd ever pay attention to anything else ever again—

Someone cleared their throat.

A moment later, they cleared it again, louder.

Reluctantly, Ivan and Tae drew apart.

Tae sat blinking for a moment before he remembered where he was and what he was doing there.

"I—I'm really sorry," said Ivan. He sounded slightly breathless, but then Tae wasn't sure how reliable any one of his senses were at this precise moment.

"Well, I'd say that was effective," said Lev, in a slightly amused voice, and it took Tae a moment to remember why Lev was here.

He drew in a shaky breath.

"Are you alright?" Ivan whispered, concern in his tone. "I'm—I'm really sorry. I don't usually—It's just that they already think that we're—I mean, and I couldn't think of anything else off the top of my head, and I—"

Tae shook his head and swallowed hard, finally remembering how to talk. "No," he said, "it's—it's fine. It—was quick thinking. I didn't —I mean, I wouldn't have—I mean, don't worry about it."

Ivan gave him a small, wry grin. "Still. I'm sorry. I promise I usually ask before I kiss someone."

"Yeah." Tae found he was slightly breathless as well. He swallowed again, hard, and pushed himself awkwardly out of Ivan's lap. "It's—fine. I—It's fine. Don't worry about it."

He stood, feeling slightly dizzy for a moment.

"Tae?" asked Lev. He still sounded amused. Tae scowled at him.

He was one to talk.

"Give me a minute to pull everything up again," he muttered, and made his way back to his seat, his legs slightly more unsteady than he was used to. He dropped into his seat, but he had to stare at his com for a moment before his brain reminded him which screen he needed to pull up, and it took him longer than it should have to navigate back into the program.

"Lev?" he grumbled.

Lev looked up sharply. "Yes?"

Tae groaned to himself. "Lev," he said patiently, "Pull up the damn holoscreen, please. Jez is going to be done at the table you gave her, and we still have about—" he scowled down at his screen, trying to force his brain to damn well recall how in the hell he was supposed to figure out what the long string of numbers scrolling across the screen in front of him meant. "About thirteen more games to rig if we want to get ten of Grigory's people in the wrong section. And if Jez doesn't have something to do for even two seconds, I don't know if even Tanya is going to be able to stop her from either getting drunk, or wreaking absolute havoc."

Lev nodded, and pulled up his own screen, frowning at it.

Tae cast a surreptitious glance at Ivan, who looked slightly stunned as well, but also, for the first time that day, like he was actually awake.

Which honestly was a very good thing, because it looked like now Tae was dealing with not only an exhausted prison escapee, a hungover lovesick idiot, and a chaotic lunatic, he was also dealing with the fact that his own damn brain couldn't seem to hold onto a single thought except the ones dealing with how warm Ivan's lips had been, and the feel of his hands in Tae's hair, and the strange tightness that formed in the pit of his stomach at the memory of his back pushed up against the arm of the couch, the leisurely urgency of Ivan's mouth on his.

He hit his com back on, in time to catch the tail end of what sounded like an impressive stream of muttered profanity from Tanya. "—and so help me, Jez—"

He drew in a deep breath and closed his eyes, the sound of Jez's manic cheerfulness in the face of Tanya's icy fury a familiar refrain that slowly brought his brain back into a functional state.

After a few moment, Lev tapped his com. "Ysbel," he murmured, "Do you know why the boyevik was here?"

"No," said Ysbel, and there was concern in her tone. "I thought I was going to have to come up with an explanation of why I was standing in the hall with Misko, but when she came out again, she just grinned at me and didn't ask." She paused. "Do I dare even ask what—"

"No," said Tae flatly, slapping his com and glaring at Lev.

"That's all well and good," said Lev quietly. "But I'm worried Grigory is getting suspicious. If he sends someone again, we're going to have to come up with something better than Tae getting snogged on the couch to explain why everyone else isn't around."

Tae dropped his head into his hands. "Lev—" he said through his teeth.

There was a moment of silence over the com.

"Hold on just a damn minute," Jez's delighted voice drawled at last. "You mean Tae just—Tae! Move quickly, don't you?"

"Oh for the Lady's sake—" he groaned, tipping his head back against the chair.

"Although, it wasn't a bad idea, really," said Ysbel thoughtfully. "I mean, he had some practice in the university, so—"

"Tae was just kissing someone?" asked Tanya, sounding interested despite the residual irritation in her voice. "Who was Tae kissing?"

Ivan looked amused, and Lev was clearly trying to hide a smile.

Tae sucked in a breath through his nose. "Can we please focus?"

"We are focusing, tech-head," said Jez, the grin apparent in her voice. "We're just focusing on the fact that apparently you were just snogging on the couch."

"Can we focus on the fact that we're all going to die if we don't bloody start paying attention to what we're doing?" he snapped. "Lev, turn on your damn holoscreen and tell Jez and Tanya what table they need to rig next. Ivan, can you go help him? I'm going to pull up the general com on the ship and see if they're saying anything about us.

He hit the com, glancing over at Lev quickly to make sure he was actually damn well paying attention for long enough to give Jez what she needed, and pulled up his hack.

A woman's voice drifted over the com. "—don't know. Boss said to keep an eye on them. Masha's in there talking to him, but he's worried about something."

"Well," came another voice, sounding amused, "from what I hear, the only thing he has to worry about is whether that tech kid is going to run off with one of the servers. I guess when Malvika walked in, they were—"

Tae closed his eyes, drew in a long breath, and blew it out again, ignoring Ysbel's snickering.

"Well," Ysbel said, "I guess it worked."

"—something in the gambling hall."

Tae sat up quickly, his heart beating slightly faster.

"Yeah, I don't know what it is, but Fyodor said there's something wrong with the games. Said to look into it."

Tae tapped his com. "You hear that, Jez?" he asked in a low voice.

"Yep." She didn't sound particularly concerned.

"Listen," he said, biting back his exasperation, mostly because there was no chance it would have even the slightest effect on the pilot. "If they're getting suspicious about the games and they come in to check it out, you'll be their number one suspect if anything goes wrong. Honestly, I think at this point half the damn mafia would kill you just for the satisfaction of it."

"Well, guess they could give it a try," said Jez philosophically.

Lev glanced up from his screen, his face grave, and for once actually focused. "We're going to have to hurry this up," he said quietly. "If they're already catching on, we don't have time to wait for the games we've set out. Give me a minute, I'm going to re-calculate this. Jez, Tanya, I want you two and Olya out of there in the next half-hour."

"Well genius," Jez drawled, but Tae could catch the slightest hint of worry in her voice. "That might not be a bad idea. Because from the looks of it, things might get pretty interesting in here in not very long."

Tae glanced up, and for a moment his, Ivan's, and Lev's eyes all met.

"I think we're running out of time," Ivan said quietly. Lev nodded.

Tae glanced down at his com, frowning at the columns of figures. "Lev," he said, "Send me the list as soon as you have it."

Lev nodded and bent over his com, seeming, finally, to be focusing on the job at hand. But Tae couldn't stop the worry tightening in his stomach.

18

"Jez." Tanya's voice was tight with strain, which wasn't really surprising, since she'd basically looked like she was restraining herself with great difficulty from actually murdering Jez since they'd sat down at the damn table.

But the look on her face now was more worry than repressed homicide, and Jez frowned.

"What is it, then?" she asked in a low voice.

"We're being watched, I think," said Tanya. "You remember Lev said they were getting suspicious. Well, I think they're getting more than suspicious right now."

Jez glanced around quickly.

It took her a few moments to see what Tanya had already seen, and honestly, she'd probably not have seen it at all if Tanya hadn't already warned her.

Then her stomach tightened.

Tanya was right. They were more than suspicious.

There were almost ten of Grigory's boyeviki, and they were watching the room suspiciously, wandering along the edges of the room with the sort of nonchalance she'd seen far too often following her in dark alleys. They didn't have their weapons drawn, but they were making no great effort to conceal the bulk of weapons under their jackets.

She took a quick breath, and grinned at Tanya. "Alright, I guess we're extra careful now."

"We've been extra careful this whole time," Tanya said in a low voice. "I'm not sure that's going to be enough."

Jez glanced around the room again and tapped her com. "Tae," she whispered. "Grigory's sent his people in here. Just so you know. How many more games you need us to rig?"

There was a moment's pause. "We're close." Tae's voice was strained. "Lev?"

"Five more games, I think," came Lev's quiet voice, but she could hear the strain under his tone as well. "It won't give us the numbers we want, but it will be close. Hopefully close enough."

"Yeah." She tapped the com off and glanced up at Tanya.

The woman looked worried.

"Alright," said Jez, and she could feel herself grinning, because damn it, her muscles were already tight with anticipation, and she couldn't keep her fingers still, and the heel of her boot was bumping gently against the leg of her chair and her whole body felt lighter and looser than it had just a few moments before. "Alright. Five more games, Tanya. We'll see what we can do."

Olya appeared beside her a moment later. "Aunty," she said, glancing up at Jez. "What's wrong?"

"What do you mean, kid?" she said, grabbing a handful of tokens.

Olya gave her a skeptical glance that didn't completely hide the slight worry in her face. "You're grinning, Aunty. That usually means something is wrong."

Jez exchanged quick glances with Tanya, then bent down. "Hey, kid," she whispered. "You're smart. Listen, I think it might be a good idea if you headed back to your mama and Uncle Lev and Uncle Tae for a bit. We're almost done here anyways, we'll catch you up."

Olya shook her head stubbornly. "No. I'm going to stay here. I'm really good at this, you said so."

"You are, kid. Believe me, you're going to be able to out-cheat your aunty soon. But look, there are only a couple tables left. Your mamochka can get those, and anyways, sounds like they need you back there. Apparently your Uncle Tae is running around kissing people when he's supposed to be working, so figure you can go back and keep them on task?"

"Uncle Tae?" The look on Olya's face was clearly skeptical now. "Because I thought usually it was you and Uncle—"

"Yeah, look, kid," Jez cut in quickly, glaring at Tanya, who was looking faintly amused. "Point is, you should get back there."

"Your aunty's right," said Tanya. "I don't want you here, my heart. You've done a fabulous job, but I'd like you to go back now."

Olya glanced between them, and there was fear behind the stubbornness in her eyes. "They're going to catch you, aren't they, mamochka?"

Tanya gave her a smile and a quick embrace. "I hope not, my heart. But they're looking for us now, I think, and they are more likely to notice a child than they are to notice me. Can you do this for me, Olyeshka?"

Olya stared at her mamochka for a moment, then gave a small nod.

"Good," said Tanya. "That's my girl. You go, but stay out of the way of those people there."

"Grigory's people?" Olya whispered.

Tanya nodded.

"Alright," said Olya in a small voice. "I will." She paused a moment, and for just that moment there was something in her face that made Jez remember that really, the kid was only eight, and it wasn't very long ago that she'd been broken out of prison, and since that time she'd hardly had more than a month together where something wasn't threatening to kill her or her parents.

"Go on, kid," Jez whispered. "Your mamochka and I will be fine. Go."

Olya nodded again, then turned and disappeared into the crowd. A moment later, they saw her slip out the exit, and Jez felt her shoulders drop in relief. She glanced up, and saw a matching relief on Tanya's face.

"Lev," she whispered into the com. "Olya's on her way. Tanya and I will finish up."

She looked up, and grinned at Tanya. "Alright. Five more tables. Next one is the one on the far right again."

She pulled up her screen as Tanya slipped off. Tae had hacked the cameras in the room, and she had visuals, but every damn angle of the visuals included some image of one of Grigory's boyeviki, scanning casually through the room. She looked up at the artificial vine in front of her.

Maybe she could actually get to like vines after all, if this one managed to keep her alive.

Tanya reappeared, but there was a worried frown on her face. "Jez," she said quietly. "I don't know how many more we'll get away with."

Jez glanced down at her screen again, and swiped to the list Tae had sent through. "Well," she whispered back, "looks like we'll have to get a few more done, or else there was no point in us coming here at all. Guess Tae's buddy Ivan's been looking through Grigory's financials, and he can afford to lose a few of his plants, and we're not quite there yet."

"I know," said Tanya in a low voice. "Believe me. But I'm not sure
—"

She stiffened suddenly, and Jez followed her gaze.

Ice formed in her stomach, and a tingle that might have been anticipation, or might have been fear, or maybe a little bit of both, spread up her arms and through her fingers.

Three of the boyeviki were making their casual way over towards the spreading artificial vine in the corner, and the table behind it.

She glanced in the other direction. Another man and a woman were strolling in their direction.

"Lev," Tanya whispered into her com. "I think they're onto us."

"You need to come in," said Lev instantly, his voice sharp with worry. "We'll figure out another way, just get back here."

"Not sure that's an option anymore," Jez muttered. "Figure the best thing for you all to do is get the hell out of the way, because once they catch us—"

"Jez Solokov."

She jerked her head up.

Fyodor stood there. He had a broad smile on his face, but it wasn't at all pleasant.

"Hey, you bastard," she said with an easy grin, leaning back in her chair. "Got bored and decided to come find me? Hell, if you're that desperate, wouldn't mind going a round with you."

From the corner of her eye, she saw Tanya move slightly, her motion so subtle that you might not have caught it if you weren't watching.

Jez put her hands behind her head leisurely, making her movements big enough to keep Fyodor's attention, and gave the woman standing beside him an irreverent wink. "Beginners luck," she said in a loud whisper. "Won every damn credit off him last time we played."

Fyodor's face had gone cold. "You're a cheater, Jez," he said. "A cheat and a useless drunk and a disrespectful nobody. But you're not stupid. And nor am I."

"Could have fooled me," she drawled.

Tanya had slipped out of her chair, and was straightening slowly. Jez had seen her move, and the woman was damn fast, and sure, there were about six of them now, but she was almost close enough to—

Tanya's posture stiffened, ever so slightly.

And then Jez noticed the barrel of the heat gun, poking through the leaves of the vine. The muzzle followed Tanya's head in a lazy way that made it clear the gun was in the hands of someone who knew very, very well how to use it.

Fyodor turned and followed Jez's gaze. Then he turned back to her, and the smile on his face this time made something cold stir in her chest.

"At least, I used to think you weren't stupid," he said. "But a little over-confident? I think perhaps you've always been that." He pulled his own heat pistol from his jacket pocket, just long enough to show it to her. "Go ahead and put your hands on the table, Jez. Your friend here too."

She caught Tanya's eye, and the moment she saw her face, she knew that it was over.

"Yeah," Jez said, finally, and she was somehow still grinning, even though she felt like the bottom had dropped out of her stomach and left nothing but a gaping hole. She put her hands on the table, and slowly, Tanya sat down and did the same. Fyodor gestured, and two of the boyeviki patted them both down quickly. They ended up with a pile on the table of five heat pistols, two knives, a garrotte-wire, and three small cylindrical buttons that Jez recognized instantly as Ysbel's explosives.

"Well," said Fyodor. "You came very well armed to a gambling game."

"Yeah, well looks like it wasn't a bad idea, seeing as six of you damn bastards happen to be holding heat-guns on us," Jez shot back.

Fyodor gestured with the muzzle of the gun in his pocket. "Come on, Solokov. Up you come. I think you've played long enough for the evening."

She stood, but her legs were shaky, and her hip bumped the table hard enough to make her wince. "What you going to do with us, enforce the damn curfew?" She was still grinning, recklessly, because hell, what did she even have to lose at this point?

Fyodor shook his head gently. "No, Jez. Nothing like that. You're just going back to your rooms, and you're going to wait the rest of the evening out with your friend. That's all."

Somehow she had the feeling that that wasn't all, but she shot him a cocky wink anyways. "Hey now, some of us can hold our tokens and our liquor, you know. Don't need to worry about me."

He didn't answer, just gestured again with the gun in his jacket pocket. "Walk nice and easy," he said in her ear as they started forward. "No point in frightening the other guests."

And for a moment she almost shouted, almost tried to break away, even though the way his gun was pointed she'd probably just end up with a smoking hole burned through the middle of her face, but—

She cut her eyes around frantically for just a moment. She could still screw this thing up for Grigory, probably, and Lev and the others might be able to—

"I know what you're thinking," he murmured. "You forget. You're on a ship that's owned by Grigory Korzhekov. Remember your friend's kids, the girl and the boy? It's not like they could hide, you know, because where are they going to hide?"

She held her breath for a moment, adrenalin rattling through her body so strongly that her hands were shaking with it.

Then, at last, she forced her too-tight muscles to relax, forced her legs to take one step after another, her movements, somehow, normal. Anyone who was damn well paying attention would be able to catch it, would be able to see that she and Tanya weren't walking out of here of their own damn volition, but this was a gambling hall, and everyone's attention was caught and held by the tokens at their tables.

And then they were out of the hall, and out of the crowd, and Fyodor drew his gun from his pocket and gestured.

A moment later her hands were bound tightly behind her back. When she cut her eyes to one side, she saw they'd done the same to Tanya.

At least they'd got Olya out. That was one thing, anyways.

Fyodor marched them down the corridor, away from the entrance to Grigory's ship, and into a lift. She probably should have realized what was happening, but it wasn't until he shoved her out onto another corridor, stretching away from her with doors set at regular intervals on either side, that she realized what she probably should have guessed from the beginning.

They were still on the side of the damn blast doors that had the explosive.

"That's your room at the end," Fyodor said, a small smile on his face. "You're lucky, really. If it had been me, you'd have come back onto Grigory's ship, and we would have talked to you for a while first. But there's too much riding on this, and torturing you to death would take time and people we don't have to spare. So you get nice and quick." He gestured her forward again, and, because she didn't actually have a choice, she went.

"I'd shoot you, but I'm not sure what exactly you've done down there," he continued as they walked. "Be a shame to kill you and then realize you had some information I needed. But this should do nicely anyways, thanks to your friend Ysbel. I've seen her work. I'm sure it will be so quick you won't feel a thing." He stopped them in front of the door at the end of the hall.

"See you gave us the nicest room," Jez said, with an attempt at a grin over her shoulder. "Sure you're not just jealous of my luck at tokens?"

"No," he said gently, as one of the boyeviki stepped in front of them and pulled the door open. "It's not that, Solokov. It's only that we needed a bigger room because there were so many of you."

Her stomach barely had time to drop at his words before the door swung open, and her eyes confirmed what her brain had just begun to guess.

The room wasn't empty.

Beside her, Tanya drew in a quick breath.

Olya sat on the bed, her arms tied tightly behind her back, Misko beside her. And beside them, Ysbel.

A quick glance around showed her Tae and Lev and Ivan against the opposite wall.

"On the bright side, you won't be dying alone," said Fyodor, pushing her through the door. She stumbled inside, too cold with shock to think of resisting.

Fyodor shot her one last smile, then closed the door, and the lock clicking into place sounded very, very loud in the silence.

19

Jez closed her eyes for a moment, fighting the panic that always seemed to well up inside her when she was locked in, the terrified, helpless panic that she couldn't seem to stop and couldn't seem to escape, that was going to actually drown her one of these days—

"Hey. Jez," said Lev, and somehow his familiar, wry voice cut through the panic enough that she could actually draw a breath, and the dizziness subsided slightly. She took a deep, steadying breath and opened her eyes.

They were all alive, thank the damn Lady, and a moment of frantic relief washed over her, but her heart was still galloping in panic, her breathing coming too quickly.

"Are you hurt?" Lev's voice was a studied calm, but there was that damn concern under his tone that always seemed to make her stomach twist, and she couldn't deal with this right now, not after what she'd said to him, even though she'd been right, she'd had to say it, and—

"Jez! Are you alright?" His tone was sharper now, and she blinked and looked up, and he was looking at her, and damn it to hell. She closed her eyes and gritted her teeth.

"Jez." It was Tae this time.

She opened her eyes and took another deep breath, trying to grin. "Don't worry, we're fine. Right Tanya?"

She glanced over, but Tanya and Ysbel were looking at each other and seemed hardly aware of anything else in the room.

"Ysbel," Tanya said quietly. "I'm alright. Jez and I are alright. Olya?"

Ysbel nodded, her movements tense. "I don't think she likes to be tied up, though."

Tanya gave her a slight smile. "I'll see what I can do. I don't think they were careful with these ropes. Olya, my heart?"

"I can help, mamochka," said the girl, her face pale and frightened, but her voice still managing its usual tinge of slight superiority.

Tanya smiled at her fondly. "I am certain you can." She crossed over to where Ysbel was sitting beside the children. Jez turned her attention back to Tae and Ivan and damn Lev. She looked them over quickly. There were no obvious injuries, but she knew the mafia well enough to know that that didn't mean anything.

"You three alright?" she asked, trying to keep the gut-deep fear out of her voice.

"We're alright," said Lev. He was still looking at her, damn it, but she didn't look away, because hell, they were probably going to all die in a few hours anyways. "They came and got us right after I told you to get out. They all had heat guns, and they jammed the coms so Ysbel wasn't able to warn us. So—" he gave a one-shouldered shrug. "On the bright side, however, it meant that none of us were injured, because we didn't have a chance to fight." He gave a slight shake of his head. "The government ships in the hanger bay have all been sabotaged, we discovered that when Tae was pulling up the vid feeds. So that means no way off the ship. And when they brought us on here, they sealed the blast doors in front of the airlock between the ships. Even if we could get out, we have no way back to the *Ungovernable.* "

For some reason, that last sentence was what finally made this whole damn thing real.

They were trapped. They were going to die. And she couldn't even get back to her ship.

She clenched her teeth hard to bite back the unreasonable tears.

"Jez," said Tanya from behind her, and she felt the ropes on her wrist tighten, then abruptly drop free. She pulled her hands out from behind her back and shook her wrists, trying to get the blood flow back into her fingers.

Tanya knelt down beside Ivan, and Olya was crouched beside Lev, and a few moments later, they were all free.

"I don't think they were too worried about us getting our hands out," said Tanya, straightening and stretching. "That would have taken me much more time if they'd been trying."

Lev stood as well, pinched the bridge of his nose for a moment, then shook his head. "Well," he said, faint, dry humour in his voice. "At the very least, as they said, Ysbel made the explosive that's going to kill us, so it won't actually hurt—we'll be vaporized before we possibly have a chance to feel anything."

"Where's Masha?" said Jez, glancing around.

"I—don't know," said Tae, and there was something in his voice that made her turn to look at him.

She frowned. "What's the matter, tech-head?"

"We—haven't seen Masha for some time," said Lev quietly. "She might be dead. Or—" he paused. "She might be with Grigory."

It took Jez a moment for what he was saying to sink in. "Wait," she said, glaring at him. "You think Masha sold us out?"

"I—hope not," he said quietly. "But—"

Something cold settled into her stomach.

"Look, genius," she snapped finally. "I know she's a damn bastard, but she wouldn't sell us out. She could have done it a hundred times, right? And she never has."

He raised an eyebrow. "Jez. I'd rather not think about it either. But —" he shrugged. "She never has. Yet. But then, she's never had what she wanted sitting right in her hands, either."

Jez was still glaring at him, but she couldn't stop the unease crawling up her back.

But—she pictured the look on Masha's face, when they'd broken into that lab in the university. The first time in her damn life she'd realized that Masha was an actual person. That what happened to street kids and poor kids and the people who the government thought were basically expendable actually mattered to her.

When Jez had stupidly blurted out how her family had thrown her out when she was a kid, given Masha a knife to cut her open with— and Masha had tried, clumsily, to patch her up instead.

She shook her head stubbornly. "Sorry, genius. I don't believe it."

He sighed and ran his fingers through his hair, then gave her a small smile. "I hope you're right," he said at last. There was something tense and tired behind his eyes, but he was still smiling, that gentle smile, like he was trying, very hard, to make sure she didn't hurt.

She took a long breath and turned away.

"Well," said Ysbel at last, "there's always the third option. If Jez is right, maybe Masha is going to walk through that door in a minute or two with the key." She gave Tanya a faint smile. "Right, my love?"

"Well," said Tanya softly, "I didn't ever believe that you would walk through the door of that prison. So I would say that anything is possible."

There was a *click* from behind them, and all of them turned. Jez reflexively kicked the loose ropes under the bed in the centre of the room and shoved her hands behind her as the door swung open.

A figure entered, and for a moment she thought maybe she was dreaming, maybe Ysbel's words had got lodged in her head and she was so out of her mind with all the crap happening with Lev that she was just standing here in the middle of the floor dreaming with her eyes open.

Because Masha was standing in the entrance, that same bland smile on her face that she always wore, that same air of slightly-rumpled competence.

And then she noticed that Masha's hands were tied behind her back, and that there was someone behind her, and that the someone carried a heat pistol.

"Go on," the man said, and he shoved Masha forward, and she stumbled, slightly, and the door swung shut behind her, the lock clicking into place.

For a long moment, no one spoke.

"Well," said Masha at last. "This is slightly smaller than our rooms on Grigory's ship, but not unacceptable."

"What happened to you?" asked Ysbel, standing up quickly, and Jez noticed, suddenly, that Masha was swaying on her feet. She grabbed a chair and shoved it behind the woman, and Masha sank into it. Her face was a few shades greyer than usual.

"I'm fine," she said, but her voice shook slightly.

Tanya was already unfastening the ropes binding her hands, and when she was done, Masha brought her arms around in front of her and began to rub the feeling back into her fingers absently.

"What happened?" asked Tae, who'd crossed over to her as well, and was crouching in front of her. "Are you hurt?"

"I'm—fine. At least at the moment," she said, with a wan smile. "I believe they just wanted me to understand that Grigory was unhappy, but they managed to break open my injury from the university. Unpleasant, but not fatal."

Her pilot's coat was closed over her shirt, so there was no way of seeing, but Ysbel took one side of it. "May I?" she asked gruffly, and Masha gave an exhausted nod. Ysbel pulled the coat back to reveal Masha's shirt stained bright red with blood.

"I'll be fine," said Masha again, and this time the exhaustion bled through into her voice. "I—don't believe there's enough time to bleed to death at any rate, if I understand the situation correctly."

"What happened?" asked Tae again, a worried frown on his face, concern in his tone.

Masha lifted her head. "Well," she said at last, "it appears that I gambled and lost. I suppose I ought to take lessons from our pilot." She pushed herself upright, wincing slightly.

"I realized they'd caught on that you were doing something," she continued quietly. "I thought that perhaps if I were to keep Grigory occupied, he might not notice until you could hide your trail. However—" She gave a slight shrug. "It appears I misjudged."

Lev looked at her and gave her a faint smile. "Well," he said, "I'm glad you didn't betray us, at least."

She raised an eyebrow at him. "Indeed."

There were a few moments' silence.

Tae sat back against the wall and pulled up his holoscreen, typing rapidly, and for a moment, Jez had a flutter of hope. But from the scowl on his face and the tension in his posture, he wasn't getting very far.

His scowl deepened. He typed something else, waited, then tried again. Then he slumped back against the wall. "They've put a lock in," he said, his voice heavy with despair. "Zhenya must have told Grigory what I can do. They've put in a specialty lock, set to our com frequencies. I can get through to the video and sound feeds, but everything else is shut off. We're completely blocked out. I—" he let out a helpless breath. "I can't hack us out of this one. I'm sorry."

"Any other ideas?" asked Lev, looking around.

"I thought you were the one with the ideas," Ysbel grumbled, but Jez noticed that she'd sat back down on the bed beside Tanya and the children and pulled Misko into her arms, stroking his hair gently.

"Unfortunately," said Lev quietly, "I don't have any ideas this time." He paused. "I suppose we wait."

Masha leaned back and closed her eyes, and from the strain in her face, Jez wasn't sure if she was resting, or if she'd passed out.

Didn't really matter, in the end, she supposed.

She took a deep breath and crossed over to where the others were sitting, and after a moment's hesitation, sank down beside Lev. If she was going to damn well be blown up, she may as well do it with the rest of the crew.

With him.

Lev turned his head and smiled at her, and she smiled back, a lump forming in her throat.

Not a bad way to die, she supposed, if you had to die.

His eyes were gentle, and there was a soft look in his face, and despite the fact that she usually went for people who looked like they could probably kill her, she'd always been a bit of a sucker for that soft look he had.

On the bright side, looked like she hadn't had time to ruin his life after all. So there was that, she supposed.

"Tae?" asked Ivan. "Are you hooked into the video feed in the casino?"

Tae nodded.

"Could you—would you mind pulling up the holoscreen?" He gave a small smile. "I suppose I haven't been almost killed as much as you all have. I'd—rather watch. I'd rather know when to be expecting it."

Tae nodded again without speaking, and pulled up his holoscreen, expanding it.

Jez glanced at it, but then, she hadn't really been paying attention when they'd talked about which of the damn plaguers were Grigory's people and which were the ones he was planning on blowing up, so it didn't really help.

She glanced over at Lev again.

He was watching her, and he had that faint, wry smile on his face, and she closed her eyes for a moment, because just a few minutes before you were about to be blown into damn space dust wasn't really the time for your stomach to tighten and something to catch in your throat when the plaguer you'd broken up with gave you that damn smile.

But when she opened her eyes, he was still watching her, and she found she'd moved towards him, just a little, was leaning into him. And he'd leaned into her just a little as well, and there really wasn't very much space in between them at all, and for some reason all she could think about was two days ago, how it had felt when he held her, and OK, she'd broken up with him right after that, and then spent the next twelve hours crying in her damn room, but—

But there was something warm in the pit of her stomach at the memory, and—well, and hell, they were all going to die anyways. Wasn't like she could freak out and take off now, first, because there wouldn't be time for that, and second, because they happened to be locked up together in a damn room.

And he seemed to be having similar thoughts, because he lifted his hand, and hesitated for just a moment, and then brushed a stray strand of hair out of her face, and her whole body went basically completely boneless at his touch. And he ran his fingers gently through her hair, and then down her jaw, cupping her face in his hand, and he didn't take his eyes off her the whole time, and she could feel her entire body shaking, and she wasn't sure if it was because of Lev's touch, or because in just a few minutes she'd lose him forever, him, and Tae, and Ysbel and Tanya and the kids, and Masha, sit here with them as the world turned white and loud and every one of them died, and—

She couldn't. She couldn't let that happen, because—well, because she loved them.

She loved him.

He had leaned towards her, and hell, it hardly mattered now, she leaned in as well, lips parting slightly.

Honestly, might as well—

She stopped abruptly. "Wait."

He paused as well, frowning. "Jez?"

"Genius. Listen to me." Her voice was shaking, from his touch and from excitement. "You know what I bet would screw with Grigory's plans? Like, even more than me and Tanya and Olya messing up his gambling rankings?"

He frowned at her.

She leaned shakily back against the wall, a grin spreading across her face. "Figure setting off a damn fire alarm might do it."

He blinked, then shook his head. "Tae can't hack us into the system, remember?"

She shrugged. "Don't need to hack into the system to set off the fire alarm. All we have to do is start a fire."

He was still staring. She pushed herself to her feet and strode over to Tae. "Hey, tech head. Pull up the camera by our table."

He gave her an odd look, but did as she asked. She squinted at the screen.

"There," she said, pointing. "Zoom in."

Her heart was beating a little faster now, anticipation bubbling in her veins.

She'd been right, she was almost certain, she'd noticed it in the back of her brain when her hip bumped the table on their way out of the gambling hall—

"There!"

Tae looked at the small button-sized cylinder, half-hidden where it had rolled into the artificial vine, then back at her.

Lev was staring too, and there was a look of dawning comprehension on his face.

Tanya came over, peering over Jez's shoulder. "That's—" she began.

"One of Ysbel's explosives you were carrying in your pocket," Jez finished. "Bumped it off the table on accident while they were dragging us away." She turned. "Tanya? Don't have a controller for that, do you?"

Tanya smiled slowly, and cast a quick glance over her shoulder at her wife. "Ysi always said to shove the controller into your cuff," she said. "They don't search there, usually." She gave the sleeve of her jacket a sharp tug, and something small and electronic dropped out into her hand.

Ysbel grinned at her.

"Wait," said Lev slowly. "We set off the fire alarm, OK. That causes mass chaos—people will be running and panicking, and there's no way Grigory gets them into position. That's a temporary solution. But he'll know exactly who's responsible for this, and five minutes later, we're all dead."

Jez was grinning even wider. "Yeah, well, that's the best part of this whole thing," she said. "See, Tae can't hack us through the lock. But if they open it for us themselves—"

Lev shook his head in slow disbelief. "I—think that might actually work," he murmured. He straightened and looked around quickly. "Alright. Tanya sets off the alarm. The rest of us get ready." He turned. "Ysbel? Tanya? I assume you can locate where on the ship they've placed the explosive that's supposed to kill us?"

Ysbel gave a faint smile. "I created that explosive. If you can give me specs for the ship, I can tell you exactly where they've put it."

"Excellent. Then the rest of us will keep the mafia boyeviki busy, and you and Tanya will get out and do whatever you need to do to disarm the explosive. Grigory is resourceful, and it won't take long to find where the smoke is coming from and put out the fire. He'll almost certainly get the panic on the casino deck sorted out eventually, but if the bomb is disarmed, we'll have a chance. He won't take the risk of his boyeviki shooting down the bureaucrats and ministers with their heat guns. There has to be plausible deniability if he wants to avoid a full-out war, something he can at least spin to look like a tragic accident. And I've seen his finances— he's not ready for a war, not right now. He's smart enough to wait and try at a better time."

"And when he finds the people he sent after us never came back?" asked Ysbel.

Lev gave her a tight smile. "I suppose we'll solve that problem when it arises," he said. "I assume it will take some time in the chaos. And by then, we'll be free, and the bomb will be disarmed, and there will be hundreds of witnesses. I'm not a gambler, but I like those odds better than the ones we're facing right now."

"Well, you do have a point," said Ysbel philosophically.

Jez gave Lev a wink. "You're starting to sound almost like me, genius," she said, and the momentary look of faint horror that flickered across his expression was actually quite gratifying.

She couldn't stop grinning, even with the tension twisting in her stomach.

Because this—this was going to be spectacular.

20

Tae jumped to his feet. Every muscle in his body was tense with a mixture of fear and desperate hope.

"Ysbel." Lev said briskly, pulling up his own holoscreen and standing. "Here are the ship specs. Where would they have planted the explosives?"

Ysbel moved over to stand next to him, and Tae felt his shoulders relax.

It was almost a dizzying relief to have the old Lev back, finally.

Ivan shot him a quick grin, despite the fear on his face. "Nice to not be pulling the entire load yourself?" he whispered, and Tae smiled back despite himself.

Ysbel glanced up. "Well, we're in luck. Or possibly out of luck, depending on your viewpoint," she said. "What I created was something to vaporize the inside of the ship first and take down the external walls afterwards. So. Unless they're complete idiots, which I suppose we can't necessarily discount, they'll have to put it as close to centre as they can, which means this floor. "

"Can you get to it?" Lev asked.

Ysbel raised an eyebrow. "Between Tanya and me, I'd be surprised if we couldn't." She glanced down again, frowning at the screen. "It looks like there will be an access port I can disable, as long as we can get a heat-gun off one of the mafia boyeviki before we go."

Lev nodded slowly, biting the inside of his cheek. "Alright. That's what we'll do then."

"Well. I suppose we'd best get ready," said Ysbel. She turned to her children. "You two. Under the bed, and your mamochka and I will drag the table in front. Olya, hold on to your brother."

"Yes Mama," said Olya. Her voice was meek, but there was excitement twinkling in her eyes, and Lev gave her a small smile.

Minutes later, the children were barricaded under the bed, the overturned table pulled in front of them, which, Tae supposed, was as safe as it was possible to be when you were on a ship scheduled to be blown into space-dust, and awaiting a hit squad from the mafia.

Tae pulled up the vid feed on his holoscreen, and Lev peered over his shoulder.

"Alright Tanya," Lev said quietly. "I think we're as ready as we can be."

She gave him a tight grin, and with a quick motion, squeezed the tiny controller.

There was the audible "pop" of the explosion, followed by a thick trail of smoke, then a lick of flame up around the artificial vine. And then the alarms shrieked, the blaring wail of them driving spikes into Tae's eardrums even from one deck up.

Jez turned to him, a huge grin on her face, and he grinned back despite himself.

The floor below was quickly devolving into complete chaos, gamblers shoving back tables and chairs to get away, pushing past each other, liquid spraying from the ceilings, soaking the expensive carpets.

And in one corner, he could see Fyodor, face furious, shouting and gesticulating at a small group of boyeviki.

"They're on their way," he said tensely, slapping the holoscreen closed.

Jez's grin grew, if possible, wider.

"Then I suppose we'd better get ready for them," said Ysbel, with a grim smile.

They didn't have weapons, but Ysbel armed them by the simple expedient of smashing one of the chairs hard against the floor, and handing out pieces of the shattered wood.

"Tae?" whispered Ivan, as they crouched behind the door. "If I happen to die in this—"

"You won't," said Tae through his teeth.

Ivan gave a slight, strained chuckle. "I'd forgotten. This is a routine part of the job with you people, isn't it?"

The door burst open.

"Go!" Lev shouted through gritted teeth. Tanya twisted gracefully around the shimmering ball of heat blasts that melted the air around them, Ysbel at her heels. One of the boyeviki grabbed for them, then crumpled as Tanya brought the edge of her hand down in a swift motion against the side of his neck.

Then they were past the boyeviki and out into the corridor, and Tae breathed a shallow sigh of relief.

"Tae!"

He spun, and brought the broken piece of wood hard across the wrist of the boyevik who'd been in the process of raising her heat pistol to his head, and at the same time, Ivan brought his makeshift weapon down across the back of her knees.

She crumpled, groaning, and he scooped up the pistol and tossed it underhand to Lev, who, while he was a good man to have on your side, didn't show off his talents to best advantage in a hand-to-hand brawl.

He could hear Jez, by the door, drawling breathless insults, and, from the sounds of things, inflicting injuries which should hardly have been possible with a piece of broken wood.

The air crackled and hissed with heat-blasts, and the temperature in the room was growing steadily unbearable.

He dropped as a heat-blast hit the wall where he'd been standing, then staggered to his feet and lunged for the man who'd shot. The boyevik took a step back, and then Tae hit him, shoulder slamming into his chest, and they both went down. For a frantic moment they struggled for the pistol, then there was a sickening *crunch*, and the man went limp. Tae glanced up. Jez, broken chair-leg in hand, dark hair wet with sweat and blood trickling from a cut across her forehead, gave him a jaunty wink and stepped over the fallen boyevik. Tae twisted the gun from the man's limp hand and scrambled up. He brushed the sweat quickly from his eyes and looked around the room.

Lev had positioned himself beside the bed where the children were hidden, and as Tae glanced over, he cooly sent a heat-blast into the shoulder of a woman who'd grabbed for the table Ysbel had set up as a shield. The woman gave a strangled scream of pain, and Lev stepped out of the way as she collapsed, writhing, on the ground.

The boyeviki seemed to have realized that now the people they'd expected to find bound and weaponless were loose and armed with heat pistols, the odds had shifted somewhat, were backing towards the door, firing indiscriminately.

Jez stepped forward and grabbed the edge of the door as one of them tried to swing it shut.

"Don't think so, you plaguer," she drawled, yanking it open. The man holding it took an involuntary step forward, tripped, and fell into her.

She stumbled, and the woman behind him kicked her viciously, and she went down on her hands, and everything seemed to switch to slow motion.

The woman raised her heat pistol and pointed it at Jez's head. Tae swore, shoving past a boyeviki, trying to get to her. From the corner of his eye he saw Lev turn, grabbing for his pistol, but they weren't going to be in time, there was no way they'd be in time …

And then Masha shoved Jez out of the way, and as Jez went sprawling, the heat blast connected squarely with Masha's chest.

And Masha collapsed in a small heap on the carpet.

For a moment Tae wasn't sure he'd seen correctly. There was no way—

Jez staggered to her feet, face bloodless, expression grim, and Lev was already half-way across the room, pistol held steady even as he ran, and Tae felt something freeze inside of him. He turned and grabbed the man behind him and dropped him with a single blow to the back of the neck, then swung and hit another of the boyeviki in the throat. The woman went down, choking for breath, and he spun to grab for the next person—

But it was over.

Boyeviki lay strewn across the floor, groaning and clutching their wounds.

Lev walked through them, disarming any who still had their weapons and methodically melting the coms off their wrists. He didn't seem to be taking particular care to avoid injuring the coms' owners as he did so. Ivan had grabbed the rope they'd been bound with, and was trying hands behind backs with impressive alacrity.

Jez crouched over Masha, tears dripping down her face.

Tae turned, slowly, and walked over to her. He knelt beside her.

"Is she—" he began.

Jez blinked quickly and brushed her sleeve across her face. "I don't know," she said dully. "I—I haven't checked yet."

He nodded, and after a moment's hesitation, reached out to pull back Masha's scorched jacket.

He'd seen heat-blast wounds plenty of times, but the thought of what he'd find under the jacket still had the power to turn his stomach.

There was a hole burned in her shirt, as well, as he'd known there would be.

And under it—

He frowned.

Jez swore, then swore again, a slow grin starting on her face. "Masha, you damn bastard," she said.

Tae, almost dizzy with stunned relief, reached out gently and touched the thin, blood-soaked heat-shield Masha had been wearing under her shirt. Masha stirred, eyelids fluttering.

"Tae?" she said after a moment, her voice weak.

"I—are you—how did—"

She groaned, braced herself, and pushed up on her elbows. "I'm fine, thank you, Tae," she said. "Are the rest of you alright?"

He glanced around quickly. "Yes. I—I think so."

"Jez?"

"Why the hell didn't you tell us you were wearing a damn heat shield?" grumbled Jez, but she was grinning. "Anyways, yeah, I'm good. Thanks to you, you plaguer."

Masha grimaced as she rolled onto her side and sat up. "I thought —" She sucked in a sharp breath, then let it out slowly, but Tae could see the pain in her expression. "I thought it would be a wise addition to my wardrobe, considering how much time I was spending with Grigory," she finished after a moment. "And it appears to have been worth my while."

Lev joined them. "Masha?" he asked, voice sharp with strain.

"She's alive, at least," said Tae, turning to him.

"You alright, Masha?" Jez asked, concern in her voice.

"Yes, thank you, Jez," said Masha. "As I mentioned earlier, Girgory's people were not impressed with my performance today, and made their disapproval known with their fists. And while a heat shield does protect you from being killed by a blast, it is still not a pleasant experience. But, it is certainly better than the alternative. And so yes, I'm alright."

Ivan came over and crouched beside her, and she let him help her to her feet. She stumbled to the bed and dropped onto it with a grimace of relief.

"Thank you," she said, at last. She looked around the room. "So. I assume, then, that we're safe until Grigory notices his boyeviki haven't come back, correct?"

Tae nodded briefly.

"And as you have not spoofed the cameras on this ship, I assume that any attempt to move to a different room would ultimately be unhelpful, correct?"

He nodded again.

"Very well," said Masha at last. "I suppose, then, we move the boyaviki we've disabled somewhere more convenient, and wait to hear back from Ysbel."

21

Ysbel and Tanya sprinted down the corridors towards the centre of the ship. Behind them, Ysbel could hear the unmistakable sound of boyeviki coming into contact with an irate *Ungovernable* crew.

She was grinning to herself.

The distance itself wasn't long, but the corridors turned back on themselves, which made sense if you happened to be trying to run a hotel/casino, but was impressively irritating if you were trying to get to the centre shaft as quickly as possible so you could disarm a bomb that was about to turn the entire place into floating space-rubble.

"Here," said Tanya, catching her arm, and they turned down a smaller maintenance corridor.

Ysbel glanced at her wife as they ran. Her face still had a hint of that hard expression she'd seen on it so often these past few days, and something inside her hurt to see it.

"Tanya," she said at last, ducking down another corridor. "What's wrong? Please tell me."

Tanya glanced over at her.

Ahead of them, two of Grigory's boyeviki stepped out of a corridor, saw them, and grabbed for their guns.

"One moment," said Ysbel, yanking her modded heat pistol out of her jacket pocket. The two boyeviki raised their guns as well.

"Let me," whispered Tanya, and slipped ahead of her. She knocked both the gangsters' gun hands up, and both weapons went off, leaving scorch marks on the corridor ceiling. She grabbed one of them and took him down with a sharp blow to the side of the neck, and Ysbel grabbed the other, twisting the woman's arm up behind her back and shoving her head-first into the wall. The woman went limp, and Ysbel let her drop as Tanya pulled open a room door.

"In here," she said, and Ysbel kicked the groaning boyevik inside as Tanya slammed the door closed.

They smiled at each other, and set off running again.

Ahead of them, a maintenance tunnel split off from the corridor.

"Down here, I think," said Ysbel. Tanya nodded, pointed the heat pistol she'd grabbed from the fallen boyevik, and sent three blasts in short succession.

The door swung gently on its hinges, lock completely melted, and Ysbel caught it with the toe of her boot, swinging it open.

They ducked inside, and Tanya hit the light on her com. The passage was narrow and claustrophobic, bare steel walls glinting in the com light. Ysbel glanced quickly in both directions, and jerked her head to the right.

"This way. We've got to get closer to the centre of the ship before we can start looking."

Tanya nodded, and followed, their footsteps echoing off the bare metal walls as they ran.

"I'm—sorry, Ysi," Tanya said at last, her voice low. "I—I felt like you weren't listening. I felt like you were making any decision you wanted to make on your own, and—" she broke off a moment, shaking her head. "And I am wondering, now, if we remember how to be married. It's been a long time."

Ysbel slowed for a moment, glancing over her shoulder at her wife.

"Tanya," she said at last. "Tanya, you were all I thought about, that whole time. Every moment, every breath."

Tanya gave a small smile. "I know," she said quietly. "It was the same with me. But it's two different things, isn't it? To think about someone when they're gone, and to live with them when they're here?"

Ysbel was silent for a moment as they ran.

They were getting closer, she could feel it. There was a gravity pull to the heart of the ship, and if she were trying to blow this herself, she could follow that feeling blindfolded.

"I—believe I see your point," she said at last, in a low voice. "You were always the one with the conscience. And I have been ignoring you, haven't I?"

Tanya glanced at her with a small, wry smile. "I know you were trying to protect our family. But—you can't do it like this. You can't do it by pretending we don't have a say."

Ysbel looked over her shoulder for a moment, studying her wife's face, the familiar lines on it and the lines that she still didn't know, but she was coming to know, because she could never get enough of looking at this woman who she loved.

"All I wanted—all I want—is for you and the children to be alright," she said at last, and the words almost choked her because of the blind, frantic panic they brought with them. "I lost you once. I lost all of you once, and I couldn't protect you that time, and I—I can't do that again. Tanya, I—"

Tanya reached out and took her hand as they ran, and squeezed it, and for a moment the tears in Ysbel's eyes blurred her vision, and she had to blink them hastily back.

"Down here, I think," said Tanya, and they turned down another side corridor. Ysbel glanced at her com.

"We should be close. They'll have to plant it near the main shaft, and—" She paused. Ahead of her, Tanya stopped.

To one side, the maintenance tunnel turned around a bulge in the wall.

Ysbel smiled. "And I think we found it."

It took longer than it should have to find a way inside. Normally, Ysbel would have simply melted a hole in the metal casing, but she couldn't predict where Grigory's men would have fastened the explosive. It was Tanya who found the way through at last, a small panel hidden in the wall.

"How's it coming?" Tae asked over the com. His voice was strained.

"I think we're close," said Ysbel. "Is everyone there alright?"

"We're all alive, and no one's attacking us at the moment," said Tae. "Which I think is the best we'll get for some time."

"I think we've located it, at least," said Ysbel. "Give us a few minutes to get the lock, and I'll be able to access it."

There was a sick feeling in her stomach as she worked, though, and she saw it mirrored in Tanya's face.

"You know," Ysbel muttered, as she clipped the lock scrambler onto the door panel that lay exposed behind the metal panels that made up the wall, "this is much easier when Tae is the one who has to get us through the locks, and I only have to worry about blowing things up."

Tanya gave a soft laugh, and Ysbel glanced over at her.

Her face was still cut with strain, but she was wearing a small smile. "We all have our talents," she murmured. "And no one can say that boy isn't talented."

The lock scrambler whirred for a moment, then there was a soft *click*. Holding her breath, Ysbel unclipped it carefully from the panel and tried the handle.

The door swung open.

Ysbel hit the light on her com, and Tanya came up beside her as they stepped through into the darkness.

They were inside a tall, narrow space, filled with the tubing and venting system that supplied the ship's oxygen and temp control, and in the mess of wires and tubing it took her a few moments to locate the familiar shape of the explosive.

Then she saw it, and almost groaned.

They'd planted it at the top of the tall cylinder, against the wall centimetres from the ceiling.

Ysbel swore under her breath.

She turned to see Tanya smiling at her, that soft, wistful smile Ysbel loved so much it almost made her ache.

"I'll be right back," she whispered. "I may have to drop it down though. Can you catch it?"

Ysbel smiled back at her.

Tanya looked up calculatingly, then began to scale the tangle of pipes and wires up to the ceiling. Ysbel watched her, and something inside her chest hurt.

Maybe Tanya was right.

It had been a long time. It had been a long, long time, and she wanted to protect Tanya, she needed to, but—maybe Tanya had never needed her protection after all.

Maybe it was herself she'd been protecting.

Tanya was up beside the explosive now.

"Has it been set?" asked Ysbel, tapping her com to the private line.

"Just a moment." Tanya's voice carried the strain of holding herself up on the pipes. A moment later, Ysbel heard her sharp intake of breath.

"They've set it, Ysi. We have half a standard hour." She paused, and there was something tight and worried in her voice. "And—I think you need to take a look at this."

22

Tae paced between the bed and the wall and back again.

He'd pulled up the vid feed of the gambling floor, and the others were gathered around it, but he couldn't seem to stand still. His blood was still pumping with the sick horror of seeing Masha take a heat blast to the chest, seeing the scorched hole in her coat.

He almost tapped his com again, but Ysbel wouldn't thank him for harassing her, and if he knew anything about her explosives, disarming them would be fiddly work.

"Tae. I think you'd better come look at this."

He turned quickly at the tone in Ivan's voice, and something about the grim expression on Ivan's face sent a cold fear through his stomach.

Lev's face, too, was set and worried.

He crossed to them quickly and peered at the screen, but it took him a moment to see what they had already seen.

And then he saw it, grim-faced boyeviki striding through the panicked gambling hall, grabbing people by the arm and dragging them from the room.

Not the people Grigory wanted to kill, though.

Instead—

"It appears," said Lev quietly, "that Grigory has given up on getting people into position."

"Where is he taking them?" asked Tae in a low voice.

"They're being taken to Grigory's ship," said Masha. She was sitting up, propped against the headboard, and there was something odd in her voice.

Tae glanced over at her quickly.

He'd never been able to read Masha's expression. But the sharp worry in her eyes was unmistakable.

"It's his own people, the ones he wants to keep alive. Looks like he's given up on shutting down the partition," said Ivan. His face had gone slightly bloodless. "He's going to get out on his ship and let this whole thing blow."

Tae gritted his teeth.

If Grigory was getting people out, he'd almost certainly started the countdown on the explosive. But Ysbel and Tanya had found it, so it should be fine.

Probably.

He hit the com. "Ysbel," he said. "How long will this take you?"

There was a short pause, and then Ysbel's voice came onto the com. "Thirty minutes," she said at last, and there was something heavy in her tone.

"Thirty minutes until you can disarm it?" he asked, glancing at his com. His stomach was tight with worry.

It would be cutting it very close, if Lev's calculations were correct. Which they usually were.

"No," said Ysbel, in that same unfamiliar tone. "Thirty minutes until it goes off. I'm sorry."

He stared at the com.

Everyone in the room was staring at the com.

Finally, Masha tapped her own com. "Ysbel. You were unable to locate the explosive? Or unable to disarm it?"

"No one is going to be able to disarm this," said Ysbel, her voice emotionless. "The thing is, they've set something into the timer. It triggers the explosive the moment the timer stops running, whether it's run out or not. We can't even run the timer backwards to add more time, because any interruption will set it off."

They were all looking at Tae now.

He stared down at his com.

The trigger woven into the timer. He'd heard of this before, never seen it.

Zhenya must have had a hell of a lot of faith in Tae's abilities.

Slowly, he shook his head. "If they've set it like Ysbel says they have, I—don't know how we'd avoid setting it off," he said, bitterness in his voice. "Even if I attempted it, somehow got through Zhenya's firewall, I'd likely blow us all to pieces."

"Could we get it out of the ship somehow?" asked Ivan after a moment.

"No," said Ysbel. "I already thought of that. But I was the one who made this. The moment it hit zero pressure, it would explode. There's no way we get it onto an escape pod, not if Tae can't get into their system to hack one. And from the specs Lev sent me, this ship's airlocks are not reinforced like Grigory's are. This thing explodes inside the airlock, and it takes the whole ship down with it."

"And even if we did manage to disarm it, it would likely only give us a few additional minutes," said Masha, in that same odd voice. "Once Grigory has everyone he wants alive off this ship, he'll destroy it. I've seen the guns on his ship. He has the gun-power to do it, and with no witnesses, he could still play it off as an accident. He spent a great deal of resources planning this, after all."

They looked at each other for a long time. Finally, Lev hit his com.

"Ysbel," he said quietly. "I suppose you may as well come back here. I think Olya and Misko would like that."

"If I had my damn ship—" Jez began, her voice tight.

Tae looked up at her.

Then he glanced down at the com again.

"Wait," he said slowly, staring at the holoscreen.

"What is it?" asked Lev, voice sharp.

"Lev," he said, looking up abruptly. "They're getting his people onto his ship. Which means—"

Lev stared at him for a moment. "Which means, the airlock doors are open," he murmured.

There was a moment of silence as they all digested that information. Then Lev turned to Jez.

"Jez," he said, "we may have a way out after all. How would you like to go get your ship?"

23

Jez stared, not quite sure she could believe her ears.

Her ship.

She could get back to her ship.

The explosive, the mafia boyeviki tied up in the room next door, the scorch-marks in the wall where the boyaviki had tried to kill them —all of it seemed suddenly unimportant.

She was getting her damn ship back.

"Alright, kids," she began, snatching a heat pistol off the chair. "Be back in a jiff."

"Wait," said Masha. "I have a pass for the one-person lifts. That should get you down more quickly than trying to melt the door locks." She reached into her pocket, grimacing at the movement, and pulled out a slim card.

Jez snatched it from her hand and turned for the door.

"Jez," said Lev. "There'll be locks on the hangar door, and Tae can't hack them. You'll need someone who can—."

"You volunteering to come?" she snapped. "Because I'm leaving right now."

Lev sighed. "Fine. I'm volunteering."

She gave him a sharp grin. "Well, genius, let's go."

They sprinted down the corridor to the lifts. When they reached them, Jez paused, glaring at the tiny pods.

She wasn't entirely sure she wanted to jam herself in there with Lev, of all the damn people in the system.

Still—

Lev took a deep breath, seeming as unenthusiastic about the prospect as she was, and stepped in, shoving himself as far into the corner as possible.

Her ship. The *Ungovernable* was down there.

She gritted her teeth and shoved herself in beside him. He shifted in a vain attempt to make more space, but she still ended up jammed up against him as the doors slid shut and the pod began to move, her back pushed up against his chest.

Which was completely fine, because they were just making do with a crap circumstance, and—

And—

She found she was losing her train of thought.

And considering they were in a race against time to save her damn ship, which was probably the thing that she cared about more than she'd ever cared about anything in her life, it didn't really make sense that she felt herself relaxing into him, the tension bleeding from her muscles, the warmth of his breath on the nape of her neck sending small shivers up her back.

The door slid open. She blinked and jerked upright, stepping out so quickly she almost tripped.

She glanced over her shoulder. Lev's face was bloodless, his hands clenched tightly at his sides.

"You OK genius?" she asked, and she found her voice was shaking.

He ran his hands over his face. "I'm—fine," he said.

She turned away quickly, before her eyes could get caught in his. "Come on then, let's go."

The ground floor of the ship had turned to utter chaos. Terrified people ran down corridors, alarms blared, doors were flung open. From the gambling hall, she could hear the tinkle of shattering glass, screams, the fuzz of a heat pistol.

She shoved her way through the people, and then they were sprinting down the passageway that led onto Grigory's ship.

The airlock doors that separated the two ships were open, but two guards were already detaching the deck from the gambling ship's airlock.

"Hey, where are you—" one of the guards began, straightening.

Jez jerked up her free arm, grinning like a damn lunatic, and swung so that her elbow connected with the guard's temple as they passed her. The woman went down without a groan. Another guard rounded the corner. "Where are you—" he began, then cut off his words abruptly as Jez scorched a hole in the wall beside him with her heat gun. She reached him before he could figure out what was happening, grabbed him by the collar, and swung him around hard. His head connected with the wall with a sickening *crunch*.

A moment later, they were at the airlock door that led to Grigory's ship's hangar bay.

"Locked," she said, glancing up.

"Hold on," Lev said, frowning at the keypad.

She tapped her foot impatiently as he scowled at the screen. From behind them there were running footsteps and shouts, and hell, she liked a gunfight as much as the next woman, but right now it was her ship they were talking about.

"Not to rush you, genius, but we're on a bit of a—"

"Got it." He hit a button on the pad, and the door swung open as two boyeviki rounded the corner.

They ducked inside as a heat-blast scorched the air above them, and Lev slammed the door behind him. She gave him a skeptical glance as they ran for the ship. "So, you Tae now?"

"No," he said. "But they armed the lock with a passcode, and I happen to be able to extrapolate from information I've been given."

She rolled her eyes at him, but she was grinning.

They reached the ship, and she hit the control to lower the loading ramp.

"Mag lock," Lev said grimly, glancing at the floor of the hanger under the ship. "They've locked the ship in."

She took a deep breath.

About what she'd expected.

This wasn't going to be pretty, which, honestly, if it was any ship except her perfect angel she wouldn't have worried about that nearly as much.

Then again, any ship but her perfect angel probably wouldn't survive what she was about to do.

She took a deep breath. "Alright, genius, I'm going in, start her up. You take this." She dropped an explosive into his hand, and he frowned.

"I—"

"When I say so, you arm it and drop it right by the mag lock. Then you get the hell in here."

"Jez, even if that actually works, and we actually get the mag lock released, how are we going to get out of the damn—"

"Leave that to me," she murmured. She couldn't stop grinning, which didn't seem to make Lev feel any better.

There were shouts from outside, and the airlock door started to slide open.

"Sorry genius, don't have time to chat," she said, swinging herself inside.

The soothing familiarity of the *Ungovernable's* old-fashioned corridors was almost enough to make her knees weak as she sprinted down them to the cockpit, and she closed her eyes in pure pleasure as she slipped into the pilot's seat, revelling in the way it fit like it had been built for her. She tapped the controls to fire the ship up, and sighed blissfully as the soft hum of the running ship settled into her bones.

"Jez—" came Lev's voice over the com, "Not sure what you're doing in there, but out here I'm about to get into a damn shootout."

"One sec." She pulled back gently on the throttle, and the ship's soft hum increased in volume. She took a deep breath and hit the shields.

"Now!" she snapped.

There was the smooth whine of the loading ramp closing, and a moment later Lev slid into the copilot's seat.

And despite every damn thing that had happened, the sight of him there felt like her entire world falling back into place.

She grinned. "Hold on, genius."

She only had a moment to register the alarmed look on his face before there was a muffled *boom* and the ship rocked with the force of the explosion. She grabbed the arm of her seat with one hand and hit the throttle with the other, and the ship groaned with the strain.

"Come on, beautiful," she murmured. "I know you can do this." She pulled back, then shoved the throttle further, and the ship rocked harder, and for half a second she felt the visceral jolt of terror, the horrifying thought that maybe she'd miscalculated, maybe her sweet angel ship would tear itself to pieces—And then there was another jolt, and the ship jumped free, and she just had time to yank back on the thrusters before they hit the roof of the hangar bay.

She pointed the *Ungovernable's* nose so it was facing the tight rows of Grigory's fighter ships.

Might as well take the plaguing things out while they were at it.

"Guns," she said through her teeth. "You know how to run them, right? Make me a door."

Lev's face was pale, and he was managing an impressive variety of swear words through his teeth, but he fumbled for the cockpit gunner controls.

"Hey you bastards, might want to get behind the airlock," Jez called over the general com line.

There was a mad scramble for the airlock doors.

"Hold on," said Lev, his voice strained. She glanced over at him. His hands were on the gun controls and his expression was grim.

"Lighten up, genius," she said, grinning. "Just a ship's gun. What's the worst that can happen?"

"It's a ship's gun. That was created by Ysbel," he said through his teeth.

"Like I said—"

He gave her a flat look. Then he took a deep breath, pulled the gun up into position, and fired.

The entire world went completely white, and the noise, inside the closed-in airlock, rose up and around them like a sort of stifling atmosphere, and she had to shove the thrusters forward to keep the ship from being thrown against the back wall of the bay.

"One more!" she shouted over the noise, and she wasn't actually sure he could hear her, but he glanced over and seemed to understand. There was that brief tension in his muscles for a moment, like he was re-thinking all the life choices that had led him to this point, and then he fired the guns a second time.

Again the world exploded around them, and thank the damn Lady for Tae's shields, because this would have been a hell of a ride without them, and then—

And then, ahead of her, through the floating debris of what was left of Grigory's fleet, there was the breathtaking, achingly beautiful blackness of deep space, and her whole body thrummed with the giddy joy of it. She whooped and hit the throttle, and the *Ungovernable* shot through the ever-widening crack in the shell of the hangar-bay, and they were out.

She was grinning so hard it hurt, and her ship was beneath her, and every muscle in her body felt loose and light, and there was a sparking happiness running through her brain that was almost too much to handle.

She hadn't realized how much she missed this.

Grigory's ship had already separated from the casino ship, and was widening the gap surprisingly rapidly. She turned the *Ungovernable*, tipping her head back against the seat, and let the feeling of flying flow through her like water, relaxing every muscle in her body, her fingers stroking the controls of her ship almost unconsciously.

"Jez?" Lev sounded slightly amused. "Do you need me to leave the two of you alone?"

She opened her eyes and turned to glare at him, but it was hard to glare when you felt this damn happy, and it turned into more of a grin.

He grinned back at her, that soft look in his eyes once more, and it took her a few moments to realize that she hadn't looked away. And that nor had he, and that she was staring into his eyes, and that the happiness that was bubbling through her brain and fizzing in her stomach was turning into—well, into something else, a familiar ache of desire that was building inside her bones, and, OK, they had plenty of other damn things to do right now, but for some reason there was another possibility that kept intruding itself into her brain —

Nope, absolutely not, this was definitely not the time to think about that.

With an effort, she wrenched her gaze away from his, and glanced down at the ship's holoscreen. It was running a red damage report, and for just a moment she felt a spike of panic, but looked like Tae's shields had held—a couple quick fixes and she should be good as new.

She took a deep breath, waiting for the shaky feeling in her muscles to subside. When her hands had stopped shaking and her breathing seemed to be mostly back to normal, she chanced a glance up. "Hey genius, thought we were in a hurry."

He glanced up as well, with a reflexive smile that dropped as soon as he met her eyes, and she noticed, in the corner of her mind, that his face was still paler than usual and something told her it had less to do with breaking out of Grigory's ship and more to do with the fact that they were here in the cockpit, sitting so close that she could easily reach out and touch him, and if they both stood up, it would only take one step, from either of them, and they'd be close enough that—

She swallowed hard, and Lev looked away quickly, turning back to his holoscreen.

"Give me a moment," he said. "Assuming we don't want to blow a hole in the casino ship's airlock, I'll need to send through the access codes we got from Grigory. I believe they should work."

He glanced up a moment later. "Got it. I've sent the coordinates of the airlock we want to your screen."

She touched the thrusters gently, and as the massive airlock doors slid open, she nudged the *Ungovernable* inside.

She glanced down at her com as she lowered the ship gently to the hangar bay floor.

Nineteen minutes left.

She took a deep breath and turned to Lev. "Well," she said. "Guess it's time to get everyone on board."

But the thought of the people inside the ship, the panic on their faces as she'd run past them on her way out—the ones who were going to die—made something tighten in her stomach.

24

"Get everyone ready to go," Lev panted into the com as he and Jez ran for the lifts.

They had eighteen minutes, and on balance, it was still likely to be faster to get everyone down the lift on Masha's lift-card than to melt through the doors.

"Lev," said Tanya through the com, her voice steel. "Listen to me. We can't leave these people here to be killed. I won't do it. And we can't leave Grigory to take over the government. That, I won't do either. I don't care if it means the minister we want to kill survives. We are going to save them."

"I don't like it any more than you do," came Ivan's voice, thick with concern. "But at this point, who we get off this ship is probably limited to who we can fit aboard the *Ungovernable*."

There was a moment of silence. Finally, Ysbel spoke.

"Listen. My wife believes that we shouldn't leave all the people on this ship to die. And yes, it means that the minister will survive this, and perhaps I don't feel exactly the same way as she does—but I support her in this. It will take a few minutes to get everyone down the lifts, anyways. Until we're on the ship, and eighteen minutes are up, we still have time to look for a solution."

Lev shot a glance at Jez, and she quirked an eyebrow at him, grinning. "Guess they always say you have to compromise in a marriage."

They'd reached the lift, and Jez pulled out the lift card.

"The *Ungovernable* has an escape pod, yes?" asked Tanya. "We could put the explosive on there, perhaps?"

"Maybe," said Lev shortly. "But as Masha said before, it likely wouldn't make any difference. I'm certain Grigory's tracking the timing on the bomb. The time limit goes and the bomb hasn't exploded, he'll simply shoot a hole in the casino ship's shell. Then everyone on it dies anyways."

"There is—one other option," said Masha quietly. She was speaking on the private line, and he glanced down at his com, frowning.

"Masha?" he said quietly, tapping his com to the private line as well.

"What—" Jez whispered. He shook his head, and she raised an eyebrow at him.

"I only wish to point out that our options are not only, leave our very powerful explosive on board, or throw it out the airlock," Masha said.

He paused a moment.

Another option. That's what they were all looking for, another option, but—

He looked up, staring at Jez.

"Wait," he said slowly. He hit his com. "Ysbel. It's not moving it that sets the explosive off, correct? It's the lack of pressure."

"That's right," said Ysbel.

"We can't throw it out the airlock into space. But we could put it on the *Ungovernable*. And Grigory's airlocks have pressure, I assume."

There was a moment of silence.

"Well," said Ysbel at last, "if you're fast enough, I suppose that would work. Although that doesn't solve the problem of—"

"I've looked at his ship specs," said Lev. "It wouldn't take his whole ship down, but if an explosive that large went off in his airlock, it would crack the hull on at least one of his compartments. That kind of breach would shunt all power to emergency systems. There's no way he'd have the capability to shoot down anyone after that."

"Well then," said Ysbel at last. "I suppose that's our solution. You'd best hurry up. You have about twelve minutes left."

Lev tapped his com off.

"Jez," he asked quietly, turning to her. "Can you do this?"

She nodded, without speaking, but he could see the stark fear in her eyes.

She'd almost lost her ship once, when Lena was after them, and it had almost killed her, and he was pretty sure that, given the alternative, she'd happily jump out the airlock herself with the explosive rather than risk hurting her ship a second time.

But it wasn't like they had a lot of options at this point.

"Alright," he said quietly, "Let's go."

"Where are we going to drop it?" Jez asked, her voice almost a whisper. "Don't know if you remember, but we blew a damn hole in the hangar bay on our way out."

He closed his eyes for a moment, picturing the ship specs. "The airlocks in the front of the ship, where Grigory and the crew are, are too heavily secured. But there's three or four airlocks near the rear of the ship. They're for loading cargo planet-side, not designed for ships, but if you can hold her steady I think we can still hook the *Ungovernable* on and get the explosive across."

She took a deep breath, then gave a tense nod. "Alright. Better get moving, then." She hit her com, and there was a forced jauntiness to her voice when she spoke into it. "Ysbel, Tanya, we're coming up the lift. You want us to take your damn explosive, might want to have it waiting."

She slapped her com as the lift doors slid open.

There was a brief moment of awkwardness, and he tried not to think too hard as they both squeezed into the cramped space.

When at last the door slid open and she half-fell out, the sudden absence of her left a lightheadedness that made him almost dizzy.

He shook his head, willing his brain to start working again, and his legs to stop being so damn shaky he wasn't sure they'd hold him up.

Ysbel arrived a moment later, cradling the explosive gently. There was sharp worry on her face.

"You don't have to worry about jostling it," she said brusquely. "Just make sure you never open an airlock unless it's pressurized, or we'll be wiping pieces of you off the outside of the ship."

He nodded. "How long do we have?"

She glanced at the explosive. "You have ten minutes."

The device was heavier than it looked, and awkwardly large. Finally, they ended up with Jez against the wall of the lift, him facing her, both of them shoved together like they were attempting a new and awkward sex position, the explosive tucked between both their legs.

He somehow managed to force his brain not to think. He wasn't sure if he actually breathed the entire slow ride down the lift, but somehow the fact that not only was he crammed into the lift with Jez, he was also crammed into the lift with an explosive that would take the entire ship apart, made it somewhat easier to stay focused.

The ground floor was utter panic now—people were screaming, muttering on their coms to family members or friends trapped upstairs, fighting with the locks between the decks—but none of them seemed to have realized yet that they were about to be damn well vaporized, so the passageway to the hangar bay was uncrowded. He hit the seal, and the moment the door slid open, he and Jez slipped through and ran for their ship.

The moment the loading ramp clicked shut, he typed in the access code. The outer doors slid silently open and the air from the hangar bay crystallized into a frozen white vapour.

And then they were out.

"Coordinates," Jez muttered, voice tense. He pulled the specs up on his com and glanced at them quickly.

"Lev," said Masha, through the com. "Listen to me. Use the airlock that's marked number two on your specs."

He frowned.

It didn't matter, specifically, but—

"I need specs, genius! Figure we have less than five minutes at this point."

He blew out a breath and hit the coordinates for airlock two into the com.

Grigory's ship was sitting just outside what he assumed would be the blast radius. The moment they came around the side of the casino ship, it was in full view.

The *Ungovernable* dived gracefully towards it, responding to Jez's touch like it was reading her mind. Her eyes were half-closed in that way she had when she was concentrating, and there was the blissful smile on her face that she always got when she was behind the controls of her ship, even, apparently, if she and the ship and everything on it was going to be vaporized in a matter of minutes.

Possibly seconds, at this point.

She hit the airlock control, and there was a faint hissing sound as it sealed onto Grigory's ship.

She turned to him. "Alright genius, I'll hold it steady. Get that damn thing off my ship."

He was already sliding out of his seat. He grabbed the explosive from the main deck, half-staggering at the unfamiliar weight as he ran down the corridor to the *Ungovernable's* airlock. The door slid open, revealing the sealed airlock of Grigory's ship.

Damn.

He shifted the explosive awkwardly so it was supported between his hip and the airlock wall and bit the inside of his cheek as he glared down at the pad.

"You done yet?" Jez's voice was strained. "Because pretty sure in about thirty seconds we're all going to be done, if you get my meaning."

He scowled, and gingerly tapped in a code.

The airlock door slid open, and he sucked in a quick, relieved breath.

He laid the explosive down gently, then hit the controls for Grigory's airlock as he stepped back through the door. The moment they were closed, he was sprinting back towards the cockpit, the *Ungovernable's* airlock doors sliding shut behind him.

"Jez, go," he shouted through the com, and there was a slight jolt as the two ships disconnected, and he reached the cockpit just as Jez hit the throttle.

The *Ungovernable* hurtled forward, and Lev barely caught himself on the back of the copilot's seat. And then a wave of energy slammed into them, hurling the *Ungovernable* sideways, spinning away at a speed that reminded him of—well, of Jez's typical flying, honestly—and the world spun around him and he clung to the copilot's seat with all his strength, and Jez was laughing in sheer delight, playing the controls between her fingers with a look of such joy that she was almost glowing. The ship slowed, slightly, as she brought it back under control, and with a sigh of relief he loosened his grip on the seat.

And then the ship jerked one final time, and he lost his balance, and landed practically in her lap.

She grinned at him with that delirious, infectious joy, and his eyes caught hers and held them, and for a moment, just one moment, he could hardly breathe.

And then he remembered, and he almost flinched at the pain of it.

Jez, too, sobered abruptly, and looked away.

"You OK genius?" she asked at last.

"I'm—fine," he said, voice unsteady. "Sorry." He pushed himself up out of her lap and slid into the copilot's seat, his legs almost too shaky to hold him.

She was still watching him. "You sure?" she asked quietly, and looking at her face, he knew she knew.

He managed a small smile, although he wasn't completely sure how. "I'm fine," he repeated. "I'll be fine."

She watched him a moment longer, then, at last, she nodded. "Yeah," she said, and there was something tired and sad in her voice. "Guess we'll both be."

25

Masha smiled slightly as she glanced around the small room on the casino ship that had been their prison.

Tanya and Ysbel and the children clung to each other, hardly seeming to notice there was anyone else present. Tae had collapsed back in his chair, shoulders slumped with relief, and Ivan was watching him, a soft smile on his face.

She closed her eyes for a moment.

They'd done it.

And right now, she wasn't gong to concern herself with what would happen next.

The door swung open, and Jez and Lev slipped inside. Jez was uncharacteristically quiet, and Lev's face was paler than usual.

Tae glanced over, then stood quickly, a familiar concern creasing his face. "Are you alright?" he asked.

Jez gave a tired grin. "Yep. Figure that worked out pretty damn well, all things considered."

She dropped into a chair, and Lev followed suit. And for just a moment, Masha thought that perhaps, just perhaps, Lev was tired enough and distracted enough—

"Masha," he said finally, turning to her.

She kept the pleasant smile on her face.

It wouldn't make a substantive difference now, of course. She'd planned for this, after all.

She hadn't planned for the slightly sick feeling in her stomach, the sudden difficulty in meeting Lev's gaze.

"Yes, Lev?" she said.

He was watching her, and there was appraisal behind the exhaustion in his eyes. "Masha. Why airlock two? You knew it wasn't going to take down Grigory's ship, Ysbel told you that, and I've seen the specs—there are blast doors separating the sections of the ship from each other. Why did it matter?"

She could lie, of course. But Tae was already pulling up his holoscreen, and any lie wouldn't last longer than it would take for him to hack into Grigory's communication system.

"I—spoke with Grigory extensively, before he caught on to your plan," she said at last. "I knew what his contingency plan was, in case his original plan failed."

"And that was?" asked Lev, his voice still soft.

It was strange, how difficult it was to say the words.

And then Tae sucked in a sharp breath, and she knew she wouldn't have to.

He turned to stare at her, and the betrayal in his face hurt more than she'd expected it would.

"What?" asked Ivan, frowning. "What happened?"

Tae didn't take his eyes from Masha's face. "Those government officials he grabbed from this ship, before he left," he said, his voice dazed and slightly sick. "All of them." He turned to glance at Lev. "How many were there?"

Lev frowned. "Forty? Fifty?"

Tae turned back to Masha, his expression still dazed, but there was a sharp hurt under it. "We killed them," he said, without taking her eyes off her. "Airlock number two was the one that connected with the room in the back of the ship where Grigory had put them for safety."

For a long, long moment, no one spoke. She could feel all their eyes on her, but she simply smiled, that bland smile that had served her so well over the years.

"Yes," she said finally. "That is correct."

For a long moment, no one spoke. Then Lev stood abruptly.

"That was stupid, Masha." His voice was harsh. "That was a stupid damn move. Is that what you were planning for this whole time? Is that why you didn't help us stop this? You wanted Grigory's plan to work, didn't you? This whole time."

"No." She shook her head. "I had no desire whatsoever for Grigory to succeed."

"Don't lie to me, Masha," he snapped. "You're not stupid enough to think I'm not going to see through it."

"I never had any question of that, Lev," she said, voice pleasant. "But you are wrong. I assumed, at all times, that you would figure out Grigory's plan, and that you would work to stop it. I had no desire for Grigory to stage a successful coup of the government. I left you to do what you do best, while I gathered information."

"But nor did you want us to succeed," Lev said slowly. There was a sharp anger behind his tone. "You never intended for us to stop the explosion. You simply wanted to control who died. Because Grigory's backup plan, to move his people to his ship if things went wrong—you knew far too much about that. What he was doing, how he was doing it. Where he'd put his people when he got them on his ship. You're smart, Masha, but you're not a mind-reader. So."

He leaned back against his chair, a small, bitter smile on his face.

"Did he tell you? No, of course not, I suspect you were the one who suggested the idea. You knew it was likely we'd manage to throw a wrench in Grigory's plans, and you needed some alternate way to gather the people you wanted to die."

She didn't bother to deny it. There was no point. He was far too clever for that.

"So this whole time, you were working behind our backs," said Ysbel, at last, her tone flat and heavy. "You planned to use us to kill fifty people. And you didn't tell us. You didn't tell us about the backup plan that you gave to Grigory. And because we didn't factor that in, we were almost killed right here in this room. My children, Masha, were almost killed." She paused a moment, her voice trembling slightly with anger. "So you won. You killed the people you wanted to kill. But understand this: you've lost your crew."

Misko, and Olya. They were watching from between their mothers' legs, faces pale.

Misko certainly didn't understand what had gone wrong. Olya, perhaps, did. She was very bright for her age.

She hadn't, of course, planned to put the children in danger. She hadn't planned for Grigory to use the backup plan when the fire alarm went off, rather than shut down the explosive and wait for a better opportunity.

But, she'd known this outcome would be a possibility.

Lev was still watching her, eyes narrowed.

And then she saw the moment he finally realized, the dawning look of disbelief and horror on his face. And despite everything she felt a quick flicker of fondness for him.

He'd always been very, very intelligent.

"No," said Lev at last, looking up at Ysbel. His voice was a detached sort of calm. "I'm afraid, Ysbel, we aren't leaving. Because that's not all Masha did." He turned to her. "Was that the plan from the beginning, Masha? Did you plan this from the moment we agreed to come with you to bring back Peti?"

"I gave you a choice," she said quietly. "You chose to come with me."

"Because we trusted you," he spat. "Because we wanted to protect you."

"What is it?" Tanya's words were as sharp as razors.

"She's marked us." His voice was hard and deadly. "You knew we'd never agree to whatever you've planned next, didn't you, Masha? And so you brought us here. Convinced Grigory that we'd help him. And then you double-crossed him. We intended to stop his coup, but if we'd pulled it off, he'd never have known why his plan hadn't worked—it could have been any of a million small things. We had to plan it that way, because Grigory's a man who'd have a man murdered for turning down his offer of work. His reputation is the only thing that keeps him alive. But what you did? There's no mistaking that. Now that we've killed his people, it's as much as his life is worth to hunt down every last one of us and make an example of us. If we split up, change course, we're all dead, and believe me, I've seen what Grigory does to people he wants to make an example of."

He gave her a bitter smile. "So, Masha. What have you planned for us next? Because I assume you have plans for us, correct?"

"I do," she said quietly. "This, here—this was only the setup."

"You killed fifty people—got us to kill fifty people—for a setup," said Lev, his voice matching hers in quietness. "You put every member of this crew, including Olya and Misko, in the crosshairs of the mafia, for a setup. And what's the sting, Masha?"

She gave him a slight smile, despite the sharp ache in her chest.

"Lev. You spoke with Grigory. Stopping this—" she gestured around. "This was never going to stop him forever. This was always going to be temporary. If we're going to take down the mafia—if we're going to take him down for good—we have to take down what keeps him powerful."

For a moment Lev didn't speak, just looked at her, dawning comprehension on his face.

"We're going to cut off his supply," he murmured, staring at her. "We're going to choke him out." He paused. "You already crippled his weapons supply, with the Vitali job. So now—"

"The pleasure planet," she said, nodding. "Since his contracts with Vitali were broken, he's switched most of his business in that direction. It now makes up a sizeable portion of his income." She could hear the hardness in her own voice, the bitterness, but again, it hardly mattered anymore what they thought. "After what we did to him here—not just embarrassed him, but took out all his government contacts—he'll follow us anywhere. He won't be able to help but take the bait now. And we're going to run the biggest sting this system has ever seen. We're going to take down Grigory Korzhikov so completely that in five standard years from now, no one will even remember his name."

There was another long silence.

"And if we refuse to work with you?" asked Tanya. There was a hint of steel in her voice.

Masha shrugged. "I will not, of course, force any one of you to stay."

"You couldn't force us to stay if you wanted to," grunted Ysbel. "In fact, if I wanted to kill you right now—"

"You are right, of course," said Masha blandly. "You could kill me quite easily, I imagine, any one of you could. However, as intelligent as you are, not one of you have the information I do on Grigory—information I gathered while you made your plans, and, I might add, saved several hundred innocent people. Or, at least, as innocent as people who work with the Svodrani System government can be." She glanced around the room. "So," she said at last. "You have a choice to make. You could kill me, of course. You could choose to take off on your own, and do your best to escape from Grigory, scavenging a bare existence on the outer rim planets until he hunts you down. And he will hunt you down. Or—" she shrugged. "You can come with me. I believe our interests, in this case at least, converge."

She paused a moment. "I—understand that you are angry. I don't blame you. But please, believe me that I did not make this decision lightly. I swear to you, what I'm doing—" She broke off abruptly, her voice shaking, something sick in the back of her throat.

She'd expected that.

She hadn't expected the desperate, aching need for them to understand.

She took a deep breath, and managed to plaster the pleasant expression back on her face.

Jez, though, was watching her, head cocked to one side, as if considering something.

"At any rate," said Masha, forcing her tone back to its usual bland calm, "we have at least accomplished something. We came here to find a way to stop the Minister from going forward with the program that would certainly kill us. I was able to convince Grigory that the Minister and her two assistants should be brought back to his ship with the others if his plan didn't work as intended. They died in that explosion. I'm certain Evka will be able to train a replacement, given time. But that is exactly what this has done—give us time.

"And Tae—" she turned to him, forcing herself to look him in the face. "There was a reason I chose the apartment building for your street-kid friends that I did. Besides having gate guards, the entire complex is shielded, and the group that the building managers pay off for protection is from Olyessa's mob. It's untouchable for any of Grigory's people. They won't be used as leverage. Additionally, the explosion that we set off in airlock two will have caused substantial damage to Grigory's ship, and I believe that Jez and Lev caused substantial damage to his guard ships when they shot their way out of the hangar bay. He'll have no choice but to find a friendly planet and lick his wounds. None of his people are left on this ship. We're safe here, for the present, and we have time to rest and plan our next move. Really, our situation is almost ideal." She paused a moment.

"Except for the fact that you betrayed us," Lev snapped. "Except for the fact you may well have killed us. You set the mafia on us, and Grigory won't stop until we're dead, or he is." He shook his head, a short, frustrated motion entirely unlike his normal calm, and turned to the others. "We need to discuss this. Figure out our next steps."

"There's a suite of connecting rooms next door," said Tae at last. He was looking at Lev, and fixedly avoiding Masha's eyes. "We can stay there tonight, at least."

Lev nodded shortly and shoved back his chair. He stood, turning to Masha for a moment. "You've won this one," he said, and the sudden calm in his voice was anything but reassuring. "But Masha —" He took a step closer.

She didn't step back.

"There will be a round two. Believe me, sooner or later there will be. And you won't fool me again."

He turned abruptly and strode to the door.

When the door shut behind him, there was silence for a few

moments. Then Tae stood, still without meeting her eye.

"I'll come too," said Ivan, standing. He did meet Masha's gaze, his glance appraising, weighing her.

Tanya and Ysbel left next, with the children. Neither of them spoke, but there was a flat calculation in the look that Ysbel cast over her shoulder as they walked out the door, and despite herself, a slight shiver ran up Masha's back.

She'd put this crew together herself. And everything she'd done, including this, had been done in full consideration of the calibre of people she was working with, and she had planned for every contingency.

But—these people were dangerous. Perhaps more dangerous than anything she was fighting.

It behooved her to remember it.

Jez was still sitting at the table, chin in her hands, watching Masha.

Masha dropped into a seat, her legs finally unable to hold her up. Blood from her old wound, re-opened by the boyevik's beating, seeped through her shirt, wetting her coat and spreading upwards and outwards.

She'd been injured enough times to know it wasn't serious—at least, it wouldn't kill her—but it was enough to make her head spin.

Finally, Jez stood and crossed over to her.

Jez, of course, was the wild card. She'd always been the wild card, and Masha had never quite been able to predict what she'd do next. And she'd tried to plan for that, tried to get rid of the restless, unpredictable pilot, before her unpredictability could cause problems.

And somehow, she hadn't been able to.

She hadn't been able to make herself.

Jez stood over her, cocking her head to one side, and for a brief moment Masha tasted a sharp, metallic tinge of fear. Because of all of the crew, Jez was the only one who might actually kill her, right here.

For a long moment, neither of them moved or spoke. Finally, Jez said quietly, "You alright, you bastard?"

For a moment, Masha wasn't sure if she'd heard correctly.

"I said," said Jez, "Are you alright, you dirty plaguer?"

"I'm—" Masha swallowed hard against something in her throat. "I'm fine, Jez. At least—" She grimaced slightly. "I'm as fine as can be expected, all things considered. I'm certainly not going to die from this."

"Let me see." Jez knelt, and Masha didn't protest as she pulled her jacket open and untucked her shirt and pulled up the heat shield. Jez examined the wound critically. "Probably should put a bandage on it, you damn scum-sucker," she said at last. She crossed to the corner of the room and pulled out the small emergency first-aid kit. She rifled through it, pulled out a bandage, and came back, kneeling in front of Masha again.

"Hold your damn shirt up," she said. Masha did so, without speaking, and Jez sealed the bandage carefully.

"There," said Jez, looking at it critically.

Masha took a deep breath and held it for a moment. Then she let it out slowly. "Thank you, Jez," she said, and she was somewhat proud of how steady her voice was.

Jez considered her for a moment.

"Listen, you dirty bastard," she said at last. "That was a scum-sucker move, what you did." She paused a moment, not taking her eyes off Masha's. "I don't know what you're after, Masha. I don't know what you're planning. But—but here's the thing. I—trust you.

For some stupid damn reason, I actually trust you. I actually think you're trying to do something good, even though I wonder if you'd recognize good if it punched you in the middle of your damn face." She paused again, for a long, long time, so long that Masha wasn't sure if she'd continue. Then, finally, she said, "Look, you bastard. I'm not good at trusting people. Don't do it very much. So don't— don't screw this one up for me, OK?"

There was a vulnerability in her expression that Masha had only seen there on the rarest of occasions.

Then she turned and left, the door clicking shut behind her.

Masha stared after her for a long time.

This was supposed to have been the easy part.

Seventeen years she'd worked in the government, worked for the very people who had been responsible for her parents' slaughter. And she'd bided her time, been pleasant and patient and agreeable. And she'd found her crew, finally picked the perfect combination of people and found the perfect job to bring them together for, and she'd pulled them together into a team, and by some miracle they'd pulled the job off. And she'd worked with them, and gained their trust, and when she'd given them the opportunity to walk away, they'd chosen to come along. Each one of them had chosen.

That was supposed to have been the hard part.

But somehow, all of that seemed to pale beside the sick, betrayed look on Tae's face when he'd realized what she'd done.

What she was doing—what she had done, what she was planning —needed to happen. She'd spent her whole life, ever moment of it since that day when she was seven years old, preparing for it.

Don't—don't screw this one up for me, OK?

She glanced down at the fresh bandage on her side, and closed her eyes for a brief moment.

Despite the bandage, she wasn't sure she'd get much sleep tonight.

295

26

Tae glanced up as Jez stepped through the door and it closed behind her. She gave him a quick smile, then dropped down against the wall in the corner, not bothering to pull up a sitting cushion.

Ysbel and Tanya had herded the children to bed, but Ysbel came out again, and pulled up a seat at the table beside Tae. Lev, too, was sitting at the table. He was scowling, and Tae wasn't entirely sure whether it was from what had happened with Masha in the room next door, or whatever had apparently happened with Jez on the ship.

Maybe both.

Tanya came out a few minutes later, and took a seat beside her wife.

"So," said Ysbel. "What do we do now?"

Lev managed a small smile. "The first thing, I think, is to figure out how to survive the next few weeks."

"She says she has a plan," said Ivan quietly. "Forgive me if I'm not reassured by this, but—" he shrugged. "As she said. I'm not sure we have many options at this point."

Lev leaned back slightly, his expression more weary than Tae had seen it in a long time. "At the moment, we're at her mercy, because she knows more than we do about Grigory, and what his likely next move will be. And she's right. We don't have a choice now. We stop Grigory, or we die. But—" he paused a moment, and there was a hint of steel under his voice. "But that advantage she has won't last forever."

Ysbel nodded. "She put all of us in danger, purposely, to get what she wanted. She put my children in danger. And I will not be surprised if one day we have to chose between killing her, or letting her kill us. But in the meantime, you're right. We don't have many options right now." She paused a moment. "Anyways, at least we have some time now, before the government fries our brains. How long do you think?"

Lev gave a despondent shrug. "Months, likely. It depends on how fast Evka works."

They were quiet for a few minutes.

Tae wasn't exactly sure when sitting around a table on a strange ship, as long as it was with these people, had become something comforting.

But somehow, nothing seemed quite as bad as long as they were still crewmates.

Not even Masha's betrayal, not even the sick feeling in his stomach that it brought.

Finally, Lev stood. "I'm sorry," he said, a trace of his usual calm returning to his voice. "I should probably get some sleep. I don't think I'm going to be much use tonight. Let's talk in the morning." He pushed back his chair and headed into one of the rooms.

"I think perhaps we should get some sleep too, my love," said Ysbel, glancing at her wife.

Tanya gave her a bleak smile. "Yes. We will have two very tired children to deal with tomorrow."

They left for their room, Ysbel's arm around Tanya's waist, Tanya's head on her wife's shoulder.

A few minutes later, Jez pushed herself up from the corner where she'd been sitting.

"Hey tech-head," she said. "You OK?"

"Yeah," he said, glancing over at her. "I—think so. I—" He trailed off.

"I know," she said softly. "I didn't think she would either. I—well, I mean, but listen. I don't—Maybe there's more to it."

He gave her a slight smile. "Yeah. Maybe. I—hope so."

She gave him a faint smile in return. "Anyways, guess I'm going to wander around for a bit. Not quite ready for bed yet, I guess."

He looked at her more closely, frowning.

She was drumming her fingers restlessly against her leg, her customary nervous energy spilling over into every movement.

"Jez?"

"Yeah?"

"If you—need something. Or get into trouble or something, just call me, for the Lady's sake. OK?"

She cocked her head at him, then grinned. "Sure, tech-head." She paused a moment, and dropped her eyes. "Thanks."

She slipped out the door, and he sighed and dropped his chin into his hands, staring sightlessly at the table.

He probably should be feeling—something. But there were too many thoughts clawing for attention in his brain, and he couldn't focus on any one of them long enough to feel anything at all, except a faint exhaustion, and a sort of desperate gratitude that the others were here, and he wasn't trying to deal with this completely alone.

"Tae."

He looked up.

Ivan pulled up a chair next to him. "It's not your fault, you know," he said quietly. "What Masha did."

"I—know," said Tae, and the words surprised him.

Ivan smiled at him. "You've changed since I met you in prison," he said at last.

Tae managed a half-hearted chuckle. "A lot has happened since then."

Ivan nodded, and for a few moments they sat in companionable silence.

"But there's one thing that hasn't changed," said Ivan. Tae looked up and met his eyes, and Ivan held his gaze, his face suddenly serious. "You're a good man, Tae. And you saved a lot of people today. Not all of them, I know. But a lot."

And looking into Ivan's face, Tae felt a sudden surge of warmth in his chest, and for some strange reason he remembered the way Dmitri had looked at him, weeks ago, and, oddly enough, that moment that he'd sat blinking up at the mafia boyevik from the couch, Ivan's arms around him.

His face was growing warm, and he dropped his eyes, but he found he was smiling, unconsciously.

"You're coming with us?" he asked at last. "To the pleasure planet, I mean."

"I'm not sure that I have a choice, at this point," said Ivan wryly. He paused. "But—I would have come anyways. I don't like what Masha did, but she's right that Gregory needs to be dealt with. And well, I've never liked the idea of the pleasure planets."

Tae nodded, and Ivan chuckled. "Go on. Get some sleep. All our problems will still be here in the morning."

Tae chuckled reluctantly as well and stood. "Yeah. 'Night."

"Goodnight, Tae."

He walked slowly into his room. It would probably hit him tomorrow, all those people they'd killed. Masha's betrayal. The fact that they were now being hunted by Grigory Korzhikov, with all that entailed.

But right now, right at this moment—he was mostly just glad he wouldn't be doing this alone.

Tanya's face was set, her head turned away, hands moving restlessly. Ysbel sat down heavily on the bed in their small room and watched her, and something in her chest hurt a little.

"My love," she said at last. Tanya's shoulders tensed, and for a moment, Ysbel didn't know if she'd respond.

Then she turned, and Ysbel stood and caught her, and Tanya, for the first time since Prasvishoni, relaxed into her embrace. Ysbel held her and closed her eyes, burying her face in Tanya's hair.

"Ysi," said Tanya at last, her voice muffled in Ysbel's shoulder. "I'm—sorry."

Ysbel pulled back slightly. "Sorry for what, my love? There's nothing to be sorry for."

"I've been so frustrated, and it's not—it's not your fault, I—"

Ysbel took her by the shoulders, gently. "My love. My Tanya. I've been so caught up in keeping you safe, you and the children. I forgot you don't need a protector, you can do that on your own. You need a wife." She paused, and gave her wife a small smile. "Perhaps you are right. Perhaps I have forgotten how to be married to you. But—I would like to remember, if you're willing to give me a chance."

Tanya met her gaze this time, and with a jolt, Ysbel realized there were tears in her eyes. "Ysi. My heart." She broke off, and Ysbel pulled her back into an embrace.

"Why didn't you tell me this sooner?" Ysbel whispered. "I should have noticed sooner."

"I—it's been so long, Ysi," said Tanya, her voice choked slightly. "I lost you for so long. And you were so alone, and I was so afraid that I'd lose you again—"

Ysbel pulled her closer. "Listen to me. I have loved you for as long as I can remember. What we built, my love—if it wasn't strong enough, it would have broken a long, long time ago. It's strong enough, I think, for you to be angry with me sometimes. If I remember, you've been angry at me before, and I've been angry at you too. And—" she found, suddenly, that she was blinking back tears of her own. "And Tanya. No matter how angry I have been, or how stupid I have been, I have never for one moment regretted marrying you."

Tanya raised her head and looked up at her, tears glistening in her eyes. Ysbel ran her hand gently through her wife's hair, marvelling at the familiar feeling of it, the feeling she'd once thought she'd lost forever.

"You can be angry at me, my Tanya," she whispered. "You can be whatever you need to be. And I will try not to be stupid, although we both know that will be difficult. I will keep trying to learn to be your wife again. To be whatever you need me to be. And we'll figure this out."

Tanya nodded, wiping her eyes, and Ysbel leaned forward and kissed her, gently. And Tanya kissed her back, and for a moment she could hardly breathe at the terrifying, desperate gratitude that she was here, holding this woman she loved.

Yes, Masha had betrayed them, and yes, because of that every member of their crew was in mortal danger and would be until they carried out Masha's sting. And yes, somehow she was going to have to find a way to stop that woman—kill her, perhaps.

But somehow, she was here, holding Tanya—and it would be alright.

Lev sat up abruptly, and tipped his head back against the wall, closing his eyes for just a moment.

He couldn't sleep. He could hardly force himself to stay still, and in the back of his mind he wondered if this was how Jez felt, all the time.

And then the thought of Jez sent his thoughts spiralling again, over and over and over, and he couldn't seem to stop them.

Jez, laughing in the pilot's seat of the *Ungovernable* as they were hurled, out of control, through space.

The look in Masha's eyes as she'd told him, calmly, what he'd already begun to guess, but hadn't wanted to believe.

Jez pressed up against him in the lift, the restless, unbearable ache of her body against his.

Fifty people. Fifty lives with that explosive. He'd been the one to trust her. He could have told Jez any of the airlocks, but he'd listened to Masha, believed her. He was supposed to be the smart one, the one who could see through the traps. But he'd trusted her, and that had blinded him. And the worst part was, he wasn't even sure, if she'd told him—he wasn't completely sure he would have made a different choice. If she'd told him, told him exactly what was behind airlock two, he might have still typed the same coordinates into the ship's com, and sent them over to Jez. And then it would be Jez looking at him with that expression of shocked betrayal.

He banged his head gently against the wall. Damn it to hell, he just needed to get some sleep, he just needed to be able to stop his brain from spinning out of control.

He just needed to stop picturing Jez every damn time he closed his eyes, stop feeling her lips on his so clearly that he'd open his eyes again to see if she was really here, stop the lightheaded dizziness of her absence, the aching need for her here, with him, somehow making sense of everything that didn't make sense anymore.

He shoved himself to his feet and paced across the room, but walking didn't seem to help, it just set his mind spinning faster, and he wasn't sure how much longer he could bear it.

Finally he stopped, resting his forehead against the wall, and swore softly.

He shouldn't do this. He knew damn well he shouldn't, but then again, after the last few weeks he wasn't even sure who he damn well was anymore.

He hesitated for a moment more, then he tapped a number into his com.

Ljubika answered almost instantly. She was awake, he knew she would be, because she'd told him her shifts, and he was pretty sure she'd be off soon.

"Hello?" she said. "Lev?"

He managed a slight smile. "Hey Ljubika. Are you alright?"

She laughed, that low, pleasant laugh he remembered from his days back in government. "I survived, anyways. I still don't know what happened, but they seem to have got it back to normal now."

"I'm glad to hear it." His smile felt a little more genuine. He paused a moment. "Um. Ljusha. I—I have a room upstairs. Would you—how would you like to come spend the night? For old time's sake?"

There was a moment's pause. Finally she said, quietly, "I'd—like that. I'm just getting off my shift, I'll be up in a few minutes."

Something like shame twisted in his stomach, but he shoved it down. "I'll send the room number to your com. There's a main room, knock when you get in."

When she'd tapped her com off, he went back to pacing for a moment.

Damn it to hell. Damn everything to hell, the point was if he didn't stop thinking about bloody Jez he was going to lose his damn mind.

Ljubika knocked on the door a few minutes later, and he opened it.

She was pretty—she'd always been pretty. More than pretty, really. And there was an air about her, a slightly-cynical amusement he'd always enjoyed, and he found himself smiling at her without even trying.

She came in and shrugged off her jacket, dropping it in a heap in the corner by the door and revealing a loose white shirt underneath. "Just got off work shift, and I didn't take time to go change," she said, with that teasing, slightly-amused smile he remembered so well. "So. You've become quite forward in your old age."

He smiled back at her and reached out, running his hand along her jawline. "I don't believe I was particularly shy last time we met, either."

She laughed and slid her hand around his waist. "True enough. I always liked that about you, Lev."

He closed the distance between them, and she smiled up at him, and damn caution and everything else because he couldn't handle it right now, he couldn't handle any of it.

He grabbed her and pulled her up against him and kissed her roughly, and she returned the kiss with enthusiasm.

Her body, pressed against his, felt wrong somehow, curvy where it should have been angular, soft where it should have been hard with wiry muscle, but her kiss brought the blood pounding through his head hard enough that he didn't have to think about anything else, and that was all he was looking for. She wrapped her arms around him, pulling his lips down to hers, and her fingers fumbled at the buttons of his shirt. He loosened his grip on her long enough to let her slide it off him, then pulled them both down onto the couch, rolling her on top of him, ignoring everything but the feeling of her body, her lips on his, her hands clasping the back of his neck, and it was almost a relief not to have to think. He slid his hands up her back, under her shirt, and she moaned in pleasure.

And then he heard a small noise at the door, and he glanced over.

Jez stood in the doorway, staring at him, face bloodless, expression stricken.

She stood there for a moment, then turned quickly and disappeared.

And despite the warmth of Ljubika's body, the pull of her lips on his, he felt suddenly very, very empty.

Gently, he broke off the kiss. Ljubika gasped and tried to pull his mouth back to hers, but he pushed her gently off him and sat up.

She looked up at him in confusion, and he tried to smile.

"I'm—sorry," he said.

"Lev?" she asked, frowning, her voice still breathless and thick with desire.

He dropped his head into his hands and forced himself to breathe in.

"Ljusha. I'm—sorry. I'm so sorry. I—I can't."

She was staring at him, and the hurt in her face cut him.

Slowly, he reached down and picked up his shirt from where it had fallen, and slipped it on.

"Lev," she began uncertainly. "Did I—Perhaps I misunderstood —"

He shook his head. "No. You didn't do anything wrong. It's my fault, and only mine. I—I'm sorry."

He stood and reached down to help her up. She pushed herself to her feet, ignoring his hand, and as she turned, he saw tears glistening in her eyes. She didn't meet his gaze as she pulled on her jacket and left, closing the door behind her. He watched her go, leaning his head against the doorpost, sickness churning in his stomach.

Damn Jez, and damn him, and damn this whole damn night.

He wasn't sure how long he stood there before he heard the click of a door opening behind him.

He didn't have the energy to look.

"Lev." It was Ysbel, and finally he did turn. She was watching him, an appraising expression on her face, and maybe with anyone else he would have tried to smile, but somehow he knew she'd see through it.

"Sit down," she said, gesturing at the table. He did as she asked, and she sat down across from him.

For a long time, neither of them spoke.

Finally, she shook her head. "Lev. That girl didn't deserve what you did to her. You are being stupid, and you need to stop it, right now."

He dropped his head into his hands. "I know, Ysbel," he said quietly. "I—I'm not sure I know how."

"You are very smart," she said heartlessly. "You'll figure it out."

They were silent for a few moments.

"What would you have done, Ysbel?" he said at last. "If Tanya had never come back from university in Prasvishoni. If she'd come back, but told you she didn't want to be with you. What would you have done?"

Ysbel gave a small snort of laughter. "What should I have done? I should have moved on, found someone else, got married, forgot about her."

"That's not what I asked," he said, still watching her.

She gave a reluctant smile. "You're right. It's not what you asked." She paused a moment, and her eyes had a faraway look. "So, what would I have done? If she'd told me she wanted nothing to do with me, I'd have respected that. Because I love her, and I couldn't love her and not respect that. But—if she'd wanted me to be a friend, instead? Perhaps a babysitter for her children, or the person she called when she needed to talk? I'd take that, Lev. I'd take it with all my heart. Because even if she was never going to be with me—I would infinitely prefer a life with Tanya in it to a life without her." She looked back at him, that soft smile still on her face, and for some reason, he had to choke back a lump in his throat.

Finally, she pushed herself to her feet. "Think about it," she said. "Think about what you want. And—I'm not as easily hurt as all that, if you need someone to shout at. Also, I will shout back."

He smiled, reluctantly, and she smiled back. Then she walked back to her room and closed the door.

It was late, too late, probably. But he sat at the table for a long time, staring at nothing.

I would infinitely prefer a life with Tanya in it to a life without her.

Jez had said she was crap at relationships. It appeared he could give her a run for her money on that score.

Hell, he was crap at friendships, apparently.

But—

But he would infinitely prefer a life with Jez in it to one without her. And maybe—well, if that was what it took, maybe not being crap at friendships was a skill he could learn.

* * *

Jez drained her glass and put it carefully down on the table.

She wasn't particularly drunk yet, but she was getting there as fast as she damn well could.

The woman sitting beside her lifted her own glass to call a server over. She turned and smiled at Jez. "This one's on me."

Jez grinned back.

They'd been sitting at conversational distance when they'd started. Now they were much closer than two people who didn't actually know each other had any right to be, and the woman's fingers were trailing down Jez's back, one leg thrown casually over Jez's lap. And Jez's hand, which had started at the woman's knee, was now resting half-way up her thigh.

She figured they were about three drinks away from getting a bottle and going back to the woman's room. Jez was pretty sure her companion had told her her name earlier that evening, but Jez had forgotten it a couple drinks back. Still—

Well, she figured getting completely smashed out of her mind and having sex with someone whose name she couldn't remember was probably a pretty reasonable way of dealing with her life at this point.

Anyways, it didn't matter. Every time she closed her eyes she could see Lev, half-undressed, tangled together with that girl, whoever she was. And it was a good thing, and it was exactly what Jez had wanted to happen. And Jez could always find someone to sleep with if she wanted to bad enough, so it was all good. It was all exactly what she'd wanted.

She had to choke back a sudden sob.

She wasn't damn well drunk enough. She wasn't sure she could get drunk enough, no matter how much she drank.

"Jez? You alright?" asked the woman, turning to her in concern.

Jez blinked hard and pasted on a grin. "Yep."

The woman raised an eyebrow at her, smiling, and nestled in closer, and Jez watched her.

She looked—nice, actually.

She looked like, besides being hot and apparently available, she was actually a nice person.

Like, maybe the kind of person who would hurt, when she woke up and found that Jez had slept with her, then taken off, like she always did.

And suddenly, she couldn't do it anymore. She just couldn't, because hell, she'd hurt enough people, and maybe it wasn't until she almost walked in on damn Lev that she realized how much it could hurt.

And this damn woman, whatever her name was, actually looked nice, and Jez couldn't do that to her.

She pushed back her chair, moving the woman's leg from her lap gently. "Hey," she said, trying to hold onto her grin. "I—guess I've probably had enough for the night. But—thanks. It was nice sitting with you."

The woman smiled up at her. "It was nice." She paused. "Give me your com number, if you want. I'll call you. I like you, Jez."

"Yeah." She held out her com and tapped it against the com on the woman's wrist. "See you round, probably."

She held onto her smile until she made it out of the gambling hall. Then she sank down against the corridor wall and put her face to her knees.

Maybe she was more drunk than she'd thought.

She sat there for a few minutes, the world spinning slightly around her. Then, finally, she pulled out her com.

"Tech-head?" she whispered.

"Jez?" He answered a moment later, sounding half-asleep and worried. "You alright? Where are you? Are you hurt?"

"I—no. I just—I think I need to go home." Her voice sounded small and lost, even in her own ears.

"Give me a sec," said Tae, sounding slightly more awake. "I'll get Ivan, we'll be right there. Send me your location on the com."

And she'd staggered home drunk plenty of times. But somehow it was different with Tae and Ivan there, walking beside her. And they didn't yell at her, or cuss her out, and when she finally broke down and sobbed pathetically, leaning against Tae's shoulder, he didn't even seem to mind.

Tae walked her to her room and helped her to her bed. She dropped onto her mattress, and after a moment, he sat beside her.

"You want to talk about anything?" he asked quietly.

And hell, if she'd been sober she probably would have pasted on a smile and told him she was fine. But she wasn't sober, and she wasn't fine, and she pulled her knees up to her chest and dropped her head into her arms and sobbed out the whole damn story.

When she was finished, they sat in silence for a few minutes. His hand rested lightly on her shoulder, and the warmth of it was comforting.

"You know, Jez," he said finally, "I don't know if anyone's ever told you this. But not being ready for a relationship doesn't make you a crap person."

She pulled her face out of her arms and stared at him. "I—" she began dully, but couldn't seem to find the words to continue.

Tae gave her a reluctant smile. "Jez. Look. You told Lev you didn't want to be with him right now. Fine. That happens. And you walked in on him kissing someone else, which—OK, but—Look, Jez. It's—it's going to be alright." He turned a little, so he was facing her. "I don't know what we have to do to convince you of this, but you're part of this damn crew. We're not going to leave you, or kick you out, or take off without you, OK? One day you're going to figure that out. And no one is going to suddenly hate you because you said you didn't want to kiss them anymore. Not even Lev, and you know how much of an idiot he can be."

She was still staring at him.

Because—well, because honestly, that had been the whole damn point of getting drunk. Because she'd screwed everything up with Lev, and everyone would hate her, and he'd hate her, and she couldn't handle that, and—well, she just couldn't, that was all. She couldn't handle her damn life without Lev in it.

"Lev won't—" she began at last. "I mean, he's not going to—"

Tae gave a soft chuckle, shaking his head. "No, Jez. He won't. He'll get over himself, and he's not going to hate you." He smiled at her. "You should get some sleep. You look like you need it."

"I—"

"Go on." He stood. "Goodnight, Jez. See you in the morning."

He left, closing the door behind him, and she collapsed back onto her mattress and stared up at the ceiling.

His words were spinning in her head.

And despite—well, despite everything—they kindled something warm and comfortable that spread from her stomach up through her chest and caught in her throat, and somehow—well, somehow, maybe he was right. Maybe things would be OK after all.

Masha sat up in bed, propping herself against the heavy headboard. After a moment she tapped her com, pulling up the holoscreen.

She'd been right—no matter how weary and battered her body was, her mind wasn't going to let her sleep.

Besides, she had plenty of work to do still. What Lev and Jez had done, planting the explosive, was just the beginning, really. The pieces were falling into place, but she still had to play them.

And she intended to.

But somehow, as she tapped away on her holoscreen keyboard, she couldn't stop seeing Tae's face, hearing Jez's last words to her before she slipped out the door.

Don't screw this one up for me.

She set her jaw.

This was what she'd been preparing for her whole life, ever since she was seven years old.

And it wasn't just her. It wasn't just a personal grudge. The fate of millions, perhaps billions of people hinged on the decisions she would make in the next few weeks. She owed it to them to make those decisions as practically and logically as possible, weighing and measuring according to calculations that she'd learned to use over her seventeen years of working in the government, never once letting her revulsion, her fear, her disgust show through the pleasant expression on her face.

All for this.

All for this, and for what would come next. Because taking down Grigory? That was something that would rock this system to its foundations. And that was only the beginning. What she was planning would take this entire system apart.

And yet—

And yet, somehow, those seven people in the room next door. Her crew.

Lev was right, she'd known they wouldn't agree to this, and so she'd forced their hands. Just like she'd planned to from the beginning.

But it wasn't like it had been in the beginning, not anymore.

For some reason, their lives—their thoughts, their feelings, Tae's look of betrayal and Jez's look of grudging trust—put a heavy finger on a scale that was supposed to be—had to be—impartial.

And the cold irrefutability of that terrified her beyond what she'd dreamed possible.

THE END

ENJOYED THE BOOK?

I HOPE YOU'VE ENJOYED Firewall, the fifth book in The Ungovernable series. Thank you for reading!

I have a small favour to ask you: Would you please leave a review? It may seem like a silly thing, but reviews are very important to authors like me, as they help other people find my book, which in turn helps me to keep writing. Even a line or two would be unbelievably helpful.

If you haven't read it yet, Zero Day Threat is the first book in the series. The sixth book is Trojan Horse.

In the mean time, if you subscribe to my mailing list, I'd love to send you an exclusive short story prequel featuring Jez Solokov, *Devil's Odds*. I'll also let you know about future launch dates, giveaways, and pre-release specials. And I always love to hear from my readers, so feel free to drop me a note!

If you'd like claim your free short story and subscribe to my newsletter, head over to my website: www.rmolson.com

Also, feel free to connect with me on Facebook: https://www.facebook.com/rmolsonauthor

or Instagram: https://www.instagram.com/rolson_author/